PRAISE FOR
A Wedding in Great Neck

"In prose as sparkling as a champagne toast, McDonough's delicious new novel gathers together one extraordinary wedding, two complicated families, and then shows how a single day can change everything. A funny, moving look at the bonds of love, the ties of family, and the yearning for happily ever after."

—Caroline Leavitt, *New York Times* bestselling author of *Pictures of You*

"In this delightful tale, Yona Zeldis McDonough limns the ups and downs of family life with a grace that brings to mind Cathleen Schine at her best. McDonough does not shirk the dark side, but her characters, as flawed as they may be, retain their humanity in the face of life's slings and arrows. A wise and witty novel from an author at the top of her form."

—Megan McAndrew, author of *Dreaming in French*

"Spirited, entertaining, and a delight to read, *A Wedding in Great Neck* offers a penetrating glimpse into the lives of one particular family, with its myriad shifting alliances, disappointments, and secrets."   —Lucy Jackson, author of *Posh*

continued . . .

"Emotional and evocative, hilarious and harrowing, *A Wedding in Great Neck* is a must read for every mother and daughter who've ever dreamed of, fought over, and loved each other through a wedding day."

—Pamela Redmond Satran, *New York Times* bestselling author of *The Possibility of You*

"Deftly handling a well-drawn ensemble cast of characters, *A Wedding in Great Neck* is a playful yet touching parsing of the tugs and tangles of familial bonds. This breezy novel offers the reader graceful writing while exploring contemporary suburban turf with an anthropologist's sharp eye."

—Sally Koslow, author of *Slouching Toward Adulthood: Observations from the Not-So-Empty Nest*

"Yona Zeldis McDonough is a born storyteller and her powers of perception are at full tilt in *A Wedding in Great Neck*. Beautifully structured around the secret longings and high emotions visited upon that special day, the book explores the fraught love between siblings, the rich wisdom of their elders, and shifting class values in one family. McDonough's *Wedding* is a page-turner—you'll feel as if you were there."

—Laura Jacobs, author of *Women About Town*

"With her trademark wit and keen eye, Yona Zeldis McDonough has created a confection that is not only a page-turner, but a poignant view of family life. This elegant novel is a must read for long-married wives and any woman who longs to be married. Book clubs will swoon."

—Adriana Trigiani, *New York Times* bestselling author of *The Shoemaker's Wife*

A
Wedding
IN
GREAT NECK

Yona Zeldis McDonough

NEW AMERICAN LIBRARY

NEW AMERICAN LIBRARY
Published by New American Library, a division of
Penguin Group (USA) Inc., 375 Hudson Street,
New York, New York 10014, USA
Penguin Group (Canada), 90 Eglinton Avenue East, Suite 700, Toronto,
Ontario M4P 2Y3, Canada (a division of Pearson Penguin Canada Inc.)
Penguin Books Ltd., 80 Strand, London WC2R 0RL, England
Penguin Ireland, 25 St. Stephen's Green, Dublin 2,
Ireland (a division of Penguin Books Ltd.)
Penguin Group (Australia), 250 Camberwell Road, Camberwell, Victoria 3124,
Australia (a division of Pearson Australia Group Pty. Ltd.)
Penguin Books India Pvt. Ltd., 11 Community Centre, Panchsheel Park,
New Delhi - 110 017, India
Penguin Group (NZ), 67 Apollo Drive, Rosedale, Auckland 0632,
New Zealand (a division of Pearson New Zealand Ltd.)
Penguin Books (South Africa) (Pty.) Ltd., 24 Sturdee Avenue,
Rosebank, Johannesburg 2196, South Africa

Penguin Books Ltd., Registered Offices:
80 Strand, London WC2R 0RL, England

First published by New American Library,
a division of Penguin Group (USA) Inc.

First Printing, October 2012
10 9 8 7 6 5 4 3 2 1

[NAL] REGISTERED TRADEMARK — MARCA REGISTRADA
LIBRARY OF CONGRESS CATALOGING-IN-PUBLICATION DATA:

McDonough, Yona Zeldis.
A wedding in Great Neck/Yona Zeldis McDonough.
p.   cm.
ISBN 978-0-451-23794-1
1. Brothers and sisters—Fiction.   2. Weddings—Fiction.   3. Dysfunctional families—Fiction.
I. Title.
PS3613.C39W43 2012
813'.6—dc23   2012002735

Set in Granjon
Designed by Beth Tondreau

Printed in the United States of America

PUBLISHER'S NOTE
This is a work of fiction. Names, characters, places, and incidents either are the product
of the author's imagination or are used fictitiously, and any resemblance to actual persons,
living or dead, business establishments, events, or locales is entirely coincidental.

The publisher does not have any control over and does not assume any responsibility
for author or third-party Web sites or their content.

For Constance Marks,
a Great Neck girl like no other

ACKNOWLEDGMENTS

For help, advice, support, and boundless goodwill,
I would like to thank Patricia Grossman,
Caroline Leavitt, Nechama Liss-Levinson,
Megan McAndrew, Paul McDonough,
Sally Schloss, Ken Silver, and Marian Thurm.

Special thanks to my gifted and utterly
unflappable editor, Tracy Bernstein,
and to my peerless agent, Judith Ehrlich,
who truly broke the mold.

A
Wedding
IN
GREAT NECK

Morning

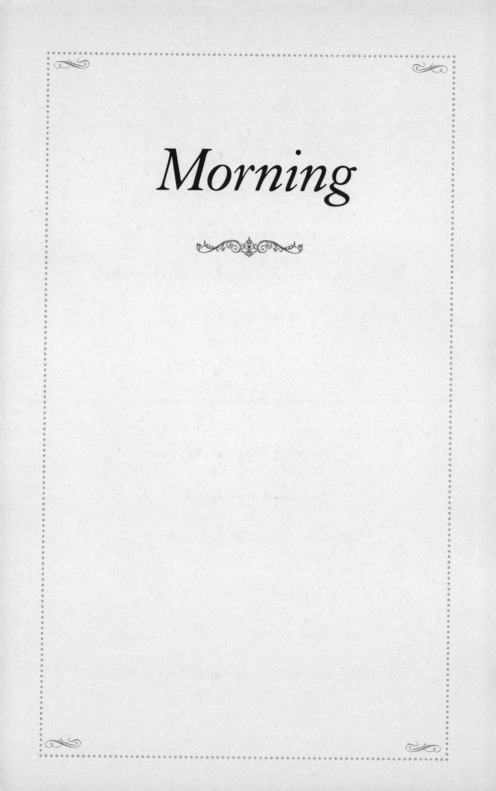

Mr. and Mrs. Donald Grofsky

and Mr. Lincoln Silverstein

request the honor of your presence

at the marriage of

Mrs. Grofsky and Mr. Silverstein's daughter

Angelica Elise

to

Mr. Ohad Oz

on Saturday, the second of June

two thousand and twelve

at seven o'clock in the evening

35 Swan's Cove Road

Great Neck, New York

Reception immediately following the ceremony

One

⌘ · ⌘

The dog. The dog was barking again, a series of clear, piercing yelps that infiltrated their way into the early-morning dreams of Gretchen McLeod (née Silverstein) and ruptured her sleep. She buried her face in the cool, polished cotton of the pillowcase in an effort to obliterate the sound. Three yips, a merciful pause in which she was lulled into thinking the dog had at last calmed down—only to be followed by three even louder and more insistent barks. The pattern cycled through three, four, five times before Gretchen yanked the blanket aside and got out of bed. She was momentarily disoriented; the house itself was still unfamiliar to her, and she had never stayed in this particular room, all English chintz and suffocating lace. But the confusion passed and she padded toward the sink; each of the six bedrooms in her mother's grand manse had its own bathroom, and Gretchen was grateful for the amenity.

The barking continued as she splashed cold water on her face and rubbed it vigorously with a plush white towel. White towels! Only people who had live-in maids would buy white towels. Now that her mother was among their number, she bought white with reckless impunity. And these were no ordinary white towels either. These white towels had a scalloped border of Wedgwood blue and matching Wedgwood-blue monograms in their centers. White towels deluxe.

Gretchen contemplated a shower, decided to wait, and instead examined her reflection in the magnifying mirror mounted above the towel ring. Slight puffiness under the eyes—check. Dark circles—check. A gradual deepening of the nasal-labial lines; small, red bump on her right cheek; slightly loosened flesh under the jawline—check, check, check. And her brows—her brows needed a major overhaul before the wedding, which was scheduled to begin at seven o'clock this evening.

Gretchen turned from the mirror. Enough. It was being under the same roof as her siblings—Teddy and Caleb with their respective partners down at one end of the hall; Angelica, the bride-to-be, ensconced in a room at the other—that brought out this distinctly adolescent form of self-scrutiny. Except Gretchen was almost forty, a significant, milestone sort of birthday, and decades away from adolescence.

The dog was still barking as Gretchen returned to the bedroom, dug out her clothes—still sloppily crammed into her suitcase—and dressed. How did Betsy endure it? This was the very same mother who, in all the years Gretchen was growing up, would not allow so much as an orange-and-black-dappled goldfish, won at the East Meadow Jewish Center's annual Purim fair, to cross their threshold.

So how, at the age of sixty-four, had her mother morphed into someone who did not simply tolerate this dog—a Pomeranian with a pointed, foxlike face and perpetually hysterical demeanor—but actually seemed to worship it? Betsy was like some freshly hatched religious fanatic. *How did I ever live without a dog?* she would say, regaling anyone in earshot about her recent conversion. *To think I could have missed this!* She spoke to the creature in wheedling, dulcet tones, fed it diced morsels of steak and roast beef, allowed it to sleep in her bed. What Don, Betsy's large, backslapping husband, thought of this arrangement, Gretchen didn't know. He seemed to tolerate it, just as he was tolerating all the hoopla—and the expense—of the wedding that was about to take place. But Don was utterly charmed by Angelica. So charmed that when Angelica wrinkled her perfect little nose at the mere *idea* of Leonard's of Great Neck— Betsy's suggestion—he immediately offered their house instead. No surprise there. Angelica was Don's favorite, just as she had been their father's. Betsy's having swapped one husband for another had not changed the essential dynamic of their clan.

Angelica had it all: the looks, the brains, and the attitude. Even the name: how to compare the celestial "Angelica" with the relentlessly earthbound "Gretchen"? Her sister had lucked out in so many ways, great and small. Gretchen's role in this wedding was, both by definition and by tradition, ancillary. It was Angelica's day, and no one cared what Gretchen thought, felt, or wanted as long as she was willing to play her assigned part, sister of the bride, in this vast, unfolding pageant. From the way everyone was carrying on, you'd think that there was no more important event in the entire nation. Or on the planet.

There had been a series of well-choreographed events at which Gretchen was expected to appear: the over-the-top engagement party at Bouley in Tribeca, the bridal shower at the Park Avenue duplex of one of Angelica's closest friends and matron of honor, the ocean-view prewedding brunch and the catered rehearsal dinner, all culminating in the nuptials this evening, when the 233 invited guests would descend on the lawn of her stepfather's five-acre, baronial, but unremittingly vulgar home to hear Angelica say, "I do."

Gretchen's own modest wedding more than fifteen years before—justice of the peace, small family party in the backyard of the East Meadow house—had not been treated with such fanfare. Of course Betsy had not yet married up, as Gretchen's grandmother Lenore liked to say. Had not yet become Lady Bountiful, with her manicured lawns, her magnificent circular rose garden—the only part of the vast property that Gretchen did not find in appalling taste—her charities, and her neurotic little dog. Everything was different now. But in another, more fundamental, and essential way, everything—that is, Gretchen's place in this family—was exactly the same.

So here she was, tetchy from lack of sleep, and ill at ease

in her mother's sprawling abode, a faux Italianate palazzo-like edifice of putty-colored stucco, with a terra cotta roof and mullioned windows. Gretchen was overwhelmed by the multitude of bed- and bathrooms, the terrace and the balconies, the pretentious curved driveway as well as the various outbuildings—sheds, greenhouse, cabana—all arrayed around the main structure. Then there was the network of brick and blue stone paths linking the various parts of the property together. Coming here for a visit required a map.

As she contemplated her options—coffee, black, steaming, and strong, or a shower—her cell phone rang. She dived for it, hoping desperately it was not her boss, Ginny Valentine, calling to annoy her with a request for some trivial bit of information that she could have found for herself if she had only bothered to get up from her padded, wheeled, and insanely expensive leather chair to look. Gretchen located her phone in the morass of her handbag. But it was not Ginny. "Hello?" Gretchen said, sinking back into the enticing softness of the bed. Silence, and then the voice of her not-yet-ex-husband, Ennis, sounding so close that he could have been standing next to her. Instinctively she moved the phone away from her ear.

"Gretchen, are you there?"

"I'm here," she said. But she wished she had not answered; she was not in the mood to talk to him today. Or any day, for that matter.

"I'm at the station."

"Station?" She didn't understand. "What station?"

"The train station. Here in Great Neck. I'll be getting a taxi to the house," he continued. "Unless you can come out and get me." He pronounced the word "out" as if it were spelled "oot"; Ennis had grown up in Glasgow, and even though he hadn't lived there in decades, he still had the accent.

Gretchen did not say anything. She knew he had been invited to the wedding; he and Angelica had always gotten along well, and their twin daughters, Justine and Portia, had begged that he be included. But he had declined, much to Gretchen's relief. All of that had been months ago, and none of her elaborate preparations for this day—mental, physical, even spiritual, for God's sake—had included Ennis.

"You still there?" Ennis was saying.

Yes, she wanted to scream. *I'm still here, but I wish you weren't!*

But Gretchen was not a screamer. Never had been and never would be. She had always been the good sport, the trooper, the one who compromised, yielded, and accommodated. She watched her sister shoot through her life with the force and direction of an arrow heading straight for the bull's-eye. Her brother Teddy had that same quality. But she, Gretchen, did not. Instead she lived her life like a handful of confetti, tossed up into the air and scattered down—gracefully, she liked to think—a little here, a little there.

"I didn't know you were coming," she said, sidestepping the question about driving to the station to get him.

"I wasn't . . ." he said. "And then I was." There was a pause. "So here I am."

"Well, well!" she said, the brittle falseness in her tone bordering on parody. "Isn't that just dandy?" She drew a deep breath for strength. "Does Angelica know?"

"Yes. I called her to tell her."

Funny, she never bothered to ask how I might feel about that, Gretchen fumed.

"Gretchen? Did I lose you?"

Did you ever, she thought. But did not say. "I'm still here," she said finally. "Though I'm really not sure why you came, Ennis. I don't think it was a good idea." She began pulling on the lace edge of a pillowcase; if she kept this up, she would tear it.

"The girls asked me to." He sounded defensive. "They kept calling to see if I would change my mind, and I didn't want to disappoint them."

"But you had no trouble disappointing *me*," she said, unable to hide her bitterness.

"That's another reason I came," he said quickly. "I wanted to see you. To talk to you."

"About what?" The lace was sturdier than she would have expected: despite her yanking, it remained intact.

"Let's do this in person," he said. "Will you come out and get me?" *Oot.*

Gretchen did not answer right away. In the past she would have gone. She would have grumbled, she would have stewed, but she would have gone. Right now, though, she felt uncharacteristically uncooperative. Why should she have to play chauffeur for her estranged husband? Would Angelica do such a thing? Angelica, who had not even bothered to let her in on this small but significant change in the guest list? Gretchen was quite sure the answer was no.

"I really don't want to, Ennis," she said at last. "I wasn't expecting to see you today, and I want to . . . prepare myself before I do." She gave the lace trim a final tug and was obscurely pleased when it tore free of the pillowcase.

There was a brief, wounded silence before he spoke again. "Fine," he said. "I'll call a taxi. See you later." He clicked off.

Gretchen was left staring at her phone. Whatever burst of spirit that had enabled her to say no evaporated as soon as the connection was severed. She felt depleted and sad. Dreamy, sensitive Ennis, with his fine, wispy hair and his adorable accent. He was the love of her youth, the love of her life. Or so she had thought. They met, they courted—he'd been so ardent back then, calling late at night "just to hear her breathe," penning verse that he slid under the door of her dorm room at school or slipped into the poetry books he was always buying for her—and they wed in great haste. Her parents had worried that they were too young, but Gretchen waved away all their concerns. He was the one, she told them. The One. Hah.

Gretchen surveyed the room to which she had been assigned. It had a cloying, virginal feel. A lace-infested bower of tiny floral prints, suffocating swags, and fancy flounces, it effectively catapulted her back to middle school, one of the more dismal periods in her life. Angelica had been given much more soignée lodgings, with a raw silk duvet the color of champagne, and a very fine, at least to Gretchen's admittedly imperfect eye, Persian rug. She had not seen the other rooms occupied by her brothers or her grandmother Lenore, though she had been downstairs to the media room with its sixty-inch flat-screen TV, piped-in sound, Wii, and latest-model PlayStation. Justine and Portia were camped out there because Betsy thought it would be "more fun" than one of the upstairs bedrooms. Portia had been delighted by all the flashy, high-tech toys, but Justine scowled ferociously.

"What's wrong?" Gretchen had asked. "Don't you like it?"

"What's to like?" Justine had said. "It's decadent beyond belief."

Gretchen had not known how to reply. Her immediate thought was that she wanted to box Justine's ears for her rudeness—*box her ears*, what an archaic term. Gretchen was not even sure she knew what it meant; besides, she had never hit her children and was not about to start now.

But on a deeper level Gretchen was worried. Justine's displeasure—with the room, with her life at school and at home in Brooklyn—had become a kind of emotional kudzu, propagating madly and strangling everything in its path. Justine was not happy with *anything,* and Gretchen's maternal barometer told her this was not just a typical adolescent need to push her mother away and in the process carve out her own identity. No, it was something more. Something, if Gretchen was willing to be stingingly honest with herself, darker and more troubling. Justine was hurting; Gretchen could feel it, smell it, practically taste it, but the barrier her daughter had erected made it impossible for Gretchen to either locate the source of the pain or do anything to help.

Looking around herself now, Gretchen felt sickened by the terminal sweetness. The urge to escape propelled her downstairs, where the kitchen was a hub of activity. Of course the crew from Elite Catering had its own state-of-the-art station set up outside, near the main tent, but Betsy's maids were preparing food to set out in the breakfast room to feed the family and, apparently, anyone else who happened to wander in.

Water ran, pots clanged, and the phone trilled. One of the maids was at the sink rinsing berries in a colander; another was pouring various juices—apple, orange, grapefruit—into colorful glazed pitchers brought back from Betsy's recent trip to Tuscany.

Gretchen heard her mother's voice: "Carmelita, could you please—" although the rest of what she said was drowned out by the noise of the food processor, which in full throttle sounded like a small jet taking off.

Gretchen paused. No one had seen her yet, and, apart from her desire for a cup of strong black coffee, there was no reason to go in. She would just be in the way. Breakfast was supposed to be laid out in the appropriately named breakfast room, but she saw no signs of it yet. Besides, Ennis would be here soon, and she still wasn't ready to deal with him.

She hurried back up the stairs and poked her toothbrush around in her mouth. Having her own immaculate bathroom for the duration of the visit was almost compensation for being here; back in Brooklyn, without Ennis's calm, orderly presence, the house had become a perpetual mess. Without any discussion or prompting on her part, he had loaded and emptied the dishwasher, dusted furniture, vacuumed with a vengeance. Now that he was gone, it seemed like there were always towels on the floor, hairs in the sink, and wads of dirty tissues and cotton puffs overflowing from the bathroom trash pail. Portia, when reminded, would make an attempt at corralling the chaos; Justine would use Gretchen's perfectly reasonable request as another black mark against her.

But it was time to stop wallowing. There was nothing she could do this weekend to address or alter whatever was going on with Justine. It would be challenge enough to get through the wedding relatively intact. She would deal with Justine when the nuptial circus had concluded and she was back home with her girls again.

Looking out the small, lace-bedecked window, Gretchen saw the four-car garage, which suddenly presented her with an escape route. Her mother had given her a set of keys to one of the cars that was housed there—not the Mercedes convertible, the Lexus or the Jaguar, but the older, admirably maintained Volvo that the maids used for running errands. She'd go find a diner where she could order coffee, a couple of fried eggs, and a side of hash browns without having to listen to anyone discuss calories, saturated fats, or the wedding of the century. If she hurried, she could be

out of the house well before Ennis and his Scottishly in-
flected but nonetheless perfidious heart arrived, before she
heard one more word about what Angelica wanted or Justine did not. Gretchen grabbed the keys. In her mind she
was already gone.

Two

❧ · ❧

Dozing lightly in a room at her daughter Betsy's Great Neck house, Lenore dreamed of breasts: big breasts and small breasts, breasts as high and firm as hills, breasts that drooped and sagged like a couple of old change purses. Breasts as pale as milk, dark as cocoa beans, and every shade in between. There was nothing erotic in her reverie; her interest was purely professional. But breasts were more than a profession for Lenore. Breasts were a calling.

Years ago, before Betsy was even born, Lenore and a friend had made the trek down to Essex Street to a lingerie shop owned by her husband's best friend's father, Sy Rosenzweig. Sy could take one look at a customer and say, "Maidenform, thirty-two-C," in a tone that brooked no discussion. If the customer attempted to argue, he would simply turn to the wall of cardboard boxes stacked up to the ceiling, yank out the size and brand he deemed appropriate, and thrust it toward her. "You can put it on over there," he would grunt, indicating a curtain—so faded a blue as to appear gray— that cordoned off the single dressing room. The woman would slip behind the curtain, try on the bra, and—lo and behold!—Sy would have been right.

Lenore had grudgingly admired his expertise, but disdained his manner. Why make a woman feel that buying a bra was somehow a shameful and dirty business, like a backroom abortion? Why couldn't the search for the right bra be a joyful, self-affirming experience? That's where Lenore had seen her opening, and she'd stepped into it with all the tremulous excitement of an aspiring actress taking to the floorboards for the first time. It hadn't happened right away; no, Lenore had had to plan and wait. But when her own sainted grandmother had died and left her a little nest egg, Lenore knew just how to hatch it: she rented a small storefront on Montague Street in Brooklyn Heights, and opened Lenore's Lingerie.

Remembering everything that had offended her about Sy's shop, Lenore set out to do things differently. The shop was painted a delicate, wistful shade of pink, like the inside of a seashell. There were pictures of lingerie ads, clipped from *Vogue* and *Harper's Bazaar* and framed in the gold-tone frames that Lenore bought on sale at Woolworth's. She had carpeting installed, and the curtains to the two small fitting rooms were made from a pink-and-green flowered fabric that she had cut and sewn at her kitchen table.

As she stitched the hems on her compact little Singer, a girlhood gift from her parents that she had brought with her into her marriage, she thought of what would take place inside these dressing rooms. She, Lenore, would do all the fittings herself. Straps. Hooks. Padding. Push-ups. All the small yet essential details that would coalesce into the perfect fit, the perfect experience. The women who came to see her would be made to feel beautiful, special, cherished. They would leave feeling confident in a way they had never felt before. And then they would return, bringing their mothers, daughters, sisters, aunts, friends, and bridge club members. Her thoughts hummed merrily in concert with the buzzing machine. There. She'd finished both panels. Now all they needed was a quick pressing with a *schpritz* of starch.

That had all been more than fifty years ago. Lenore had opened her shop, and then another in Midwood and a third in Bay Ridge. They'd been successful, every single one of them, and she'd reluctantly had to accept that she could not do every single fitting herself. But she trained her fitters personally and would perform surprise spot checks, sweeping in unannounced to see how Myra, Susie, Ruby, and Precious were getting on. Even now, she still made her weekly rounds to the different shops, though Betsy had been hinting that she ought to give up driving. Give up driving! Lenore seethed just thinking about it. She loved to drive almost as much as she loved to breathe, and she still kept a drawer filled with silk scarves—only silk, never cotton or, God forbid, polyester—that she tied over her head when she was behind the wheel. Not only did she like to drive, but she liked to drive fast, and the scarves provided the necessary protection for her carefully wrought coif.

The sun was brightening behind the shades, and Lenore

woke herself with a little snore. How rude! She was glad that no one, not even Monty, had had to hear that. One more indignity of aging, these crude, piglike snores; she had never snored when she was young. Or if she had, she had slept so soundly that she had never heard herself.

Mildly disgusted, she got out of bed and went to the window. A light tug caused the shade to snap up with a satisfying ping and allowed her to survey the scene below. Two gardeners were working around the edges of the lawn; another trimmed the hedges across from the kitchen door. Someone she didn't recognize—maybe from the catering crew?—hurried across the lawn, avoiding the path. Lenore hoped Betsy did not see him; she was very particular about people using the paths, not the lawn.

Several large potted hydrangeas—all of them creamy white and at the peak of their form—sat in terra cotta urns on the terrace, awaiting their ultimate deployment. Angelica, God bless her, had superb taste; Lenore had to concede that, even though she was still slightly rankled by her granddaughter's refusal to invite Lenore's old friends Bunny and Tess to the wedding.

"Grandma, we've been through all of this before," Angelica had said last night when Lenore brought it up again. "The guest list was getting too big. We had to rein it in."

"But to leave out Bunny! And Tess!"

"Didn't I invite Arlene and her new husband? And what about Celia, Claire and Doris? All with escorts?"

"Well, yes, but . . ." said Lenore, beginning to be mollified but not wanting to let go of her grievance just yet.

"Also the Blooms, the Kremers, and the Steins. Your guests, all of them, Grandma."

"That's true," Lenore admitted.

"So Bunny and Tess were really at the bottom of the list anyway. Besides, Bunny's not even here. You said she was on that cruise."

"She would have canceled it for this," said Lenore, eager to start fanning the flames of her resentment again. "I know she would have."

"It's too late, Grandma," said Angelica gently. "Sometimes you just have to admit defeat gracefully."

"Do you?"

"Do I what?" Angelica had said. Her dark eyes looked genuinely curious.

"Admit defeat gracefully?"

But Angelica had elected not to answer that; instead she leaned in and deposited a light kiss on her grandmother's cheek—what delightful perfume she wore; Lenore would have to get the name of it—and was gone.

The kitchen door opened, and Betsy's furry little dog ran out, squatted, and ran back in again. At least it hadn't relieved itself in the house. Like it had at least twice before. Lenore loved dogs, but this one tried even her patience. It yapped; it quivered; it puddled. She had seen it bare its sharp little teeth more than once (the last time she was here, the dog had snapped at one of the maids), though fortunately not on this visit. Yet Betsy was enamored of the creature and simply ignored any and all complaints lodged by her family against it.

Turning from the window, Lenore looked at the room and its adjoining bathroom; she approved of her lodgings. Betsy had finally done well, though Lenore had wondered occasionally about the mental acuity of her new son-in-law. *Not the sharpest knife in the drawer* was what her beloved Monty, may he rest in peace, would have said. Though Don certainly was what would have been called, in Lenore's day, a good provider. Where had all his money come from? Lenore had asked Betsy this very question. When Betsy told her that Don had made his fortune with a patent for a particular kind of cabinet hinge, Lenore had felt a flash of kinship. She understood how some seemingly ordinary, even inconsequential item—a hinge, a bra—could spawn an empire. Granted, Lenore's Lingerie was not exactly an empire. But three successful stores, a new car every couple of years, a brownstone on Pineapple Street in Brooklyn Heights where she still lived, a summer place on the Island, which she had sold when Monty died—those things were not exactly chopped liver. Lenore, a Brooklyn girl raised in a modest Flatbush apartment—her parents had slept on a fold-out sofa and allowed Lenore and her sister, Dottie, to have the single bedroom—and educated at Erasmus Hall High School, had done pretty well for herself. But Betsy, God bless her, had done even better: Hunter College, and then Columbia, no less, for a MSW. Well, that was the plan, wasn't it? That the children should do better than the parents, and the grandchildren better yet?

Lenore thought about her own grandchildren as she

made the bed, with its ivory sheets and gaggle of small fringed pillows. Betsy would have chided her for this—*That's why I hired the maid, Ma!*—but Lenore, who liked comfort as well as the next person, had her standards. Certain things should be done for yourself and by yourself. Making a bed you had slept in was one of them.

Judging from this wedding, Angelica certainly was doing well. Yes, Betsy and Don were contributing a sizable amount, but Angelica and her fiancé, Ohad, had also pitched in. Such a handsome young man, that one. Like a movie star, with those teeth, that hair. A good match for Angelica—their babies would be drop-dead gorgeous. Ohad had been born and raised in Israel. Jerusalem, no less. He'd been in the army. Of course they all were: the young men and the women too. But Ohad had been both a pilot and a commanding officer. Angelica had revealed this with something akin to embarrassment, but to Lenore, a staunch supporter of Israel since the nation's earliest days, it was heroic. Yes, Angelica had made the right choice. This lavish wedding was the sort of solid proof Lenore sought: big, showy, and public, it confirmed, in her eyes, that Angelica was proud of her decision and wanted everyone to know it. Lenore was not worried about Angelica.

Then there was Teddy, head of his own company and seeing a very nice girl who was a lawyer. Of course she did go by a boy's name, which Lenore had trouble remembering. She stopped what she was doing to think. Marti, that was it. Now why would such a smart and pretty girl let herself be called Marti, especially when her given name was Martine? Lenore was stumped; she could not fathom the ways of the young. But, still, Teddy had found himself a prize. Teddy too was on his way.

But it was different with Caleb and Gretchen. Caleb was the sweetest boy on God's earth. Tender, considerate, always thinking of someone else. Yet he was, it had to be said, a *faygele*. Not that there was anything wrong with that; Lenore knew you loved who you loved. End of story. But other people were less understanding, and she worried about him, her boychick. When he was a child, she had wanted to protect him—from the world and from the obstinate vulnerability of his own gentle soul—and though he had not been a child for years, the impulse was still there, strong as ever.

So Lenore had been instantly on guard when he introduced her to Bobby, the glib young man whom he had invited as his escort to the wedding. She didn't trust him, not for a second, and while the rest of the family fairly swooned for his muscled, blond good looks, overplayed Southern accent, and slightly risqué jokes, Lenore was not charmed. *Can't you see that he'll take Caleb's heart and break it in two?* she had wanted to yell. *Break it and stomp on the pieces?*

Lenore gave the pillows a final smack. It was still early, though there would be plenty to do today. She wanted a long, soul-restoring soak in the tub before the wedding. And she planned to steam her dress, since the steaming of special garments was another task that Lenore felt a person should not entrust to anyone else. Angelica had offered the services of the visiting hairdresser, manicurist, and makeup artist to anyone who wanted them. Betsy and Marti had signed on, of course, as had Lenore. So had two of the bridesmaids, friends of Angelica's, who were due here soon. But Lenore was not sure that Gretchen would take advantage of this generous offer, and the girl's refusal vexed her.

Gretchen was the other worrisome grandchild, the one who could or would not take her place in the world. Oh, she had gone to college, where she had done quite well, though Lord only knew what it was she had studied; it seemed to change every other month. And after she graduated, she continued to bounce around from this job to that, never settling on any one thing in particular. Lenore could smell the indecision on her, ripe as the scent that emanated from a bunch of soft, spotted bananas.

One thing Lenore had approved of was that her granddaughter had married young and given birth to twin girls shortly thereafter. Lenore remembered feeling relieved that Gretchen seemed to be acquiring some heft, some substance, even if the husband—a poet, of all impractical things—was never going to be a good provider. Still, he'd had a job teaching poetry (imagine *paying* for your children to *potchke* with such a thing!) at Brooklyn College, which was where Monty had gone; he and Gretchen owned a pretty brick house not far from Lenore's Midwood store. The house had a backyard, a deck, and a wood-burning fireplace.

Lately, though, there had been some major trouble

between them, and it all went to pieces: Gretchen and the
girls were alone, while the husband—for he still was her
husband—had found himself a room in an apartment that
he shared with two other men, both strangers. Now where
was the progress in that? The situation was clearly not good
for the girls, Lenore's only great-grandchildren. One had a
four-inch streak of hot pink running through her hair; the
other had a pierced eyebrow, nostril, and God knew what
else; both went to a *meshugenah* school where such things
were not only permitted but encouraged.

But none of this would deter Lenore from fighting
back, because she was a fighter by nature. She would fight for
Gretchen, whom she pitied as well as loved. And for Caleb,
whom she flat-out adored. Ostensibly she was here to celebrate Angelica's wedding, and celebrate she would. She had
new shoes—gold—and a brocade dress with rhinestone buttons and a matching coat, though she did not think she
would need the coat today. She had big glitzy earrings, satin
gloves, and a satin evening purse. She had . . . what was that
word she had just learned . . . bling, that was it. She had
bling. She could see herself all decked out in the front row,
weeping delicately into her hanky. Later she would make a
champagne toast to the newlyweds and dance with any and
all of the available gentlemen at the reception.

But Lenore had other less visible, though equally compelling, agendas. This wedding provided her with multiple
opportunities to deal with her wayward grandchildren. She
would find a way to prove to her grandson that this Bobby
person, this opportunistic schnorrer, was not for him, and

that he should give his tender, trusting heart to someone who would cherish it.

And unbeknownst to her granddaughter, there was a man she was destined to meet at this wedding, a man whose presence had carefully been orchestrated by none other than Lenore herself. He was forty-one, divorced, with a daughter, and he was the only son of Lenore's old friend Celia, that very same Celia whom Angelica had finally deigned after much pleading on Lenore's part to invite. And since Celia's husband was dead, it was perfectly appropriate to ask her son Mitch to be her escort. Lenore did not, however, tell Celia about her matchmaking scheme. Celia was funny that way; she might not like the idea. No, better to just invite him, introduce them, and see what happened next.

So Lenore had made sure that Gretchen and Mitch would be seated at the same table. She would not be at the table herself, but she would stop by to make sure the two met and to point out the many things they had in common: both divorced, with teenaged girls. . . . Lenore couldn't think of anything else at the moment, but that was a start.

Then tomorrow, after the wedding, she would find out if Gretchen liked this Mitch person—he was an ophthalmologist, a profession that did not exactly rank with the sort of medicine practiced by Angelica or her young man, but still—and perhaps coax the girl into making something like a plan.

Plans were what kept you going; plans were what kept you alive. Lenore understood this as surely as she understood anything, and she hoped to make Gretchen understand it too. With her own plans quickly gelling in her mind, Lenore opened the door and stepped out into the hallway, ready once more to face the glorious day—one of the nearly thirty thousand that life had so far granted her—that quivered and danced just ahead, just beyond the range of her still-avid, still-seeking vision.

Three

꧁ · ꧂

Just as Gretchen's hand touched the smoothly carved banister for the second time that morning, she heard her name and turned. There was her grandmother Lenore swathed—that was the only word for it, really—in a ruffled pink garment whose enormous collar—seemingly borrowed from a clown's costume—made her head, with its shellacked blond waves, appear small and doll-like

"Good morning," Gretchen said, sorry she had been caught. Conversations with Lenore were never short; by the time this one was over, her chance to escape from the house for a little while would have disappeared.

"Good?" Lenore fairly accused. "I hope it's more than good. I hope it's great. No, even great is not enough. It should be spectacular, magnificent, and life altering."

"That's a lot for just one morning, don't you think?" Gretchen smiled. Her grandmother was a piece of work, all right. But a lively piece of work. How old was she now, anyway? Eighty-five? Eighty-six? Whatever it was, she showed no signs of slowing down.

"It's not just any morning. This is the morning of the day that Angelica's getting married. Married! I can hardly believe it. Just yesterday she was a little *vildechaya*, running around the house without her underpants, and grape jam smeared all over her face."

"I'm sure she'd love it if you reminded her of that," Gretchen said.

"Are you making me fun of me?" Lenore leaned closer and peered into Gretchen's eyes.

"Only a little," Gretchen admitted. She took her grandmother's hand and squeezed it briefly; slightly gnarled by arthritis now, the fingers were still covered in rings, and her nails were painted a pale, impeccable peach.

"Only a little!" Lenore repeated. "No one has any respect these days, none at all."

"I was just going out to get some coffee," Gretchen said. The lack of respect in the younger generation was not a topic she wished to tackle before her daily caffeine infusion. "Come with me?"

"You want me to go out now?"

Gretchen nodded, ears attuned to the bustle below.

"But why? There's coffee right here. And good coffee too. That man your mother married, he's no skinflint. You eat well in his house. Did you know that tonight they're serving three entrees? Three! And one of them is filet mignon."

"Exactly. The place is a madhouse. We'll just be in the way."

"Betsy said there would be food in the breakfast room," said Lenore.

"There was nothing there when I last checked," Gretchen said. *And even if there was, she still wanted to get the hell out of here for a little while.*

"Maybe it's there now," said Lenore.

"Let's go out," Gretchen coaxed. "It'll be fun."

It was the word *fun* that persuaded her; Gretchen could see that. "All right," Lenore said. "But first I have to get dressed."

"You are dressed." Gretchen knew from experience that getting dressed for Lenore was something that might take an hour. Or more.

"In this? I couldn't possibly go out in this." She fluttered her hands, indicating the vividly colored garment.

"Put a raincoat on over it."

"I couldn't do that."

"Yes, you could. We're just going to a diner. Some people go in their pajamas. Or what might as well be," she amended.

"You ought to know by now that I am not *some people.*"

Which, of course, was true. "Well, all right," Gretchen said. "But please—*hurry.*"

Lenore went back to her room and promptly reappeared in a pair of brown linen pants and a flowing leopard-print blouse whose buttons glinted with rhinestones; a square silk scarf in a brilliant flame color was tied under her chin. "So my hair doesn't get mussed from the wind in the car," she explained.

Gretchen doubted the windows had ever been opened in the Volvo; her mother was a believer in heat during the winter and air-conditioning at all other times of the year. But she saw no reason to say this to Lenore. Instead she made sure her grandmother was safely buckled into her seat, and then they were off.

The diner was more crowded than Gretchen would have liked. Oh well. She had escaped, and the waiter, clearly experienced in handling a crowd, had them in a booth within minutes. Plastic-coated menus and thick white mugs filled with steaming coffee appeared almost immediately after. Lenore took a sip, leaving the vivid, striated imprint of her lipstick on the ceramic surface. She scanned the menu and then snapped it decisively shut.

"Do you know what you want?" Gretchen asked.

"I *always* know what I want," Lenore countered. "But what about you, darling? What do you want?"

"I thought I'd have fried eggs and hash browns. With toast and a side of sausage." Gretchen set the menu aside and tried to make eye contact with the waiter.

"That's not what I meant."

Gretchen continued looking for the waiter. She had an abiding tenderness for her grandmother, and recalled the many afternoons spent companionably on Lenore's ice-blue satin comforter, eating handfuls of Poppycock with a scoop of Breyers vanilla ice cream on the side, and watching the soaps or working a crossword puzzle together. But all that was a long time ago, and now, when Lenore slid into her meddlesome mode, it made Gretchen itch to be somewhere, anywhere else. The waiter was embroiled with a party of eight, two of whom were squirming toddlers. Gretchen sighed and turned back to her grandmother.

"No? Then what did you mean?"

"What you want. From life." Lenore removed the scarf from her head and reached up to pat her lacquered hair, as if she wanted to make sure it was all still there.

"To be happy?" Gretchen ventured. She sipped the coffee, which was not at all bad.

"Well, of course you want that, darling! We all want to be happy. Happy as songbirds, trilling our happy little hearts out. But that's so vague, don't you see? Wanting to be happy." Lenore knotted her ruined fingers tightly and placed them on the table in front of her. "No, you have to decide what it will take to *make* you happy. And then you have to go out and get it."

"It's not that easy, Grandma," Gretchen replied. She had believed that Ennis would make her happy. And now look.

"Who ever said it was?"

Just then the waiter appeared to take their order, so Gretchen had a reprieve. But as soon as he left, Lenore began again.

"Tell me this: are you happy now?"

"Happy about what?" Gretchen knew perfectly well what Lenore meant; she was simply stalling.

"Happy with yourself, your life. What you're doing, where you're going."

"Sometimes, yes."

"And the other times?"

"No one is happy all the time. You know that."

"I know what I know," Lenore said cryptically.

Was Lenore losing it, or could she really tap into what Gretchen was feeling? Because most of the time Gretchen wasn't very happy at all. She was unhappy about her separation from Ennis—not even the soul-rousing, clean break of divorce—and the reek of disappointment and bitterness that trailed along in its wake. She was unhappy about her job, at which was she pedaling in place, and unhappy about her disorderly, decaying house—leaks in both bathrooms, an invasion of ants in the kitchen, and, just last week, the sudden collapse of the deck out back—which seemed a perfect metaphor for her life. And she was perhaps most unhappy about her daughters, who had somehow been turned from two impish, adorable girls into a pair of opaque, critical, and, in the case of Justine, increasingly difficult strangers.

Thinking of Justine was like touching her finger to a hot iron; Gretchen needed to quickly snatch her thoughts away or she would be seared. And while she knew her mother—who was already paying the tuition for the private school the girls attended and had made clear her intention to pay for college as well—would have gladly helped with repairs on the house and even with a maid, Gretchen was aware that allowing her mother's rich husband to subsidize her life would be just one more thing about which she would not be happy. She looked around desperately for the waiter.

"I don't mean to pry," Lenore continued. *Really? You*

could have fooled me, Gretchen thought. "But I'm an old woman and I don't have much time left, so I might as well be blunt. I worry about you."

"I'm sorry I worry you," Gretchen said. It was true. She didn't want to be the cause of anyone's worry; she just wanted to slip under the radar of her family's notice and live her life without hewing to their standards, their expectations, their whole way of seeing the world. Was that so terrible? So she was unhappy. Her unhappiness was hers alone; she was entitled to it. But looking at Lenore's fretful old face, Gretchen softened. "You don't have to worry, Grandma. I'm all right." She tried the words on to see whether she could make them fit. "I was promoted at work; did you know?"

This last comment was a bit of a stretch; Gretchen's professional life was as crammed and disorganized as her suitcase. In school she had studied subjects as wide-ranging as medieval Norse poetry (the fateful class in which she had met Ennis), silent film, Russian literature, and environmental science; she'd had a host of jobs since graduation, but not one of them could have been considered a career.

Ennis had been the artistic one, the one with the calling. Gretchen had been willing—no, eager—to hover around the periphery of his creative flame. If there had been something she wanted for herself, she would have described it this way: she wanted to be of use. This was, she knew, a quaint, old-fashioned concept, especially when compared to the goals of her classmates, who were busy angling for fast-track corporate jobs and admission into the trifecta of professional schools—law, medicine, business—or of Ennis, who sought to add his humble drops to the vast and coursing river of Literature.

Her first job after college was teaching English to a group of well-educated Russian women—pharmacists and chemists, accountants and psychologists—who desperately wanted to be able to work at something other than menial labor in their adopted country. When the grant money that funded the program dried up, it left the Russian women adrift in a confusing sea of unfamiliar conjugations and verb tenses, and Gretchen unemployed. She moved on to a day care center in an impoverished Bronx enclave, but after months of watching the parents—many single women—trying to juggle too many children and too little money, she was nudged in a different direction. Ennis had applied to an MFA program in Syracuse and she followed him there, landing a job in what was euphemistically called a family planning clinic.

It had given Gretchen a quiet, radiant sense of competence to be able to show a nervous teenager how to use a condom (unfurling it over a slender green wand of zucchini while the girl nodded her head in fierce concentration) or to counsel an overburdened mother of five about her options concerning her sixth—accidental—pregnancy. But then the clinic was bombed by a group of fanatic right-to-lifers; the building was severely damaged, and the doctor who performed the abortions had three fingers blown off in the explosion. Most horrific was the fate of a technician Gretchen had especially liked—sixty-three and only months from retirement, the woman had been left legally blind after her corneas were scorched in the blast.

Gretchen could not—would not—go back to such a place. So she was massively relieved when Ennis completed his MFA and was offered the Brooklyn College position. She had taken time off when her girls were babies and toddlers—twins were a major handful, and, besides, she had wanted to be there *with* them, *for* them—and since then none of her jobs had the altruistic aspirations as those of her youth. Thanks to Ennis's many connections, she'd dabbled in the arts: she had been the office manager for an experimental theater company, worked on the set of an indie film and as an assistant at a now-defunct literary magazine.

Her present job had sounded interesting, even exciting, when she first signed on. She had been hired by one Virginia Valentine, a former principal dancer with the New York City Ballet. Ginny, who was now married to a brilliant—and quite wealthy—neurosurgeon, was writing her memoirs, spurred on by the fat six-figure advance she'd received from a very important New York publishing house; it was Gretchen's task to assist her in this undertaking. Ginny was vastly entertaining, and over many wine-fueled dinners, she regaled Gretchen with tales from her storied past. The two of them sat in her dining room, table swathed in raucous red linen, as the maid brought in course after course of rich, delicious food; no wonder Gretchen had been packing on the pounds. It was especially annoying since Ginny, slender as a stick of chewing gum, seemed to be able to down the duck and the veal, the cheeses and the desserts with no apparent effect at all.

Gretchen would both record her subject and take notes as well; later she attempted to turn all this material into a coherent narrative. But Ginny would not leave one single thing to Gretchen's discretion and instead would excise, alter, or curtail Gretchen's every vaguely felicitous turn of phrase, every original thought or word. The project, which had been in the works for more than two years, had yielded exactly eighteen pages thus far, pages so arid, clichéd, and devoid of interest that Gretchen was certain the big important publisher would soon find out, and when he did, he would cancel the contract. Immediately.

Since Gretchen was the only employee and worked out of not an office but the maid's room of Ginny's expansive Riverside Drive apartment, telling her grandmother that she had been promoted was something of a lie, albeit a white one. Still, as long as she was lying, she might as well use the lie again—get her money's worth, so to speak.

Lenore brightened. "Your mother didn't tell me!"

"She's been preoccupied," Gretchen said. "With the wedding." As if that needed clarification.

"That's another thing," Lenore said, quickly seizing on this new topic.

"Angelica is getting married; Teddy has someone, and so does Caleb. But you—you're alone."

"I have Justine and Portia," Gretchen said, stung. "I wouldn't exactly call that alone."

"But you're not living with your husband. And you don't have a boyfriend." She paused. "Do you?"

"No, but there's still time," Gretchen quipped. She reached for a packet of sugar; what if she tore it open and poured the white crystals right down her throat? Or maybe she could tackle the waiter the next time he sped by?

"Not as much as you think," Lenore said; her usual bravado seemed to crumble slightly around its edges. "You'd be surprised how fast it goes."

"I know," Gretchen said, thinking of Justine and Portia's astonishingly rapid transformations from babies to girls and now to perplexingly aloof and self-contained young women. Sometimes she pined for their infant days, difficult though they had been. "I really do know."

"Then *do* something," Lenore implored. "Do something, and don't let it all pass you by."

"Let what pass me by?" Gretchen said, moved despite herself by her grandmother's urgency.

"Everything, darling! Everything!"

Gretchen looked into Lenore's slightly cloudy blue eyes; were those tears, or were her eyes simply watering? Before Gretchen could decide, the harried waiter appeared with breakfast.

"Finally!" Lenore said, releasing her knife and fork from the napkin's cocoon. She looked up at the waiter and batted her lashes in a gesture she must have perfected seventy years earlier. "We thought you'd never get here!"

"Sorry for the delay," he said, setting the plates on the table.

Gretchen tore into her eggs and eagerly mopped the plate with bits of toast. She was so hungry. Even though she would consume a lavish meal tonight, she felt incapable of depriving herself now despite the extra pounds she was toting. She'd even had to buy a new dress, black of course, for the wedding; nothing she owned fit anymore.

Lenore, who had ordered blueberry pancakes, was pouring the syrup into concentric circles on their speckled brown surfaces; she added a pat of butter—softened and fluffy as whipped cream—on top. Unlike Betsy or Angelica, Lenore never included the caloric content of what she—or anyone else—ate in her conversational repertoire.

"Do you want a bite?" Lenore looked up from her plate and held out her fork, on which she had impaled a large and particularly tempting wedge. Gretchen wavered for a moment before leaning forward to accept a mouthful.

"Delicious," she said and felt her annoyance with her grandmother dissolve along with the warm, maple-laced morsel that slid so easily down her throat.

She suddenly remembered a time nearly thirty years ago when Lenore had taken her to Bloomingdale's, where she bought Gretchen a cranberry-colored dress trimmed with a black velveteen collar, and a tiny pot of iridescent pink lip gloss, something Gretchen's mother would not have bought her in a million years. Later there had been grilled cheese sandwiches and chocolate milk shakes in a coffee shop—the shopping bag with its new dress tucked tightly between Gretchen's knees, and the lip gloss in her coat pocket, where it seemed to give off a subtle electric charge. She loved that lip gloss so much that she barely permitted herself to use it. She was so successful that she still had the nearly spent pot, its lid dinged and crazed from its tumultuous life inside her various book bags, backpacks, and handbags, when she went off to college.

So magnanimous did this memory cause Gretchen to feel that she actually let her grandmother drive home, something that would have made Betsy, had she known, crazy. Gretchen sat beside Lenore, whose eyes never left the road. There was little traffic, and Lenore seemed perfectly competent, if a tad prone to speeding, in the driver's seat.

"Slow down," Gretchen told her at one point.

"Slow down?" Faded eyes blazing, Lenore turned to her. "At my age, there's no time to slow down!"

Gretchen almost reached for the wheel, but then the speedometer slipped back a few crucial numbers, and besides, here they were with the car nosing right up to the house like a horse finding its way home.

Ennis had not yet arrived. Good. She needed more time to ready herself. She had not thought to ask whether he was bringing a date, and when the possibility occurred to her, she felt physically sick. But she did not believe Ennis would be so brazen or so cruel, and Gretchen banned the thought from her mind.

Back in the bathroom of her flowered quarters, she took a long, indulgent shower. There were three kinds of body wash, two shampoos, and two conditioners from which to choose. And then—the dreamy white towels. Afterwards she reached for her dress, which she had bought without trying on; those pesky new pounds made any dressing room mirror a small smack to her self-esteem. Pretty risky, but it was black, and although black was hardly the ideal choice for a June wedding, the dress was also stretchy and had looked very forgiving on the hanger.

Her first full-length view of herself was, then, a surprise, though it turned out to be a welcome one. The dress was more than forgiving: it was downright flattering, making her look curvy, not fat. The low-cut neckline highlighted her cleavage—always a strong component of her physical arsenal—and against the black, her skin looked creamy and lush. In this dress she wasn't just some overweight, not even properly divorced loser; in this dress she was a babe, a piece, a cougar. She experimented with a small, predatory snarl in the polished glass.

The unexpected success of the dress started her mind thrumming, her synapses snapping. So what if Ennis would be here? He had no claim on her, none at all. Maybe she would meet someone tonight, here at the wedding in Great Neck. Someone whose identity was as yet unknown to her, but who would have a profound effect on her life. She could almost feel the aura. It might be a guy—wouldn't *that* would be nice? But it might also be a professional contact, someone to whom she might turn for guidance, counsel, advice—or something more concrete, like a new job. A job in which she would be both immersed and engaged, not just spinning her wheels.

Maybe she could parlay her most recent experience with Ginny into something better. An arts organization or some other culturally minded nonprofit? She could see herself in development or PR; she was good at writing grants and at igniting a spark in the hearts and minds of those with money to burn.

Still gazing at her not-at-all-shabby appearance in the mirror, Gretchen coiled her wild mass of hair into a loose topknot. The added height made the line of her neck look longer—a welcome and slenderizing effect. She let her hair go, and it sprung loose from her fingers, as if glad to be free again. Surely that stylist downstairs would have some bobby pins; Gretchen would go downstairs and find out. She'd inquire about having her brows done too. Nothing like a well-waxed pair of eyebrows for facing your future.

And even if she didn't meet someone tonight, Gretchen resolved to start making calls on Monday, putting out some feelers. She knew a few people, and those few might know a few more. She might even sign up for an online dating service, though she had shunned the idea in the past. But her best friend, Shelby—divorced three years this month—had done so and met a sweetheart of a saxophonist, who had been wooing her with intimate weekends at his beach house and his lush, fruity music.

Gretchen thought about what her grandmother had been trying to say earlier. That her approach to her own life was too vague, too diffuse. According to Lenore, she needed to know what she wanted and go after it, like a panther stalking its prey. Like Teddy. And Angelica.

Well, maybe Lenore was right. Maybe Gretchen had been too vague, too soft, too willing to let things happen instead of making them happen herself. Her eyes went once more to the mirror. Was it ridiculous to think that a becoming new dress could signify a change of mind, a change of heart? Gretchen didn't know. But she fully intended to find out.

Four

～ᴥ · ᴥ～

Standing in the crowded Continental arrival lounge at JFK, Lincoln Silverstein bit down on the stale, brick-hard granola bar and cracked his back molar. Blame, like debris from an explosion, shot out in all directions. He blamed the stingy airline for not providing any food, thus driving him, in his ravenous state, to foolishly attempt to eat the year-old granola bar that he found lodged deep in the recesses of his carry-on bag. He blamed Jerry, the tightwad owner of the telemarketing company where he was currently employed, for excising the dental coverage from the already meager insurance plan. Without insurance to help defray the cost of the dentist's visit, Lincoln had studiously ignored an intermittent pulsing in that molar, a pulsing that, it was all too clear now, was a signal of the impending dental calamity that had now befallen him. While he was at it, he blamed the manufacturers of the granola bar—brittle, sugary excuse for food that it was—his ex-wife, Betsy, for divorcing him, and Aaron Schulkind, his best friend throughout grammar and middle school, who had defected to the cool crowd when they reached the ninth grade, leaving Lincoln to eat his dust. Blame, once you got started, was viral: pretty soon it was everywhere.

Gingerly, Lincoln touched his tongue to the cracked tooth; pain shot through his head like a bullet. He pulled his tongue away, and the pain retreated a millimeter or two. Now what? He didn't want to have to deal with this, not when he was on his way to Angelica's wedding. It seemed wrong, selfish even, to complicate the day—*her* day—with his damn tooth.

Lincoln glanced at his cheap Timex watch. Caleb should have been here by now, and Lincoln was getting antsy. But he did not want to call his son, not yet. He viewed this visit like an audition or a job interview: he was going to be judged by a lot of people, most significantly by his children. He didn't want to start out by sounding petulant and whiny, so he'd suck it up and wait for Caleb without complaint.

Lincoln knew that he had screwed up with his kids in so many ways great and small. His son Teddy had told him so more explicitly than the rest of them. But over the past decade Lincoln had put his life back together, piece by excruciating piece: he'd kicked the booze habit, moved out to LA, gotten an apartment, and held a series of jobs, none especially gratifying but still they were jobs. The latest, working for Jerry, had actually offered a glimmer of possibility: it turned out Lincoln was excellent at making the cold calls required for the time-share telemarketing position. With his low-key humor and ability to listen as well as gab, he'd been the top-selling employee four months running, and Jerry was tossing words like "promotion" and "supervisory responsibilities" into their conversations with some frequency.

Lincoln dug through his carry-on bag again, found the bottle of Advil he had hoped was still there, downed two gelcaps dry, and hoped they would kick in soon. If he was careful about what and how he ate, maybe he could get through the wedding without telling anyone about the tooth. It would be his own private triumph, a little gift he could give Angelica without her ever knowing.

Because he was doing this for her, that was the crucial thing. Angelica was getting married and she wanted him to be there. And for his other kids—Teddy and Caleb and Gretchen—he was doing it for them too. He hadn't seen any of them in more than a year now, and no matter what they might think or like to tell each other, he did miss them. And his granddaughters too—Justine and Portia. A year made a huge difference at their age; they'd be grown-up before he knew it.

The rest of the crew—his former wife, Betsy; her new husband in his hot-pink Ralph Lauren sweater (a six-feet-four, three-hundred-plus-pound guy in hot pink? Who knew they even made the damn sweaters, with their damn little ponies dancing across the nipple, so big? That sweater could keep a hippo warm), his erstwhile mother-in-law, Lenore; the friends he'd had from his marriage who'd dropped him like a clod of horse dung when he'd moved out, lost his

job and had to spend those months in rehab—he was not doing this for any of them, so he would put them out of his mind. Zap. Gone.

There would be no other members of Lincoln's family present at the wedding. His parents were long dead, and his brother, Bruce, had died of cancer five years ago this August. In the years he'd been drinking, he'd lost touch with his remaining aunts, uncles, and cousins, and even after he'd stopped, he somehow never reestablished the ties.

His cell phone buzzed. Caleb, no doubt, to say he'd gotten tied up in traffic. Lincoln was glad he had not broken down and called. But when he answered the call, it was not Caleb. It was Angelica, the dream daughter herself. "Hi, Daddy," she almost purred into his ear. Nearly thirty years old, about to be married, and she still called him *Daddy*. Lincoln lapped it up.

"What's up, sweetheart?" he asked, ready as ever to do her bidding.

"I need your help," said Angelica.

"Just tell me where it hurts." Lincoln felt puffed with pleasure. Despite everything, Angelica still felt she could turn to him. Not Betsy, not Don with all his money. Him. *Daddy*.

"It's about Gretchen. You see, Ennis *is* coming after all. And Gretchen is not going to be happy about it."

"That's news," Lincoln said. Which was more neutral than the *uh-oh* that he wanted to say.

"I know. But he called to ask if it would be all right. And Justine and Portia really did want him there. So I

thought in terms of the big picture and hoped Gretchen
would understand."

"But you haven't actually asked her?"

"No," Angelica said. "I haven't."

"You want me to talk to her, then? Smooth it over?"
said Lincoln, assembling all the pieces in his mind.

"Could you? I would, but there's just so much left to do
before tonight. And besides, you know how it is with
Gretchen, Daddy. She's jealous; she always has been. I think
she begrudges me this wedding. Do you know I asked her to
be my matron of honor, and she turned me down?"

"I'm sure she's happy for you," Lincoln lied. He was
sure of no such thing; he had not talked to Gretchen in quite
some time, although he had heard about her refusal to be in
the wedding party. Since both the boys and her daughters
were, her decision seemed, well, strange. He hadn't dis-
cussed it with her, though. "But you can understand how she
feels about Ennis. I mean, he did behave like an asshole."

"I know. Which is why I thought it would help coming
from you. Because you're a man. So do you think you
could?" Her voice was coaxing and soft.

"Of course," Lincoln said. He was a man, all right.
Right now, he was *the* man. "I'll talk to her."

"Thank you, Daddy," Angelica said. "I knew you'd
come through for me."

"Always, sweetheart," Lincoln said. But she had already clicked off. Lincoln stood staring at the cell phone as if
he could summon her back by the force of his gaze. Angelica.
His cupcake, his muffin, his dolly girl. She'd been dazzling

him—and the whole world—with her strategically situated dimples, her thickly fringed dark eyes, her gleaming curtain of black hair since she was a half-pint.

He and Betsy already had a daughter and two sons—Gretchen had been nine, Teddy seven, and Caleb five when Angelica was born—but she was the one who did him in, the one who, with the merest lift of her delicately arched brow, yanked at his heart like it was a big, fat flounder on the line, the one who pierced him with the pooch of her pursed, pink baby lips. He could still remember the hot weight of her pressed against his chest as he'd paced the living room with her in his arms, the velvety feel of her head as it tucked so neatly under his chin, the avian melodies of her gurgling. Gretchen had been solemn and phlegmatic; she soon turned into an oversized, galumphing girl. Teddy was red faced, colicky, and squalling; Caleb was so introverted that they thought for a while he might be autistic. Angelica, however, lived up to her name: she was a dream baby dropped into their lives at just the moment when the marriage had begun to show its first ugly and eventually fatal fissures.

Betsy was already griping about money, and about his drinking, which at that point was hardly out of control, but she was such a puritan that she couldn't let a guy get a little buzz on without huffing and hissing about "dependency" and "enablers"—by the former she meant his nightly beers; by the latter, the drinking buddies with whom he'd liked to kick back a few at the end of a long, dreary, commute-propelled week. Angelica had been an accident but a happy one, and for a while they really thought she was a sign that they were meant to remain together and a family. Whatever his problems with Betsy and with the booze, Lincoln loved his children, loved them in a way that stretched, broke, and entirely remade him. And Angelica he loved most of all.

He put the phone away. She was not going to call back, not now. But he would keep his word and speak to Gretchen. Right away. Now if only Caleb would get here already; Lincoln was mighty tired of waiting.

Just then something shifted in his mouth, and a piece of the tooth broke off; he felt a sharp edge scraping the surface of his tongue. Discreetly he spat the fragment into his palm. How worn and yellowed a bit of bone it seemed. The sight of it made Lincoln want to cry. But of greater concern was the now-jagged edge of broken tooth in his mouth, as well as whatever raw pulp or nerve might be newly revealed. The Advil had blunted the pain, but Lincoln knew the respite would not last long. There were not that many capsules left in the bottle; he'd have to replenish his supply.

Tucking the fragment into his pocket, Lincoln looked around at the milling crowd. JFK was now foreign turf; he had not lived on the East Coast in more than a decade, and he seldom visited. Several times he was jostled by the people hurrying past, and the strap of his carry-on bag—secured the night before with duct tape—broke, so he was forced to tuck it under his arm, which was awkward at best. His only other piece of luggage was the garment bag that contained his tuxedo; he handled the rented garment with slow, exacting care. When he got to the motel, he would steam it out in the shower. Even though the place was sure to be a dump, he had no desire to stay with Betsy, despite the offer. *We've got so much space, after all,* she had said, and he'd thought, *Rub it in a little more, why don't you? And how about adding a little salt too?*

Betsy had finally landed the big kahuna, the one she'd wanted all along, a rich guy who could afford the fancy spread in Great Neck, along with a pair of his-and-hers Mercedes—no kidding, the vanity plates read *His* and *Hers*—as well as maids who washed her delicates by hand and cleaned up after the snappish, noisy little dog that she had acquired. He knew all these particulars from Teddy, who, though not averse to sharing in his stepfather's largesse, nonetheless enjoyed poking fun at the to-the-manor-born pretensions of both his mother and her second husband.

Lincoln cautiously began circling the lounge in case Caleb had come in and he'd not spied him yet. In addition to being in pain, Lincoln was also ravenous, for he'd never actually eaten that granola bar. He badly wanted a coffee but was worried the heat would cause the tooth pain to spike, so he settled for an overpriced corn muffin purchased from a vending machine. In vain he attempted to peel back the film of hermetically sealed plastic as his frustration mounted. Finally he clawed the damn thing open. Once the sticky-surfaced, doughy-centered blob was revealed, he took a big bite, avoiding the side where the broken tooth lay in wait. He looked at his watch—again—and then anxiously scanned the waiting area.

Still no sign of Caleb. He quickly finished the muffin,

which was bland and gummy; when he looked down, he saw a festive sprinkling of crumbs all over the front of his shirt. He brushed them off. The tooth fragment was still in the pocket, and he pulled it out to inspect it more carefully.

It could have been a piece from a 3-D puzzle; the companion piece was in his mouth, still attached to his gum, still a blessed part of flesh and bone—*his* flesh, *his* bone. This broken bit was the future, though, an intimation of what was to come: decay, loss, the inevitable shedding of the mortal skin. He ran a pinky over the fragment one more time before pinging it into the trash. It didn't even make a sound when it hit. Yeah, death awaited him, like it awaited every single other living creature on the planet. But not today, damn it. Today Angelica was getting married. Woo hoo! Now where the *hell* was Caleb? Lincoln was just about to pull out his cell phone when he heard his son's voice—"Dad! Over here!"— hailing him from a few feet away. Finally!

"So sorry I kept you waiting!" Caleb said.

Lincoln's annoyance dissolved as he drank Caleb in. He was deeply, unnaturally tan and wearing an expensive-looking blue-and-white-striped shirt—Lincoln knew he shopped at places like Paul Stuart and Thomas Pink—and a pair of artfully weathered jeans. Keds so white they must have been bleached, no socks, hair slicked back from his high forehead with some kind of gel. Lincoln had once stayed at his Chelsea apartment, and in the small but well-appointed bathroom, with its stack of thick folded towels and glass canister of bergamot-scented soaps, he found enough hair-care products to stock a small salon. Caleb took his appearance very seriously. He always had. His predilection in boyhood for pressed khakis worn with neat leather belts, three-button polo shirts, and argyle sweater-vests had worried Betsy. That and his interest in baking; by the age of eleven, the kid was turning out coconut layer cakes, Key lime tarts, and butterscotch blondies by the panful. But what the hell? If the kid was gay, the kid was gay. Or at least that's the way Lincoln saw it.

"Hey, Dad," Caleb said now, simultaneously smiling at his father and reaching for the bag still wedged uncomfortably under Lincoln's arm. He examined it before tucking it under his own. "Little mishap in transit?"

"The strap broke," Lincoln said, falling into step beside him.

"There's a place in town that repairs shoes and luggage. We could stop."

"Not worth it," said Lincoln.

"How about getting you a new bag?"

"Caleb." Lincoln put a hand on his boy's shoulder. "It's okay. Really."

"If you say so," Caleb said, and smiled again.

When they reached Caleb's car, parked at the far end of the lot, Lincoln stowed his bag in the trunk and laid the garment across the backseat. Then he turned to envelop Caleb in a big, crushing hug. "I missed you," he muttered against Caleb's tightly muscled back. He knew his son was serious about his weight training. "I missed you all."

"Missed you too," Caleb said, gracefully extricating himself from the embrace. Lincoln felt tears—sudden, hot, wholly embarrassing—welling in his eyes. Jesus, it was hours before the wedding was even scheduled to start, he hadn't touched a drop, but here he was, weepy as a five-year-old on his first day of kindergarten. He didn't want Caleb to see him like this, didn't want to burden him with his own rush of feeling. Abruptly he yanked open the car door and slid inside.

"How are things back at the ranch?" he asked, hoping the hale-fellow-well-met tone would mask any lingering traces of emotion. For the twentieth time he ran his tongue over the surface of the broken tooth but resisted sticking his finger in to further the probe.

"Well, let's see," Caleb said, hands on the wheel, not looking at Lincoln. "I haven't seen Angelica; she's been sequestered. But that's all right: Grandma has taken over her role as family diva at least for the day."

"Really?" Lincoln had not seen Betsy's mother, Lenore, in years, but he remembered her self-dramatizing flair quite well.

"Last night she was in a state because Tess Kornblatt and Bunny Epstein won't be there."

"That's old news; Angelica showed her the guest list months ago." Lincoln took advantage of the opportunity to observe his son in profile: the familiar curve of his forehead; the full, almost girlish lower lip; the tiny, blurred scar, a faint reminder of his childhood bout with chicken pox, at the corner of one eye.

"That's what Mom—and Angelica—kept pointing out. But you know Grandma."

Lincoln let that one slide. "So, what else is going on?" he asked brightly. "Work all right?" Caleb was in retail; he had job in the men's department at Barneys. "And weren't you talking about moving? With—with . . . that guy—" Damn, why couldn't he remember the name of his son's new boyfriend?

"Bobby," Caleb supplied. "And, no, we haven't moved yet. We're still looking for a place." He kept his eyes fixed on the road, as if he was intentionally avoiding Lincoln's gaze. "Work's fine." Clearly, it was an afterthought.

"Bobby," Lincoln repeated. "Bobby, Bobby, Bobby."

"That's okay, Dad," said Caleb, finally turning to face Lincoln. "You'll meet him today, actually. He's back at the house now, sound asleep." His expression relaxed into a smile. "I think you'll like him."

"As long as you like him," Lincoln said. "That's what counts."

"I love him," said Caleb. He sounded serious, even grave. "I love him more than I've ever loved anyone in my entire life."

Your entire life? Lincoln wanted to say. *And how long has that been? You're a babe, a pup. A* pisher, *as Lenore would have said. Still wet behind the ears.* Something cautioned him against speaking, though, and he was grateful for the slender thread—Of self-control? Of respect for his son's admission?—that kept him from blurting out that first thing that came into his head.

The car slowed, and Caleb turned in to the entrance to

the motel. It was outside Great Neck proper, and with its gamely planted circle of weed-choked grass, empty, flaking swimming pool, and hideous pus green façade, every bit as seedy and derelict as Lincoln had envisioned.

"This is it," Caleb said. He pulled up in front of a sign that read CHECK IN HERE and parked. "Hey, are you all right?" he asked, swiveling around to look at Lincoln.

"Me? I'm fine," Lincoln lied, though the Advil did not seem to be doing the trick, and he felt the refrain of the earlier pain begin a faint chorus in his mouth.

"You don't look fine," Caleb said. He was staring. "You look kind of gray, in fact. And you're sweating, Dad. There's sweat all over your forehead."

"People sweat," Lincoln said. However dismal the room was going to be, he longed for Caleb to leave so he could be alone in it, alone with his pain.

"I feel kind of bad leaving you here," Caleb said, shifting his gaze from Lincoln to the cruddy motel. "Why don't you let me drive you back to the house? You could stay there—Mom said it was okay."

"No!" Lincoln said, and when Caleb looked taken aback, he tried to soften it. "I just wouldn't be comfortable staying there. But I appreciate your concern."

"Dad, I don't think you're making a good choice, and I am not leaving you here." Caleb leaned back in his seat and crossed his arms over his chest. "Either I take you to Mom's, so I can keep an eye on you, or to a doctor. Your call."

Lincoln debated whether to tell Caleb the truth and

finally decided it would be easier than continuing this stand-off. "It's not a doctor I need," he said. "It's a dentist. Only I'll wait until I get back to the West Coast to see one."

"You have a toothache?"

"I have the mother of all toothaches," Lincoln said. "I was ambushed by a stale granola bar, and I broke a molar."

"Ouch," Caleb said. "That must hurt. But we can find you a dentist; Mom must know someone who'll squeeze you in for an emergency visit."

"I'll be all right," Lincoln said. "I've got Advil."

"Dad, you broke your tooth and you look terrible. Why don't you want to see a dentist? It's no big deal; I'll drive you."

"No dentists, no driving," Lincoln said firmly. Now that the cat was out of the bag, he was free to dig around in his bag and pop another couple of Advil. So what if he'd taken the last ones only an hour or so earlier. Clearly he needed reinforcements.

"You take those things dry?" Caleb said. "Jesus." He shook his head. "Anyway, why are you being so stubborn? I don't get it."

"Because this is Angelica's day, and I don't want to add any, and I mean *any,* stress to what is already a very stressed-out situation."

"Ah—so this is about Angelica the princess," Caleb said. He uncrossed his arms and raked his fingers through his hair. "What else is new?"

"What is that supposed to mean?" Lincoln said. The car was hot and stuffy, but he made no move to get out; he did not want to bring Caleb into the motel room.

"Just that some things never change. Angelica was always your favorite."

"Not true," Lincoln said, though of course it was, it was. But he thought he had hidden it better. Wrong, wrong, wrong.

"Dad, who are you trying to kid? Of course she was your favorite. She still is."

"I love all of you," Lincoln said. God, he was practically croaking. "Very much." Guilt snaked through the pain, lacing in and out of it like a braid. Had he really been so transparent, so obvious? *Everyone knows everything all the time*, his mother had been fond of saying. Well, it looked like she had been right.

"I know you do," Caleb said and leaned over to give Lincoln a kiss on his clammy, ashen cheek. "Only you love her more." He started the car up again. "Why don't you go and lie down for a while?" he added kindly.

"Will I see you before the wedding?" Lincoln said, confused but moved by the sequence of events these past few minutes: the accusation followed by the unexpected gentleness.

"Of course. I'll check in with you later," Caleb said.

Lincoln nodded. Clutching his meager baggage, he got out of the car. The broken tooth throbbed, almost musical in its iteration of pain. Watching Caleb as he pulled away, Lincoln remained where he stood long after the car had disappeared down the road.

Five

❧ • ❧

A wedding in Great Neck, fumed Justine. *A Great Neck wedding. Nuptials in the Neck. The bride wore green.* Justine imagined many thousand-dollar bills pasted to the had-to-have-cost-a-fortune wedding gown that no one, not the bride's mother, not her stepfather—who had paid for the damn thing—not her husband-to-be had been allowed to see. How predictable, how lame, how wasteful. And to think it was her aunt Angelica—formerly so hip, so cool, so smart—who had not only consented to but was actively embracing this whole over-the-top, show-offy business. Justine was awash in righteous revulsion. She'd agreed to be in the wedding party only because Portia had pitched a small fit when she had expressed her disgust at the idea.

Yesterday when they had arrived, Don, Grandma Betsy's husband, had insisted on going into town for a walk along the main drag. In one shopwindow Justine saw watches so big they must have weighed half a pound, their bulbous faces crammed with so many dials, needles, and numbers that telling the time would be impossible. In another window was a monstrous choker with a cluster of jewels the size of a golf ball in the center; a third featured a leather-trimmed canvas tote that cost 945 dollars; the price tag looped around the handle faced outward, toward the street.

She turned away, disgusted. Had she a rock, she would have pitched it through the glass. Her own clothes were gleaned from stores like the Salvation Army or Goodwill. She told Don she wasn't feeling well—not a lie, actually—and so was able to beg off the trip to Häagen-Dazs in favor of driving right back to the house.

Justine looked over at Portia, who was still asleep in the room that they had shared last night. With its massive television screen and series of serpentine leather couches (several of which opened into beds), it seemed like the perfect place to stage an orgy: just dim the lights and break out the Ecstasy. But Justine highly doubted that the room had ever been put to that particular purpose. Her grandmother, Betsy, and her husband were way too old. And it was clear her grandmother was more besotted with her dopey dog than with any being possessing a mere two legs.

Justine wandered into the bathroom and back out again. Portia slumbered on. Ordinarily Justine would have woken her twin, and together they would have found a way to make this day bearable. But right now Justine was actually glad of the time alone. She had a few things she had to work out before the wedding of the century unfolded tonight, and for once she was not letting Portia in on her plans.

This was a departure from form, and a radical one. Portia had always been her partner in everything. When they were little, they had their own language, which they called *twinspeak*. It had driven everyone within earshot crazy—much to their mutual delight. More recently they had had to deal with their parents' stupid and messy separation, and try not to take sides, which was pretty impossible. They pooled their intellectual resources to do their schoolwork (Portia was better in math and science, while Justine was the literature/history/politics maven) and they resolutely defended each other against mean girls, bumbling administrators, boring teachers, jerk-off guys—in short, the world as they knew it.

But lately Justine had felt subtle tremors, the sort of occurrences that might signal an earthquake or a tsunami, beneath the tectonic plates of her bond with Portia—this was exactly the sort of metaphor Portia would have employed. Justine could not really put a name to it; every time she tried to analyze it—What exactly were signposts of the change? What between them was actually different?—she failed.

Maybe the problem was not Portia at all, but Justine herself. She was the one who had changed. That was the nasty little secret she'd been trying to push away or ignore. Lately she had been prone to these—What to call them? Moods? Trances?—that descended on her out of nowhere. She was powerless to predict when they would arrive or with what intensity, but when they came, they ruled. The *dread reds* made her seethe with a low-level but deadly kind of anger: at her parents, at her circle of friends and their petty concerns, at her teachers, who encouraged their asinine ruminations. If, in the throes of this thing, she could have banished them all permanently with a blink to some unseen parallel universe, she would have done it.

Then there were the *moody blues*, when the smallest thing—a news account of someone shot and killed in a holdup, the sight of a dead pigeon in the street—could make her eyes flood and her chest heave with hiccupy sobs so that she could not catch her breath; she'd have to curl up alone in the dark (light was intolerable when she felt like this) until the sensation passed. The *mean greens* were similar though not identical to the dread reds; when she was in the grip of them, she was compelled to commit small, spiteful deeds, ones that she hoped would go unnoticed. She'd yank a button off a coat that someone at school had left hanging over a chair; she'd steal something dumb, something she didn't even want—dental floss, a gross wad of beef jerky—from a store as her pulse roared in her ears at the possibility of being caught. Afterwards she'd feel sick with shame, which in no way prevented her from doing it again when the urge seized her.

She looked over at Portia, still sleeping, oblivious to her sister's turmoil, and she felt simultaneously furious and bereft. Better to get out of here now, before she was tempted to wake Portia and tell her everything after all.

Justine emerged from the media room and went quietly up the stairs. She could hear the activity coming from the kitchen. They had all been instructed to take their breakfast in the breakfast room, where food would be laid out for them, but Justine wanted to do a little scouting around first.

A television—tuned in to a weather channel—was announcing the possibility of a thundershower this afternoon. Could she detect the sound of someone—her grandmother, possibly—moaning, or was she imagining this? There was a tent, of course; two tents, in fact—one for the ceremony, the other for the dinner. Justine had heard all about them, with their laminate flooring, chandeliers, and cathedral-style "windows," several times. But she got the feeling that, even with the tents, Angelica would consider it a personal affront from God if the sky opened and it poured on her wedding day.

Neatly skirting the activity, Justine continued up the stairs to the second floor. The hallway was wide and long, and the floor covered in a deep, plush carpet that did feel nice on her bare toes. The carpet, chosen by her grandmother, Betsy, no doubt, made her feel guilty. Grandma B. was not a bad person; she was amazingly generous to Justine, Portia, and plenty of other people besides. Justine was fully aware that what she planned to do today was going to hurt Grandma Betsy. But knowing this did not change anything; she was going to do it anyway. Collateral damage, isn't that what they called it?

The way Justine saw it, she was rescuing Angelica from marriage to a man who was an oppressor, a colonizer, and even a murderer. Angelica was too blinded—by love, by lust—to see him for what he was, but Justine was not. So it was up to her to unmask him and show Angelica—along with everyone else—just what kind of a person he really was. No one would thank her for it—not immediately, anyway.

But years from now Angelica—and everyone else—would see that Justine had been a hero, the only one in the family with the vision to see the truth and the courage to do something about it.

Once in the hallway Justine was faced with a number of doors, all of them closed. Now, this was a problem. She knew her mother was sleeping up here, along with Angelica, her grandmother, her uncles and their various partners, and Great-grandma Lenore, with her constant talk of boobs and whose bra did or did not fit correctly. But Justine didn't know who was in which room, and it was essential that she find out; could she hang around and wait to see who emerged?

Ohad, Aunt Angelica's fiancé, wasn't even staying in the house; he and his large, noisy Israeli family—the dark-skinned, black-haired mother, siblings, aunts, uncles, and cousins—were all checked in at a nearby hotel. So it wasn't even clear to Justine what she was doing; she wanted to find Ohad, and she wanted him to be alone. It wasn't likely that either of those aims were about to be accomplished by prowling around up here.

Still she crept along like the inept spy that she was, staring at the doors. There were voices coming from behind one of them; she pressed her ear to the wooden panel to listen. The words were not clear, but she thought she could hear her uncle Teddy. Major douche bag. Also pompous, status obsessed, and self-important. Last night at the rehearsal dinner, he must have asked her three times where she planned to go to college.

"I've just finished my sophomore year; I have a little while to decide," she had answered.

"Not all that much," he shot back. "You'd be amazed at how the time flies."

"Would I?" she said. She raised her left eyebrow, the one with the piercing in it. She could tell that this piercing, even more than the stud in her nostril, offended him deeply, and from this she derived a rich and enveloping sense of satisfaction. "I'm not so sure."

"Well, you should be," he said. "Getting into college is the whole point of high school. And not just any college—the *right* college."

"Really?" she asked with feigned innocence. "I thought the point of high school was to get an education." In fact Justine was quietly obsessed with the topic of college in general, and the *right college* in particular. She was maniacal in her quest for good grades and spent most of her allowance on scoring Adderall—the cheery yellow 30-milligram capsules were the most coveted of the lot—which enabled her to study with a magnificent and single-minded ferocity. When she was deep in the A-zone, her mind became a highly powered leaf blower whose roaring blasts sent all extraneous thoughts scattering; she could hunker down and work for hours without a break. But she had no desire to share any of this with her uncle Teddy, who had clearly decided that she was not worth another nanosecond more of his precious energy and moved off in search of someone else to badger.

Justine pressed her ear closer to the door. Yeah, that was Teddy in there, all right. Teddy had gone to Dartmouth as an undergraduate, and he managed to twist and stretch virtually every conversation to include this fact. What if she told him that these days Dartmouth was considered the bottom of the Ivy barrel, filled with dumb-ass frat boys who probably had sex with cows in their downtime? Justine had set her own sights on Yale.

She continued along the hall. At the far end was her grandmother's room; she knew that, but even if she hadn't, the sound of the dog—it had started barking *again*—would have clued her in. So she had eliminated two of the possibilities. Then it occurred to her that she could simply knock on the doors or, if no one answered, go in. She could say that she was looking for her mother. Why had she not thought of this sooner? She rapped on the next door she came to.

"Come in," quavered a voice she recognized as belonging to her great-grandmother, Lenore. Justine opened the door a crack and peeked inside. "I said to come in," Lenore said. She was standing next to a complicated-looking steaming device planted in the center of the room; she wore something flowing and gauzy that involved leopard print and lots of it. Shiny buttons winked their way down the front. With both hands, Lenore directed the nozzle at an olive-green dress. "Ow!" she added. "That's hot."

"Are you okay?" Justine asked. Maybe Grandma Lenore shouldn't be handling the steamer by herself.

"I'm fine," Lenore said, sucking on her finger. "Don't you worry about me."

"I was looking for my mom," Justine said, though Lenore had not asked.

"Other direction," Lenore said. "Down the hall."

"Thanks," Justine said, feeling awkward. "Thanks a lot."

Lenore looked up at her as if only just realizing who she was. "What bra are you wearing?" she asked. "To the wedding?"

"I don't know. Just a bra." Grandma L. truly was obsessed by the topic of other people's underwear.

"The dress is shantung, right? And very fitted?"

"I guess," said Justine. She didn't know what shantung was, though she actually liked the dress Angelica had chosen, which was dove-gray and had a silvery sheen in the light. But she disapproved of it on principle. Meant to be worn once and then never again, it offended both Justine's sensibilities and her morals.

"You have to have the right bra, sweetheart. You can't just wear any bra under a dress like that. You need something with shape but smooth too. No seams in front. No little bows." She put down the steamer's nozzle and used her gnarled hands to gesture across her breasts.

"I have the right bra. You don't have to worry." Justine smiled. Grandma Lenore was doing fine. Just fine. She turned to leave the room.

"Well, I hope so!" Grandma Lenore said, frowning slightly. "Your whole look can be spoiled by the wrong bra." She appeared to be thinking and then added, "Sweetheart, there'll be a couple of girls here later who'll be doing hair and makeup; you'll go see them, right?"

"Definitely," said Justine, though she had no intention

of going anywhere near either of them: she didn't wear makeup, period, and she would not allow her hair to be sprayed, moussed, gelled, or fluffed by a stranger with a possibly lethal pair of scissors in her hand.

"And Portia too?" Lenore had resumed her steaming.

"Portia too." She glanced again in the direction of the steamer. "Nice dress, Grandma Lenore," she added.

"Isn't it?" Lenore said, turning to gaze at it as well. "And it has a matching coat." She gestured to a garment that was spread across the bed. "Do you know how long I've had that outfit? Thirty-five—no, forty years. I bought it at Loehmann's, just off Flatbush Avenue. Those were the days . . . not like now." The comparison made her frown, but then her expression softened. "Anyway, this dress is quality goods. And quality lasts." Lenore nodded for emphasis; her head on her delicate neck seemed to wobble even after she had stopped.

"Sweet," said Justine. She was definitely good with the idea of wearing old clothes rather than depleting the poor earth's waning resources by buying new, new, new all the time. She blew a kiss to Lenore and closed the door softly behind her.

There was no answer at the next door, so Justine very quietly tried the knob. The room was empty. Right away she knew she had found the place she had been seeking. The closet door was flung wide-open, and the few articles of clothing it contained were shoved together on one side. There, encased in an enormous black plastic garment bag, was what could only be Angelica's wedding dress.

Score. Because she had found Angelica's room, and wherever Angelica was, Ohad was sure to follow. Those two couldn't keep their hands off each other; it was like one of those parties where the parents were out, the lights were low, and a bunch of kids coupled off, sucking face and God knew what else. Not that she, Justine, was against sex—although she hadn't actually *had* it yet; this was all in theory—but she thought there ought to be some mystery to the whole business, some magic. Not this public groping for anyone and everyone to watch.

Justine approached the closet; should she unzip the bag and peek? Angelica would be upset if she found out. No one was supposed to see the dress until the wedding. But, then again, if everything went according to plan, there wasn't actually going to *be* a wedding. Justine stood there, hand on the zipper, for several seconds. Finally she backed away. She didn't want to violate—there, that was a good word, an SAT-worthy word—Angelica's wishes. She just wanted to save her from making what was the worst mistake of her life. And she knew just how to do it too.

She would find Ohad. And she would seduce him. Oh, not for real, of course. There was no way she would have sex with him. She just had to make it *look* like he was coming on to her and that they were about to have sex. She would have to get him to take his shirt off, to kiss her or something. Her shirt would have to be off too. She had gone back and forth about this a hundred times and decided that much as she disliked the idea, she would have to do it anyway. Both of them shirtless would make the evidence—the picture she planned to take with her cell phone—that much more incriminating. All she would need to do was to show that picture to Angelica, and then, shalom, Ohad. The wedding would be off, and he could go back to bombing Palestinian children or whatever it was that he had been doing before he came here. He would deny it, of course. But it would just be his word against hers. Hers and the picture. The picture would tell the whole story.

Sitting down on the bed, Justine felt a flash of fear. More than two hundred people were coming here today to see Angelica get married. Then there was her family; her great-grandma, Lenore; and Betsy. Her grandfather was coming too; her mom had told her that he was flying in from LA. They would all be hugely, monumentally disappointed. And what about Angelica herself? She was going to be crushed when she found out about Ohad. Her heart would be broken, and Justine would be the cause of her misery.

Abruptly Justine got up. She wouldn't look at the dress, but she couldn't resist what seemed like an innocent bit of snooping. It wasn't snooping anyway. It was worship, pure and simple. She and Portia had always adored Angelica; yes, she was their aunt, but since she was only thirteen years their senior, she really seemed more like some exotic older cousin or even a glamorous sister than anything else.

Pulling open a drawer, Justine saw a jumble of underwear. She dipped her hand in and pulled out a peach thong, which she looped over her thumb. Well, thongs were hot; why shouldn't Angelica wear one? More searching revealed a matching bra as well as a ribbed silk tank top with a tiny rosette at the neckline, and a long satin nightgown in the most beautiful shade of chocolate brown. Now, who but Angelica would think to have a brown nightgown? So much more interesting and less predictable than black. Justine held it up, admiring it, before carefully folding it and placing it back inside the drawer.

When Justine and Portia were little, Angelica would swoop down from college in Cambridge and later from medical school for the weekend, and take them to the kinds of places for which their parents never seemed to have the time or energy. They went downtown to see a collection of amazing, intricately wrought eggs made by this guy named Fabergé. Justine still remembered the gold and the pearls, the jewels and the glossy enameled surfaces. She took them to a place in Soho where they got to make their own paper from recycled rags. They had dim sum in Chinatown, frozen hot chocolate at Serendipity, pizza at V&T on 110th Street and Amsterdam Avenue. They went to Shakespeare in the Park, and rock concerts at outdoor plazas in Midtown. She took them Rollerblading along the Hudson River, to Coney Island, and to a stable out in Queens where they got to ride their horses along the beach. She talked nonstop, asked them a million questions, and really listened to the answers, infected everyone around her with her particular energized glow.

She and Portia had only to hear the words *Angelica is coming*, and they would break out into what they called their *happy dance*, which consisted of chasing each other around the house in a wild syncopated gait accompanied by lots of whistles and hollering. Their mother, overwhelmed, would go into her bedroom and shut the door until they had worn themselves out.

Angelica was just beginning her career as a gynecologist and obstetrician. "Women's health is one of the most pressing concerns of our collective medical future," she told Justine, who had just sat there, wide-eyed. "And delivering babies—what more joyful work could there be on earth?" She went on to describe the births at which she had assisted: the baby born to a mother with a gunshot wound to her abdomen, or the one who was blue and still, the cord wrapped around the tiny neck, or another so small as to fit in the palm of your hand. And she, Angelica, was part of the miracle that extracted the baby safely from the mother who had been shot, who breathed the air back into the lungs of the baby who was still and blue, who quickly whisked the preemie to the neonatal unit where it would be fed and warmed to have a chance at life, the life that she, Angelica, had helped usher into the world. Who could not love her?

Justine closed the drawer. She picked up a bottle of perfume—it was from Chanel and had the intriguing name of Cristalle Eau Verte—sniffed and set it back down again. There was a cosmetic bag, partially open, sitting next to the perfume, and although she knew she shouldn't, Justine peeped inside. Mascara, a trio of eye shadows, several lipsticks, pressed powder in a midnight-blue compact. Even though she kept her own face pure of makeup, all this stuff was perfectly familiar to her: it could have been the property of anyone in her grade at school or even Portia, who had lately taken to wearing goop on her eyelids and something slick and repellent on her lips. Then Justine saw the round blister pack of pills and knew immediately what they were.

Her heart started beating more quickly. She picked up the birth control pills and examined them closely—not that she hadn't seen similar packages, either brought in by the school nurse and passed around during sex ed class or flashed by some precocious classmate in the girls' bathroom. But those anonymous rectangles or rings carried no weight, no meaning, and were utterly unlike the package of pills—four were already missing—actually used by her aunt. Her heart sped up even more, and Justine felt a little queasy. Now, *that* was dumb. Angelica was a grown-up. Of course she was having sex with Ohad. But knowing this in the abstract and seeing the intimate, indisputable proof were light-years apart.

Large grayish spots quivered in front of Justine's eyes; a headache instantly bloomed, causing her left temple to throb horribly. She was having an attack of the mean greens. Right here, right now. That was the only explanation for this behavior and the grip of her compulsion. She adored Angelica; rummaging through her things was not only crazy; it was despicable. Despicable, yes. Another good SAT word. Justine let go of the package. It fell to the floor, and after she had retrieved it from under the dresser, she put it back where she had found it. She had to get out of here—immediately.

But before she could escape, her attention was snared by a tangle of jewelry that sat in an open leather case. Here was the heart-shaped locket Angelica always wore, and her braided gold chain, and her charm bracelet. How Justine had loved that charm bracelet when she was little; Angelica told her it had been a gift from Grandma Lenore, who had worn it when she was young.

Why was all this stuff sitting here? Then Justine remembered: last night, after the dinner, Angelica had gone to a local spa for something called a brown sugar scrub and a facial; she had invited Justine and Portia to join her. Portia had gone, but Justine said no. Not that she hadn't wanted to spend time with Angelica. But not if it involved the idea of allowing a stranger to slather nasty brown sludge all over her body. Anyway, Angelica must have taken off all her jewelry and not put it back on yet.

There, at the center of the case, winked a diamond ring. Not just any diamond ring either; it was Angelica's engagement ring, which had been shown to and admired by all the women in the family. All except Justine, who thought that the mining of diamonds was a *truly* despicable act, even worse than snooping through someone's stuff. As far as she was concerned, the glittering stone might as well have been dipped in blood. The mean greens were not over, no; they were just hitting their full stride. Justine's hand, an appendage not governed by her rational mind or will, reached over to pluck the ring from its nest. She held it for a moment, felt its cold, hard weight, before she tucked it into the pocket of her denim shorts.

Pumped by the audacity of the act, she sped to the door, but before she could seize the knob, it flew open, and there stood Angelica. She was dressed in a pair of ancient, faded jeans and an oversized white linen shirt with the sleeves rolled up; the latter must have belonged to Ohad. At the base of her white throat was a tantalizingly crude hunk of turquoise that hung suspended from a smooth black cord. She looked the way she always looked: perfect.

"Justine, baby!" Angelica said. "What are you doing in here?" Mute with remorse, Justine opened her mouth and then closed it. She was horribly aware of the ring jammed into her pocket; she could almost believe it would start to beep or squawk or something. She wanted—oh, oh, how badly she wanted!—to put it back, but obviously she couldn't do that now.

Angelica, however, seemed oblivious to her distress. Without waiting for a reply, she breezed by her niece into the room, depositing a quick peck on Justine's flaming cheek as she passed.

Six

Reaching for her reading glasses—their cherry-red frames the exact color of a Charms lollipop—Betsy consulted her master list for the tenth time that morning. Pippa Morganstern, the wedding planner, was due at the house any minute, but that didn't lighten Betsy's load, not one single bit. She dreaded Pippa's arrival and could not fathom why Angelica had ever hired her. Surely there was someone else she could have chosen. But, no, it was Pippa and only Pippa who would do, and Betsy had been Angelica's mother long enough to know that what her daughter wanted, she almost invariably found a way to get.

Betsy despised every single thing about Pippa, from her cloying singsong voice to her obnoxiously officious manner and her name, which, coupled with the woman's emphatic Brooklyn accent, seemed insufferably pretentious. Pippa. True, the new Princess of Wales had a sister with that name. But she was British, after all. Not some phony putting on airs.

Pippa thought that she and only she was capable of

making any informed decision about this wedding and that
Betsy's input was superfluous at best, an impediment at
worst. It was a new experience in humiliation for Betsy, who
prided herself on her competence, and she was privately
smarting about the fact that her daughter had chosen to in-
flict it on her.

The front doorbell chimed, and Carmelita went to answer it. "Morning, morning, morning!" trilled Pippa. Betsy's
jaw clenched. *Here it comes*, she thought. *Here we go.*

"Good morning, Pippa," she said, striding into the
foyer and willing her expression into some tolerable facsim-
ile of a smile. "I have my list right here."

"Oh, that!" Pippa said with a dismissive flick of her
wrist. She was a small woman, but with her upswept hair,
four-inch heels, and enormous bust, she seemed larger, more
menacing. Betsy thought she resembled a puff adder, inflat-
ing herself to scare her enemies. And she was sure that Pippa
was not wearing the correct bra to contain her ample assets;
she was surprised that Lenore had not told her so yet, but,
then again, the day was still young.

Pippa approached Betsy and made a kissing gesture
somewhere in the vicinity of Betsy's face. "I'm sure your lists
are very useful to *you*, but I have all the information we need
right here." She tapped on the iPad she was clutching. "I've
got the master list on this baby."

"Fine," said Betsy, determined not to start an argument, not today of all days. "May I see it?" Never mind that
she had a master list of her own; she would be cooperative, a
team player.

"Well, actually, I wanted to go over a few things with the bride herself," Pippa said. "Is she around?"

"She's upstairs," Betsy said. "But I'm sure I can have a look."

"Now, Betsy, you know that there are some things that are just too *important* to *delegate*, even to your mother! Let me just give her a little ringy-dingy and see if she has a minute for me." Out came her iPhone.

Ringy-dingy, thought Betsy, taking deep, calming mouthfuls of the surrounding air to keep from screaming. Why was she even having a conversation with a person who thought *ringy-dingy* was an acceptable substitute for *phone call*?

"Angelica?" Pippa said conspiratorially into the phone. "I've just gotten here, and I wanted to touch base with you." There was a pause while she listened to the response. "Uh-huh, uh-huh." She screwed up her face into a parody of concentration. "Got it. I'll be right there." Powering off, she shot a look—was it really triumphant, or did Betsy's loathing cause her to interpret it this way?—in Betsy's direction. "I'll just be a jiff," she said. "Is there something you can take care of until we need you?"

Something she could take care of until they needed her? How about dealing with the caterer, ensconcing the hair and makeup girls in the den downstairs, and finding a private spot for the final fitting of Angelica's dress? Or dealing with the florist, who would be here any minute, the two bridesmaids who had just arrived at the station, and the photographer? Did any of those things count *at all*? How was it that this interloper had managed to usurp Betsy's authority and make her feel unwanted and peripheral right in her very own home?

I am not going to make a scene. I am not going to make a scene, Betsy chanted to herself. Instead she thought of her daughter, resplendent in a dress that even she had not been shown, and she tried to be calm. Angelica was getting married today, and all would be well. She firmly turned her mind to the things she could do: check the weather *again* to see whether that afternoon shower that had been predicted was still in the forecast, and ask Carmelita to make up another bed, this one in the small study off the media room downstairs; Gretchen's husband, Ennis, was going to be joining them after all, and he would need a place to sleep.

Betsy looked down at the list that Pippa hadn't even deigned to glance at. *I am not going to make a scene.* There. It was working. Sort of. So Pippa had demoted her. That didn't mean she wasn't useful, that her help was not necessary. Betsy had always been a list maker and knew the value of lists within lists—sublists and sub-sublists that broke the world and its staggering array of tasks into manageable bite-sized bits. For a project of this magnitude, Betsy knew she needed one master list with at least six sublists, all of which she kept track of in her yellow spiral-bound notebook, completely ignoring the expensive, exasperating iPad with which Don had presented her—elaborately wrapped and beribboned—on her last birthday. Exactly the sort of iPad that Pippa had and had just used to insult Betsy.

"What color sheets, Mrs. Betsy?" Carmelita asked, when Betsy mentioned the bed.

"What do we have down there?" Betsy asked. "Ivory? Light blue? Whatever you think works will be fine," she said and then checked the item that said *Carmelita, bed* off her list. Even if Pippa had no use for her, checking off an item still gave Betsy a sense of accomplishment and satisfaction.

Upstairs the dog barked. Betsy momentarily considered asking the maid to bring her downstairs but remembered that the dog often snarled at poor Carmelita, so she decided to go up instead. She was perfectly aware that no one in her family could stand the creature and that they made fun of her—an aging empty nester besotted with a small, spoiled dog—quite openly. But Betsy did not care. After years of forbidding pets of all kinds—she had categorically said no to kittens, puppies, rabbits, hamsters, snakes, mice, and even goldfish—she felt as if she had been born again, and now found her heart overflowing with love for this diminutive creature who adored her to the exclusion of every other being on earth.

Betsy mounted the stairs quickly. She was in excellent shape: five feet five, 122 pounds, and a perfect size four. She watched every morsel of food that passed from fork to lips, adhered to a routine that included regular sessions with a trainer, laps in the pool, and weekly tennis games or long, brisk walks with her little coterie of friends. She might not be young, but she could certainly stay trim.

Angelica understood the importance of this kind of

self-discipline, but Gretchen unfortunately did not. Betsy had noticed with some mild disapproval that her older daughter had put on some weight recently. Not that she was going to *say* anything about it, but it did concern her. She'd seen the way Gretchen had eaten at the rehearsal dinner last night: diving into the bread basket, slathering butter on every bite. Two helpings of the pasta; an indecent mound of whipped cream on the peach pie. It was clear she was not even trying to control herself.

It was a pity too, because Gretchen was an attractive woman. Not a beauty like Angelica, true. But she was impressively, majestically tall (almost six feet; where in the recesses of the gene pool had *that* been hiding?) and with her mass of dark, curly hair (Betsy did wish she would let someone shape it, even just a bit) and her white skin—both of her daughters had inherited her mother's creamy skin, which had, alas, skipped Betsy entirely—she had a real presence, if only she would stand up and claim it.

The dog was on the king-sized bed Betsy shared with Don—sprawled on her back, thumping the mattress with her hind paw in a soft, but insistent rhythm. The taut pink belly, the exposed throat, the look of utter bliss that seemed to descend slowly over her canine features when Betsy began to stroke her—all these things knotted the cord of love and attachment to the animal even more tightly.

"Who's my girl?" she said softly. "Who's my puppy?" The dog's ears flattened, and her mouth opened slightly, revealing the tip of her long pink tongue and her sharp, dainty teeth—teeth that had never, ever been used or even shown in aggression towards Betsy. So what if her children thought she was a doting fool? Betsy was happy with the dog, just like she was happy with just about everything else in her present life. And the kids were filled with plenty of scorn for that too.

When Betsy and Lincoln were young, Great Neck was a place to which Betsy had longingly aspired. The beautifully tended homes, the lovely leafy streets, the excellent school system. East Meadow had always felt to her like the poor relation and never quite measured up. She projected the various dissatisfactions of her marriage onto the external grid of the place, and the phrase *if we lived in Great Neck*...was a familiar refrain in her mind. If they had lived in Great Neck, they wouldn't be scrambling for the money to buy a new washer/dryer or to have Teddy's woefully misaligned teeth straightened. If they lived in Great Neck, Angelica could be in the honors program and take four years of Latin, Gretchen would hang out with a better crowd, Caleb might have found that he enjoyed sports after all. If they lived in Great Neck, they would have a pool, belong to a tennis club, mingle with an altogether more interesting, more successful group of people. Lincoln wouldn't need to drink; Betsy wouldn't need to be so bitter.

This was pure fantasy, she knew, and yet she had stubbornly clung to it. So when she learned that Don's house was in Great Neck, on the coveted Swan's Cove Road, no less, some atavistic flame had leapt up in her heart. Even if the Great Neck of today, filled as it was with Iranian Jews, was a different place than the Great Neck of her youth, it didn't matter to Betsy. The life she lived here was closely enough allied with her fantasies, and she felt as if she had at long last arrived.

Her children either didn't know or didn't care about any of this. They teased her about Don's house, the pool, the maids, and the posh, pampered world that she had suddenly entered, like Alice, as if she had gone through the looking glass. She knew too how snide they could be; she'd heard the little asides, the faintly hostile observations. Heard them all and didn't care, because Betsy loved, loved, *loved* money and loved the untrammeled freedom it permitted her. The breast cancer and AIDS research she regularly—and generously—contributed to? Funded by money. The repaired cleft palates in Ecuador and the literacy programs in those grim neighborhoods in Queens and Brooklyn? Money made those possible too.

That old adage about money not buying happiness? Dead wrong. Money did buy happiness, just like it bought comfort, security, and ease; money was love; yes, it most certainly was. And Betsy was intent on spreading the love—along with the money that intoned its name—around liberally.

Did her scoffing children know, for instance, that Don had put both Carmelita and Esperanza on the pension and health insurance plans of his company? Or that she was making sure both women got their GEDs and hosting study sessions in her kitchen on the weekends? And that she paid for Esperanza's daughter's new flute and soccer camp for Carmelita's two boys? Then there was private school for Justine and Portia, and the repairs to Gretchen's house she would have happily funded had not her daughter been so stubborn in her refusal. When Teddy needed money to start his new business or Angelica needed help with her lavish wedding, it was Betsy's well-manicured hand with its platinum and diamond eternity band that wrote the checks.

Just last week she had met Caleb for their monthly lunch at Bergdorf, just a short distance from Barneys, where he worked. The restaurant on the top floor overlooking Central Park was sparkling and airy, opening onto the city like a little jewel case; it was their favorite spot, and their lunches always had a festive quality. But as Betsy nibbled at her Cobb salad and sipped her iced tea, she noticed that Caleb seemed glum; he barely touched his seared scallops and was oddly silent, not offering her any of the little work-related tidbits that were often the staple of their conversations.

"Are you all right?" Betsy ventured after he had declined the waiter's offer of dessert. "Things with Bobby okay?"

"Bobby's great," he said, his whole face brightening. "But there is something else. . . ." He lowered his voice and leaned in closer. "I'm just not very happy at work, Mom." Then the full story tumbled out: the promotion he'd been hoping to get that did not materialize, the frustration with his present position, his increasing boredom.

"Could you look for another job?" she asked. "At a different store?"

"More of the same," Caleb said. He speared a scallop, no doubt stone cold by now. "The thing is, I want to leave retail entirely."

Betsy, well schooled in conversations with adult off-spring, said nothing but took what she hoped was a contemplative sip of her tea and waited.

"I want to go to cooking school," he announced and then guiltily looked around the room, as if someone he knew from work might have been listening. "To become a pastry chef."

Betsy remembered the period of intense baking when Caleb was a boy; she and Lincoln had called it the Year of the Scone because Caleb had tried—and perfected—no fewer than sixteen varieties before it passed. They had eaten raspberry scones in the morning, currant scones in the afternoon, pumpkin ginger scones before bed for weeks; Betsy had gained three pounds and was relieved when his interest moved on.

"A pastry chef!" she had said. "What a wonderful idea." And of course the conversation—now much more effervescent—concluded with her writing the check for the first tuition payment at the culinary institute in the south of France (because where better to study pastry making?) Caleb had selected. So let them tease. It wouldn't stop her from giving the money as long as she had it to give. And it clearly wouldn't stop them from taking it.

The ten or so minutes Betsy spent bent over and petting the dog were like a tonic. When she straightened up, she felt refreshed and even more ready to tackle the day with all the complexities it held: ex- or almost-ex-husbands, eccentric and worrisome mothers (Gretchen had actually allowed Lenore to *drive* this morning), potentially volatile new in-laws

(Ohad's family seemed so intense, it made hers look like the most reticent of WASPs in comparison), and the evil mutant wedding planner who had bewitched her daughter. She took the nightgown she had worn last night and spread it out across the bed; the dog liked to nestle in her clothing in her absence. Giving the pink tummy a final pat, Betsy left the room and closed the door quietly behind her.

As she walked briskly down the hall, she caught a glimpse of her granddaughter Justine skimming down the stairs. In the past her twin granddaughters had liked fooling people about their respective identities and had insisted on dressing identically. But this had changed, and now Portia sported a streak of fuchsia in her long hair, whereas Justine had gone for the piercings, something that made Betsy shudder. Of course that was the whole point, wasn't it? To make the adults cringe? Betsy remembered the overalls she had worn the better part of her freshman year at college; she knew that Lenore had wanted nothing more than to burn them.

But where was Justine going in such a hurry? Where did she have to be, other than outside under a gorgeous rented sailcloth tent at seven o'clock this evening? Even with all the myriad people and demands making claims on Betsy's attention, something about the girl's demeanor—and not just right now—made her want to know more. Was she having trouble in school? Or with a boy? Betsy knew that the separation had been hard on the girls; they loved their father and had blamed Gretchen when he moved out. Wasn't that often the way? Her own kids had been furious when she'd made Lincoln go, even though he had been an out-and-out drunk for years.

Betsy glanced at the Mickey Mouse watch on her wrist—another gift from Don—and wondered when Ennis would arrive. Lincoln had already gotten here; Caleb had gone to the airport to pick him up. But she wouldn't see him until the wedding; though she had invited him with great sincerity to stay at the house, he had declined, choosing instead some fleabag outside of town. That was Lincoln all right: so filled with his cockeyed principles. It was defensible to escape into drink, essentially abandoning wife, kids, and all semblance of a responsible life. Yet it was compromising to stay under her roof and bury the hatchet for the sake of their children. The door slammed, and the dog commenced upon a frenzy of yapping. "Gretchen?" called out Betsy.

"I'm downstairs," Gretchen called back. "Ennis is here. I just let him in."

Betsy hurried in the direction of her daughter's voice. She knew it would be difficult for Gretchen to see Ennis, and she wanted to help smooth over the rough edges. But the sound of laughter—Pippa's distinct, wheezing *chee, chee, chee,* the more melodious peals emitted by Angelica— stopped her. It was coming from Angelica's room; Angelica and Pippa were behind the closed door, giggling like a pair of teenagers on a sleepover. Why did this make Betsy feel so utterly bereft, as if she too were a teenager, an unpopular one, condemned to remain outside the charmed circle of their intimacy?

"Mom?" Gretchen called up. "Are you coming?"

Betsy forced herself to move away from Angelica's door. She knew she was being ridiculous. Angelica was her daughter, for heaven's sake. Pippa was nothing, no one. By tomorrow, once the wedding was over, she would disappear from their lives, vanishing as if she had never been.

This cheering thought propelled Betsy down the stairs into the foyer, where Gretchen, Ennis, and Justine had gathered. Ennis was looking well—hair neatly cut and a pressed, pale blue shirt—if a bit awkward. Gretchen was studying with rapt interest the black-and-white marble tiles that composed the entryway floor.

"Hello, Ennis," Betsy said. She leaned in to give him a quick peck on the cheek.

"Isn't it *great* that Dad's here?" Justine said. Her voice had a manic edge. "I mean, I didn't know he would be coming, but I'm so glad he did." She grabbed his hand.

"Does anyone want anything to eat?" Betsy said brightly. Once a Jewish mother, always a Jewish mother. "Esperanza set out croissants and fruit in the breakfast room."

"Coffee would be great," Ennis said, putting his battered olive drab knapsack on the floor.

"You can leave that there," Betsy said. "Someone will bring it downstairs."

"Where's Portia?" asked Ennis.

"Sleeping," Justine snorted. "But I'm going to wake her up."

"It's okay, baby," Ennis said. "Let her sleep. I'll see her later." He walked into the dining room with Justine, who was still clutching his hand.

Betsy, left alone with Gretchen, watched them go. "I know this is hard for you," she began.

"It's all right," Gretchen said. "He's their father. And it would be worse if he'd deserted them."

"That's true," Betsy said. She had an urge to smooth the tangle of Gretchen's curls, but she refrained. Her daughter was a grown woman with daughters of her own. Too old to have her hair smoothed by her mother.

"They still blame me," Gretchen said in a low voice. "They don't know everything. I haven't told them yet."

By *everything* Gretchen meant this: Ennis, who taught poetry at Brooklyn College, had slept—only once, he swore—with one of his students in the MFA program. But the single indiscretion had had major consequences. The girl—she was in her twenties but still, truly, a girl—had gotten pregnant. And she had refused to have an abortion. When Ennis had told her—kindly, gently, he swore—that he would not marry her, she had become so hysterical that she had shown up at their house after downing a bottle of Ambien, and because Ennis had not been home, Gretchen was the one who had called 911 and accompanied her to the emergency room.

"You were protecting them," Betsy said. "That's what mothers do. Good mothers, anyway."

"I tried," Gretchen said. She ran a hand through the tangle; it didn't seem to help. "Not that they're grateful at all."

"No, of course not," Betsy said. "What makes you think children are ever grateful?"

"What about us, Mom?" Gretchen said. "Were we grateful? Did you have to protect us from Dad?"

"Whatever your father did, you all knew about it. There was no hiding anything." This was true: how many times had Teddy or Caleb or one of the girls come upon Lincoln, dead drunk on the bathroom floor or passed out by the front door, after he'd stumbled in at four in the morning? How many times had they heard the excuses, the promises, the pleading?

"What did Dad do that we all knew about?" Teddy asked; he must have come through the kitchen, where either Esperanza or Carmelita would have let him in. Teddy, Betsy observed, seemed to be in the pink: sleek and well attended to. It must be that girl he had brought with him.

"There's no time to go into all that now," Betsy said, consulting Mickey Mouse again. Good God, it was already after eleven. Just then Betsy looked up and saw Angelica and Pippa descending the stairs. They had linked arms, and though it hardly seemed possible, they were *still* giggling. And as absurd, childish, and embarrassing as it was, the sight of them together caused a scrim of tears to cloud Betsy's eyes. She would not let them fall; she rarely did. But she knew that they were there, and she turned her head so no one else would see.

Seven

❧ • ❧

Gretchen jackknifed off the side of the swimming pool and straight into the blue. She was a good diver and a good swimmer too, swimming being one of the few—okay, *only*—sports she could not just tolerate but actively enjoy. Down, down she went, slick as a seal, until she had traversed the length of the pool—interior walls painted a haunting shade of indigo—and burst up to the surface at the other end. God, that felt good. She needed to do this more, she decided. There was a free public pool out in Red Hook and another in Sunset Park. Or she could join a health club with a pool. That was another thing she planned to look into next week; her list was growing. She gathered her hair—now flattened against her skull and pasted to her neck and shoulders—into the elastic she had around her wrist and began to swim: long, even strokes, back and forth, back and forth. *Work off some of those breakfast calories*, she thought as she swam. *It couldn't hurt.*

After Ennis and Justine had disappeared together

downstairs, where presumably they would take on the chore of waking Portia (the girl would sleep all day if allowed), Gretchen faced the inevitable *now what?* The rest of the household would be consumed by wedding preparations; the women who were doing hair and makeup had arrived, along with the florist, and Betsy had disappeared in a flurry of instructions, directives, and imperatives.

Gretchen decided against having her brows done after all; she'd seen the alarming mask—a gleam of purple shadow, false lashes as thick as fur—on the young woman assigned to the job and decided she did not want this person anywhere near her face. She planned to steer clear of the hairstylist too. Her long, wild curls may have been a mess, but they were her mess, and she liked them just the way they were.

Outside, the gorgeous June day had beckoned. Even though the weather report, which had been a constant, feverish topic of conversation since her arrival, was predicting a thunderstorm in the late afternoon, there was no evidence of it yet: the sky was a limpid cerulean blue, and only the gentlest of breezes wafted over the fat pink roses that bloomed along the stone wall outside the kitchen door.

And so here she was, clad in the sensible black maillot, a trusty, tried-and-true staple of the Lands' End catalog that did not let her down, even with the extra poundage she was carrying. Spread out across a chaise longue was one of her mother's heavenly white towels, ready to receive her when she finished her swim. Swimming was good: it cleared her mind of Ennis, of Justine, of Angelica, and of just about everything else. She focused instead on the movement of her body as it sped through the water, arm over arm, legs kicking vigorously behind her.

She had swum the pool's length about six times when her solitude was broken by a buff, tanned guy with a smoothly shaved head who was walking purposefully across the lawn, past the pool. He gave her a friendly wave, and she waved back, though she didn't know who he was. He looked good though. He wore cutoffs, and he was shirtless; an amazing pair of tattoos—huge blue-black wings whose rippling feathers were filled with slashes of purple, scarlet, blue, and green—covered his shoulders and draped down his back.

Gretchen, who was a secret admirer of such bodily markings and, though she would never have told her daughters, was contemplating having a small tattoo—A flower? No, that was such a cliché; perhaps a bee or a mushroom would be better, more original—inked on her ankle or her hip, was mightily impressed by the whole package. She remained at the deep end, treading water as she watched him disappear into a shed and then emerge again with a red wheelbarrow. Mystery solved. He was clearly someone her mother had hired, part of the grounds crew, no doubt. Not that such a thing would bother her. Not a bit. Hadn't she just been fantasizing she might meet someone at this wedding? Well, she hadn't imagined anyone this hot. Gretchen continued treading water and hoping that her sodden ponytail did not make her look too foolish.

"How's the water?" he called out.

"Fabulous," she replied.

He nodded as if this were important information worth weighing and considering.

"I'm Gretchen," she added.

"Jon," he said. He adjusted the wheelbarrow. "You're here for the wedding, right?"

"Sister of the bride," she said. The treading was tiring, but she didn't want to move down to the shallow end, where the water would no longer cover her. She wasn't ready for him to see her in her bathing suit. Not yet, anyway.

He nodded again. "Big day for your family."

"Oh, you have no idea," she said. She was aware that she sounded too effusive somehow, as if she were drunk. But she hadn't met anyone who had appealed to her in the longest time, and she was seriously out of practice.

"Well, have fun," he said, resuming his walk with the wheelbarrow. The sun gleamed on his head; maybe he oiled it.

"See you," she called back lamely. But would she? She certainly hoped so.

She tried to resume her swimming, but her concentration—and with it her sense of pleasure—was broken, so she climbed out of the pool, unbound her hair, and settled with the towel on the chaise longue. She wouldn't stay out here, of course; she was always mindful of her pale skin, which burned easily. But, oh, the sun felt so good. She closed her eyes and drank in the warmth.

"That's an upstairs towel."

Gretchen squinted up at Caleb, who was leaning over her.

"What are you talking about?"

"Your towel. It's from the bathroom upstairs."

"So what?" The point of this exchange eluded her.

"Mom said the upstairs towels should stay upstairs. Towels for the pool"—he shook a turquoise-and-yellow-striped towel in her face, as if he were the matador and she the bull—"are in the cabana. Over there." He let the towel go limp and pointed.

"Big deal," she said, rolling over and away from him. "Who even cares?"

"Mom. She made a point of telling me."

"So what is she going to do about it? Dock my allowance? Ground me?" She was annoyed; ordinarily she got on well with Caleb, but right now he was deliberately baiting her. *Regression*, she thought again. That was what happened when all four adult siblings were under a single roof.

"No need to get all huffy," he said. "I was just stating the rules of the manor. Milady's pleasure, if you know what I mean."

"Grow up," she muttered. *Fuck you*, was what she really wanted to say, but why go there? She closed her eyes and, because she'd left her sunglasses upstairs in her room, pressed her forearm over them. Maybe if she pretended to be trying to nap, Caleb would go away. No such luck.

"You remember Bobby? From last night?"

She opened her eyes to see her brother's new boyfriend standing at his side. Naturally she remembered Bobby; did her brother think she was senile? But she just propped herself up on her elbows and said, "Sure."

"I told Caleb that you were the smart one," he said in a low, confiding voice. Despite her annoyance with Caleb, Gretchen smiled. Bobby was charming; she would grant him that. Charming and good-looking too, with a thick sheaf of blond hair that fell across his intriguing, amber-colored eyes.

"Going in for a swim?" she asked.

He nodded. "Looks like you've been in already."

"I was. And the water's just fine." She settled back down.

Caleb and Bobby laid their striped towels—their *cabana* towels—on the pair of chairs flanking the chaise longue and jumped into the water. They didn't so much swim as frisked, splashed, dunked, and cannonballed; they made quite a racket. Gretchen could have easily left. She'd had her swim, and she'd had her flirtation. But she found herself wanting to stay, so she got up and dragged the chaise longue into the shade, where she would not have to worry about sunburn. Caleb and Bobby were swimming now, gracefully in tandem across the glittering blue surface of the water.

Her brother looked so—well, so *happy* that Gretchen's earlier irritation evaporated, leaving a tender and protective glow in its place. Caleb had been a sensitive, nervous kid. He cried easily and took even the smallest things very hard. So it was nice to see him enjoying the giddy little intoxication of this nascent romance. Caleb was a honey. Oh, he could be prickly, but that was only in self-defense; he was so easily hurt and needed some sort of armor. She hoped Bobby would understand this.

Finally the two men climbed out of the pool and lay panting side by side in the sun. Gretchen saw Caleb reach for Bobby's hand and give it a squeeze; Bobby leaned over to whisper something in Caleb's ear that made him burst out laughing. He was still laughing when Bobby got up, crossed the lawn, and headed back toward the house.

After a minute Caleb opened his eyes and waved at Gretchen.

"Come sit with me," she called. "I'm in the shade 'cause I don't want to get burned."

"You and Angelica, always shunning the sun," he said, but he got up and ambled over, striped towel trailing along behind him, to where she sat.

"When we're old ladies, our skin will still be radiant and dewy, while yours will be all wrinkled, like a raisin."

"No, it won't," he said, nudging her leg with his.

"Why not, smarty-pants?" she retorted. "Do you have an antiaging secret you're not telling me about? No fair."

"Didn't I tell you? I'm not going to get old."

"And how are you planning to avoid that?" Gretchen scanned the sky overhead; it must have been noon or just about. She was getting hungry, damn it. The downside of physical exertion.

"I'm planning to die young."

He looked so serious that Gretchen wanted to hug him and say, Shut *up*, in that way she heard her daughters say it, the emphasis on the second word. Instead she said, "You're really crazy about this guy, huh?"

He nodded, and the smile widened until it consumed his face.

"That's wonderful, Caleb. Really wonderful."

"We're moving in together." He leaned forward as he spoke.

"Really? I didn't know." Gretchen considered this for a moment. Was it too sudden, or was Caleb really ready to commit?

"We just decided."

"Any thoughts about where?"

"It's complicated." Gretchen said nothing, waiting for him to go on. "I haven't told this to anyone but Mom yet," he continued, voice growing more animated. "I haven't been happy at work for a long time now, and I'm ready for a change. So I'm going back to school. To become a pastry chef."

"You're kidding!"

"Not."

"Well," Gretchen said. "Well."

"So everything's a little unsettled now. I'll be starting school in September, and I want Bobby to go with me."

"Go with you where?"

"This is the best part: the cooking school is in the south of France. A town called St. Jean Cap Ferrat; it's on the Riviera."

Gretchen was silent.

"What? You mean you don't think that's a little slice of heaven?"

"Mom's paying for this, isn't she?"

"What difference does that make?" He looked hurt.

"None, I guess." Why had she even *said* that? She let her mother pay her daughters' tuition, didn't she? Who was she to throw stones?

"It's not like she can't spare it," he said, gesturing to the pool and all that went with it.

"You're right," she said, shamed now by her ungenerous response. "You're absolutely right. She has the money, and she wants to give it to you. Why shouldn't you take it?"

"Exactly," Caleb said. "And if I become really successful as a chef, I can pay her back, right?"

"Right," she said, and in that moment he was her little brother again, dripping chocolate batter onto the pages of the *Joy of Cooking* as he pored intently over its stained pages. "Anyway, all this talk about pastry is making me hungry," she added, swinging her legs up from the chaise and reaching for her towel. "Why don't we go inside and see if we can find some lunch?"

Caleb got up, and together they walked back along one of the paths that led to the house. Along the way they passed a quaintly decaying stone well—nonfunctional—and a bronze fountain of a dolphin spewing water from its bronze mouth. Her mother did love her garden ornaments. They also passed the little shed; Gretchen noticed that the red wheelbarrow was standing by its door, which was partially ajar. That meant Jon, the sexy grounds crew guy, was somewhere nearby. She sucked her stomach in as she ever so casually glanced around in the hope that she might see him. And in the next instant she did, but then just as quickly wished she didn't: still shirtless, he stood just inside the shed, his wonderfully tanned and muscled arms locked tightly around Bobby as the two of them kissed as if they would never stop.

The sensation she felt, that slow drop of her heart from its perch of high, eager anticipation was nothing—and this she knew from cruel experience—but *nothing* compared to what her brother must be feeling. She put her hand on his arm, trying desperately to think of something, anything that would be of comfort to him now. But he recoiled from her touch as if he'd been singed, and ran without looking back or stopping toward the shelter of their mother's house.

Gretchen was still standing there wondering what to do—follow Caleb or give him some privacy—when Teddy came out, wearing a garish pair of baggy flowered swim trunks that extended to his knees. *Once a frat boy, always a frat boy,* she thought. Walking alongside him was the elegant and self-contained Marti, her smooth brown hair in a twist, her well-cut black bikini—she had the body for it, that was for sure—at once sexy and sophisticated.

"What was that all about?" Teddy asked. He removed his dark wraparound sunglasses. "Caleb just went streaking by; boy, were *his* knickers in a twist."

"He was upset," Gretchen said. How much to tell Teddy? He and Caleb were not especially close, and she did not want to expose her youngest brother, especially in front of Marti, whom none of them knew well.

"I could see *that*," Teddy said witheringly. "I was wondering why."

"Maybe Gretchen does not wish to say," Marti said, putting a hand on Teddy's arm. She had a slight French accent and a low, pleasant voice.

"It's true, I don't," Gretchen said gratefully. Teddy's main squeeze was both attractive *and* sensitive, a winning combo in Gretchen's view.

"Hey, I'm his big brother. He has no secrets from me," Teddy said, looking back and forth from Gretchen to Marti.

"We all have secrets," Marti said airily. "Don't we?"

"Whatever," Teddy said, taking Marti's hand. "He always was a drama queen."

"That isn't nice, Teddy," said Gretchen.

"Nice? Who wants to be nice? Nice is for losers."

Gretchen stared at him. Had Teddy always been such a jerk?

"No, that's not true, Teddy." Marti smiled, but there was something firm, even directive in her tone. "The losers are the bitter ones. It's the winners who can afford to be gracious and kind, no?" She cocked her head in Gretchen's direction, a small Gallic gesture that completely won Gretchen over; if she'd been inclined to like her before, she was inclined to love her now. Her brother should *not* let this one get away.

"Touché," said Teddy, looking at her with open adoration. "I promise to be nice from now on."

"You should be as good to your family as you are to me," Marti continued.

"Of course," Teddy said, and he actually bowed at the

waist and playfully kissed Marti's hand. "Your wish is my command."

Marti smiled serenely. Gretchen was amazed at how this woman had so deftly handled her brother; why, he didn't even know he'd *been* handled. *Touché,* indeed. Then Marti and Teddy continued down the path toward the pool. Marti turned back to give Gretchen a final smile. Was she winking too? Marti was not close enough for Gretchen to be sure, but somehow she thought that, yes, that was *exactly* what Marti was doing.

Afternoon

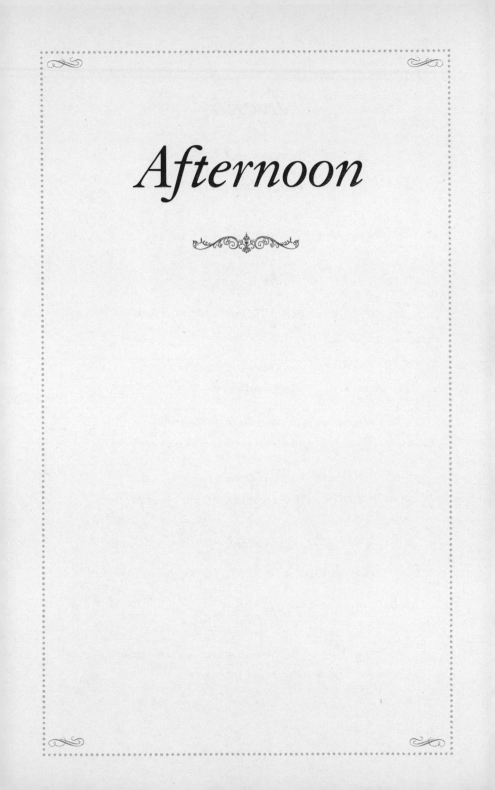

Menu

Angelica and Ohad
Saturday, June 2, 2012

SELECTION OF COLD HORS D'OEUVRES

Main Course:

FILET MIGNON WITH SMASHED YUKON GOLD
POTATOES AND HARICOTS VERTS

POACHED MONKFISH WITH QUINOA AND
ROASTED BEETS

PAPPARDELLE WITH A MEDLEY OF ZUCCHINI,
TOMATO, ONION AND ROASTED RED PEPPER

GREEN SALAD WITH SLICED LADY APPLES,
WALNUTS, AND AGED BALSAMIC VINAIGRETTE

Dessert:

LIME MOUSSE, PETIT FOURS, SUGAR COOKIES

Wedding Cake

SELECTION OF HANDMADE CHOCOLATES FROM
LE COUP DU CHOCOLAT

Eight

❧ · ❧

Why had she taken the ring? This was the question that kept ricocheting off the walls of Justine's mind and getting in the way of the precious time she got to spend with her father. It wasn't like she planned to keep it. She hated diamonds. And she didn't want to hurt Angelica, did she? Then again, maybe she did. Maybe Justine was angry at Angelica: for being in love with that warmonger, for planning this big, dumb wedding, and for betraying everything Justine had ever believed about her.

"So, you girls nixed the camp plan this year?" her father was saying.

"What?" Justine had not been following the thread of the conversation.

"Camp," her father repeated. "Portia said you had decided not to go."

"Right, right," she said. Could anyone see the ring's bulge in her pocket? Had Angelica realized it was missing yet? What would she do when she did?

"I was hoping maybe you girls would want to come and spend some time with me in August. I've rented a little cottage in New Hampshire. It's on a lake."

"New Hampshire," Justine parroted, still not really paying attention. "Lake."

"We should go," Portia said to Justine. "Anyway, *I* want to go, Dad. When will you be up there?"

Justine's thoughts returned to the ring while her father and sister tossed dates back and forth. She had to put it back, that was all. She just had to go upstairs, slip into Angelica's room, and put it right back where she found it. Easy. Angelica would be having her dress fitted, her nails painted—whatever. She would be out of the room most of the afternoon.

"Okay, then we'll talk to your mother," her father said, getting up from the long, curved sofa. He leaned down to kiss her forehead and then Portia's. "I'm going to put my things away," he added. "Then maybe we'll have a swim before the wedding, hey?" Ennis often said *hey* at the end of a sentence, a little conversational tic that Justine and Portia loved, just like they loved his Scottish accent and his uncanny ability to create a whole gallery of shadow puppets—clowns, witches, wolves, birds with flapping wings—on the scuffed lilac wall of their childhood bedroom. Why did her parents have to go and get separated anyway? Now Justine had to, like, *schedule* time with her father. Like he was an orthodontist's appointment or something.

"So, what's with you?" Portia said when Ennis had left.

She picked up her hairbrush and began to pull it through her hair. Tamed, the hot pink streak grew smooth.

"What do you mean, what's with me?"

"You're acting all weird."

"I am not," said Justine. But she averted her eyes. It was the ring, of course. The stolen ring, with its ugly nugget of a stone, which was still in her pocket. Portia could sense it.

"Justine, this is me, remember? Portia, your other half. Your *better* half. There is no way you can pull this shit with me, okay? So don't even try."

"Are you going for a swim with Dad?" Justine decided that changing the subject was a better plan.

"Maybe," Portia said. The brush sat idle in her lap. "I thought I might go to that hairdresser Grandma Betsy hired."

"Whatever for?"

"I'd kind of like a streak of blue right next to the pink." She touched her head with the tip of the brush handle. "Or maybe green. What do you think?"

Justine turned to scrutinize her sister. "Green," she said. "Add a strip of green. But do you really think any hairdresser Grandma hired is going to have the stuff she'll need to do that?"

"You're right," Portia said. She stood, and the brush clattered to the floor. "She won't." Justine picked up the brush from near her foot, where it had landed, and handed it to her sister. "Still, I'm going to see her anyway. Maybe she'll have some other ideas. You never know."

Justine highly doubted this, but "Okay" was all she said. "We can swim later if you want."

"Mom and Uncle Caleb were out earlier," said Portia. "Are they still there?"

Justine shrugged. "I don't know." She felt ready to implode. She wished she'd brought along a little something to help her wind down; she did have a couple of her beloved Adderall capsules, but they would do nothing to calm her.

She stood and stretched, a phony stretch that allowed her to run her hands across the front of her thighs to feel the subtle bump the ring made in her shorts. God, she wished she could show it to Portia. She had never, ever in her life kept something this major from her before. It felt terrible, as if in hoarding her secret, she had somehow been cut loose from her sister and was left adrift in some strange and hostile new atmosphere.

"As long as Uncle Teddy isn't around," Portia said, moving toward the door. "He's *such* an ass wipe. Has he been hounding you about college yet? Oh—excuse me. I mean, the *right* college. If I hear that again, I'll barf."

Justine grinned a broad, face-splitting grin. All at once she felt drenched in relief. "Let's tell Uncle Teddy we've decided not to go to college at all," she said. Portia was still Portia. The cord was not severed. "You can say you want to go to some technical school and learn to fix refrigerators. Or air conditioners. And I'll tell him that I want to go to . . . dog grooming school! I'll learn to groom nasty little lapdogs like Grandma Betsy's. Listen." She paused. "I can hear it barking now." And it was true: the dog was at it again, the high-pitched sound penetrating the windows and walls with insistent, irritating clarity.

"Can you believe she puts up with that?" Portia said. She shook her head. "I'll look for you at the pool later."

Justine nodded, still smiling. "Green," she said. "Definitely green."

As soon as Portia had left, Justine changed into her bathing suit—navy, one-piece, kind of like her mom's, in fact—and topped it with a short navy-and-white terry robe. She actually thought the robe, a present from her grandmother, was dorky, but it conveniently had a pocket, into which she slid the diamond ring. She'd just amble back upstairs, put the ring back in its leather case, and no one would ever know. She still had to find Ohad; she had a whole other plan to put into action. But somehow the urgency of that had receded a bit in the face of this new imperative.

Justine managed to avoid the activity in both the kitchen and dining room, but as she breezed through the entryway, the bell chimed, and one of the maids answered it. Grandma Betsy was right behind her, saying, "I'm so glad you're here. I was beginning to worry!" The young woman who entered—small, with a bunch of tiny reddish-brown pigtails that poked up all over her head, and a neatly pierced septum in which a gold hoop shone—looked scarcely older than Justine was. It was only the load of equipment she carried—camera cases, tripod, lights—that identified her as the wedding photographer. Interesting. Maybe Justine should have had her septum done, instead of just the puny nose stud.

Though curious to find out more about the photographer, Justine had no time to stick around. Still thinking about the pierced septum, she ran up the stairs, down the hall, and, in her haste to accomplish her mission, flung open the door to Angelica's room. Bad move. There, stretched out on the wide bed with its crinkly duvet cover, was Ohad. He wore jeans and a white shirt like the one she had seen Angelica wearing. Except for the chunk of turquoise around her neck, they were dressed identically.

"Oh!" said Justine. "I am, like, so sorry! I should have knocked." She had wanted to find him, hadn't she? But not here, not now. She didn't even have her phone, damn it. She slipped her hand into the pocket of her robe. She had the ring, though. The ring that she needed to return, like, this second.

"It's all right," said Ohad. Although his English was good, his accent was heavy.

"I didn't mean to disturb you or anything," she added. "Were you having a nap?"

"Just closing my eyes for a few minutes. I can't get any peace back at the hotel," he said. "Someone always wants or needs something. A question, a problem, a piece of advice." He swung his legs around and off the bed. "Families. What can you do?" He smiled up at her, and she felt like someone had socked her in the stomach. He really was drop-dead gorgeous, just like Grandma Lenore kept saying. All at once Justine was overcome with a new sensation. This one was an intense, smoldering shade of violet. Hot. Sizzling. The *very violets*, that's what she would call this new, electrified state.

Flustered, Justine tried to fight the heady cloud that swirled in her brain. But it was hard. There was that dark skin and the white, white teeth, for starters. There was also the sculpted nose and the scary-sexy eyebrows over the nearly black eyes. The hair, black too but totally unlike Angelica's. While hers was smooth and glossy, his was matte and coarse; it stood up from his head like a pelt.

But no matter how hot he was, he could not be trusted. Forget the looks. Looks could lie. She imagined his life back in Israel: the army, the fighter planes, the firing of rockets and bullets into defenseless villages and towns where innocent people—babies, little kids, pregnant moms, and old women like Grandma Lenore—were wounded, maimed, killed. Legs and arms blown off, skulls crushed, blood everywhere, everything on fire. And he, Ohad, was the cause.

"You have a big family too," he said. "Do you sometimes feel like you need to get away from them?"

"I guess," she said. She could barely sustain this conversation. The violet feeling was sucking at her, making her imagine all sorts of wildly inappropriate things. What if she did let him kiss her, like, for real? And take off her shirt and touch her boobs? Suddenly this seemed like a very compelling scenario.

But she could not let herself think this way. She had to get rid of him. Now. *The ring, the ring. Return the ring.* Then she could deal with the rest of it. Of course she would have to get her phone somehow so she could take the picture. The picture was crucial.

"But, still, families are important, right?" he said.

"Families are the starting point of . . . everything. Good or bad, they hold us like glue. Don't you think so?" He rolled his shoulders back a couple of times as if he were getting the kinks out.

"Yeah. Sure. Whatever." She knew she sounded rude. Also stupid—he would think she was a total moron. But what could she do? This was making her crazy, especially because Ohad was being so, well, nice. More than nice, actually. He had that way of talking *to* you, not *at* you, like so many people, especially adults, did. Angelica had it too; it was one of the things she and Portia loved about her. So Justine guessed it wasn't such a surprise that she loved him. Even if he was a missile-launching baby killer.

"Were you looking for Angelica?" Justine nodded. "She's downstairs, I think. I'm not sure what she's doing, though." He flashed her that smile again. The violet haze grew thicker.

"Angelica. Right." She backed out of the room.

"If she comes up here, I'll tell her you were looking for her, okay?"

"Okay." She gave him a weak little wave and then instantly regretted it. God, *why* had she done *that*? Now she would really look lame. But he didn't seem to mind, because he waved back. Except when he did it, it didn't seem lame. Only friendly.

Justine went down the stairs as her heart smacked around in her chest like a tennis ball. She was so confused. Ohad. Angelica. The ring. And no one to talk to about any of it. She passed the room where the hair and makeup business was going on. Well, not the makeup. Not yet. But there was Portia perched on a stool and wearing a hideous flowered smock. She lifted her hand out from under it to motion Justine into the room. Justine shook her head, but Portia gestured again.

"Teeny, please," she said, using one of the many childhood nicknames they had devised for each other. It was the *Teeny* that got her. It always did. Reluctantly she entered the room.

"She wants to cut it," Portia said. "What do you think?"

"Your hair?"

"Duh!" When Justine did not reply, Portia asked, "Do you think I should?"

"It will be fantastic," said the stylist. She had the kind of artfully applied blond highlights Justine despised.

"How short?" she said, turning back to her sister.

"Maybe to here," Portia said, indicating her collarbone.

"Dull," Justine said. "Megawatt dull."

Portia looked questioningly at the stylist.

"Well, we could go shorter if you wanted . . ." the stylist said.

God, but she was useless. "Cut it short," Justine said to Portia. "Really short."

"A pixie cut?" ventured the stylist.

"A buzz cut," Justine shot back. "Bzz!" She made the sound of the electric razor as she drew her hand along Portia's head in an imaginary swath.

"I don't want a buzz cut, Teeny," said Portia, looking alarmed. "I really don't. But I do like the idea of going shorter."

"Pixie, then," Justine told her sister. "Think of what everyone will say; it will be such a surprise." Too bad about the buzz cut; maybe she should go for it herself. But then she looked again at the stylist, who was blinking in an especially clueless way, and she decided, *Not.*

"Okay," Portia said. "Pixie."

"Sweet. I'll be back in a little while to see how it's going," Justine said before leaving. She stepped out of the house and headed in the direction of the pool. No sign of her mother or Caleb, though there were plenty of other people around, moving potted plants, setting up chairs under an enormous, pennant-capped tent.

There was one guy, shaved head and shirtless, with the most amazing set of tats on his shoulders: big wings that seemed to undulate when he moved. She'd have to make sure Portia saw him; they were both into tats, though neither of them had actually gotten one yet. They were still trying to convince their mother to let them. Maybe Justine would sneak off to St. Mark's Place and have it done without telling anyone, even Portia. There was a guy at school who, for the right price, could come up with a highly convincing fake ID.

Justine approached the pool. No one was in it. Carefully she folded the robe and put it on a chair with the pocket facing up. She patted it just to be sure the ring was inside. Then she dived in and sped along the surface. Like her mother, she was a strong swimmer. So was her dad; Portia was the only one in the family who didn't like swimming.

Justine flipped over and did a backstroke until she got tired of that and simply let herself float, looking up at the sky. A few clouds had rolled in; would they bring the rain that everyone had been talking about? Hard to tell. They were puffy and white, not gray or black. But, still. The sky— like everything else—could change in a nanosecond.

"Having a swim, hey?"

Justine lifted her head out of the water. Dad. She had not heard him approach. He wore faded, baggy swim trunks, and he seemed, oh, a little thinner, maybe. A little thinner and a little older too. More tired than she remembered. But still her dad. She was glad to see him.

"Come on in," she called. "I'll race you." He dove in with a minimal splash and joined her at the shallow end. "On your mark, get set," she said, positioning herself in the water. "Go!" She shot ahead, arms slicing the water in clean, even strokes. She was aware of him at her side, stroking furiously. His arms were longer, true, but he was older. He had strength and size on his side; she had youth and speed. She kept her pace and touched the wall only a second before he did.

"The winner!" he said and, grasping her hand, pulled it into the air for a victory pump.

"The winner," she echoed, and let herself surrender to the feel of his hand as it closed around hers.

They swam back and forth a few more times at a more leisurely pace before getting out.

"So, how are things?" he said as he toweled off. "You seemed kind of quiet before."

"Oh, everything's fine." The lie slid out easily.

"School's okay?"

"School's great," she told him. "I mean, it was great. We just finished finals."

"But no grades," he said, wrapping the towel around his shoulders.

"Not yet. But I'm in good shape. My average so far is 3.98. I'm getting an A in my British and American Poetry class; the teacher already told me." Justine knew he'd care about that grade above all the rest.

Her father whistled his approval. "I'd say that's pretty terrific." He rubbed the towel across his back and legs. "But it's not a surprise. Not to me. Always knew you were my poetry girl from way back, hey? Remember when you memorized Blake's 'The Tyger'? You must have been seven."

"I was eight, Dad," she said. "Maybe even nine." But the praise made her beam like a tensor lamp inside.

"Eight, seven, same thing." He scanned her face. "So you'll come to New Hampshire with Portia, hey?"

"I will. But I want to start my SAT prep this summer; I'm taking a course, and I'll have to fit it in around that," she said, reaching for her robe.

"Kind of early, isn't it?" He sounded concerned.

"Never too early for SAT prep," Justine said. God, but

she sounded like her uncle Teddy. Hideous thought. "Not if you want to aim high."

"You do aim high," her father said.

Why did he sound so wistful? Justine shook off the feeling. She would not let the moody blues come over her; she would *not*. Belting her robe tightly around her waist, she added, "Anyway, don't worry so much. I'll come see you this summer."

"Promise?"

"Promise."

They started toward the house and passed the tent where the ceremony was to be held. Justine had to admit it looked pretty, the opening framing a green expanse of lawn behind it. That was where Angelica and Ohad would exchange their vows. Rows of white folding chairs had been set under it as well, and a long roll of white carpeting had been unfurled, creating a smooth aisle down which the couple would walk. Justine knew that Angelica had a pair of killer heels and clearly was not going to risk tripping.

But then Justine remembered, as if waking up from a dream, that none of this was going to happen, not if she had her way. The tent, the chairs, the ribbon of white—all wasted, beside the point once she had presented Angelica with the proof.

She started walking more quickly now, eager to get back to the house so she could change, grab her phone, and begin the hunt for Ohad. She had told Portia she would come and check out her haircut. And the ring—she had yet to return the ring. Damn it! She'd let herself be distracted by the water and a little face time with her father. How dumb was that? She broke into a trot.

"What's your hurry?" her father called. He was lagging behind, still clutching the towel like a sad cape around him.

"I'm starving," she called back. "I haven't eaten a thing all day." Which in fact was true, but she had been way too jittery to eat. She went into the breakfast room to see whether there was still anything there. And, yes, there was food arranged on the table and the sideboard; Justine helped herself to a banana and began to peel it. But before she had taken the first bite, she practically ran into her grandmother, who had come striding in. Right behind her was Angelica.

"I didn't see it; I wasn't even in your room this morning," Grandma Betsy was saying.

"I left it right there on the dresser, in my jewelry case," Angelica said. "I can show you the exact spot."

"Then it should still be there," Betsy said.

"But it's not. That's the whole point. Everything else is there—my chain, my locket, my bracelet." She gave her hair an impatient shake. "Do you think it could have been one of the maids?"

"Carmelita or Esperanza?" Betsy stopped, hand pressed to her chest. "Absolutely not. Not even a chance."

"Can we at least ask them, Mom? I'm not saying one of them took it. But maybe it got moved or tucked away somewhere."

"We can ask, of course we can ask, but I don't see how that's going to help." Betsy sounded exasperated.

"What are you looking for?" Justine asked. Like she didn't *know*. She only hoped her voice did not betray her guilt, which was quietly sucking the air right out of her lungs. She squeezed the banana so tightly she felt it turn to mush in her fingers. Ew.

"My diamond engagement ring," Angelica said. "It's missing."

No, it's not, Justine wanted to say. *I have it safe and sound right here. Look.* But when she dipped her other, non-banana-smeared hand into the pocket of the now-damp terry robe, it came up empty. She froze, unable to believe it, so she checked again and a third time. Then she checked the other pocket, thinking she might have been mistaken about where she'd put it. But that too was empty. Impossible as it seemed, the ring—glittering, expensive, and much exclaimed over—was gone.

Nine

⁓ • ⁓

Lenore laid out her entire ensemble on her bed: brocade dress, matching coat, earrings, purse, gloves, and panty hose in a flattering shade of celadon. She hated having to wear hose on such a warm day, but she was an old woman, and no one wanted to see an old woman's legs. Not even her. Decades ago she had scandalized her mother-in-law by running around in saucy cuffed shorts. "Cover yourself!" she'd cried. "It's a *shandah*!" But Monty had loved the shorts and the generous expanse of pale skin they had revealed. "You've got the gams of a showgirl," he had always said. "The gams of a showgirl."

Placing the gold shoes on a hand towel, Lenore set them alongside the pieces she had already assembled. Next she selected her foundation garments: Lily of France lace bra and matching panties, half-slip with a delicate scalloped border. Then she went into the bathroom—it had been cleaned *again* in her absence—to find her cosmetics: the powder blush, eyebrow pencil, frosted lipstick, and the travel-sized bottle of Shalimar, which had been her evening fragrance for the past forty years.

When she came back into the room, she noticed that the panty hose were no longer on the bed, where she had left them. Odd. Had she put them somewhere else and forgotten? Old people were forgetful; that was the cliché. But not her. Not yet, anyway. Her memory was good, her mind sharp. So where were the panty hose? They couldn't have just vanished.

Then she saw something pale green fluttering along the floor near the end of the bed. Lenore walked around to see Betsy's little dog; the creature had the panty hose in her mouth and was shredding the sheer fabric with her white, pointed teeth.

"Bad dog!" Lenore scolded. Bright black eyes unblinking, the dog looked up at her. She did not seem perturbed by the admonishment and continued her shredding. "You give me those right now," said Lenore. The shredding ceased, and the dog cocked her head. Progress. Lenore inched closer and seized the hose. The dog shook her head, but she did not let go. *She thinks we're playing,* Lenore realized. *She thinks this is a game.*

But it was not a game. Lenore needed the panty hose to wear tonight; she had not brought an extra pair along with her. She yanked the hose from between the dog's clenched teeth. Startled, the dog jumped up and began circling furiously. Then she squatted, leaving a small, dark puddle on the rug.

"Oh, for heaven's sake!" Lenore said out loud. How had the dog even found her way into the room? How she'd gotten the panty hose—now ruined—was not a mystery: Lenore remembered that she had left the legs hanging over the side of the bed. The dog, while small, could have easily pulled them down.

Lenore tried to grab the dog, but the creature eluded her easily. She may have been small, but she was speedy. Lenore lunged again, nearly losing her balance. But she caught herself and sat down. This was ridiculous. Betsy would have to coax the creature out of here. And then one of the maids could help with the cleanup.

Now, where was Betsy? She'd better go and find her before that stain had a chance to set. Lenore cast a last glance at the dog, now sitting on the rug and panting slightly with a sorrowful look on her face. *Why are you going?* The black eyes seemed to contain a question. *Can't I go too?* For a moment Lenore understood why Betsy was so taken with the dog. Such an intense, focused expression. Like she wanted something. *Knew* something. Then the moment passed.

At the top of the stairs Lenore nearly collided with Angelica, who was clearly in a big hurry; Betsy followed in her wake. "Neither of them touched the ring," Betsy was saying. "They didn't even go into the room."

"How can you be so sure?" Angelica whirled around to ask. "Were you keeping watch up there all morning?"

"No, but I know both of them, and I am positive that neither one of them took it."

"Took what?" Lenore asked, looking first at her daughter and then her granddaughter. "What's missing?"

"My engagement ring, that's all!" said Angelica. She sounded impatient, and Lenore was hurt. Well, she'd always been an imperious girl.

"There's no need to snap at Grandma," Betsy said. "None of this is her fault."

"Oh, so it's my fault? Is that what you're implying?"

"I never said that," Betsy said. "Honey, you're twisting every word I say. I know you're tense because of the wedding—"

"That's exactly right! I am tense! Exceedingly, extremely tense! It's my wedding day, and my beautiful ring, my *engagement* ring, is missing. And it doesn't seem like you care very much."

"Of course I care! I don't see how you can say that when I've gone to such trouble and expense for this wedding. You're being unreasonable. And rude."

Angelica did not answer but marched down the hall in the direction of her room. Betsy followed, and Lenore decided she ought to go along too. The delinquent dog remained behind, but given these more pressing concerns, she supposed it wouldn't hurt for the animal to stay there a little while longer. As for the stain on the rug, Lenore thought that a little seltzer—or was it white vinegar?— would take care of it. She hurried along behind her daughter and granddaughter.

Lenore knew that losing an engagement ring on the

day of the wedding could be viewed as a bad omen. But she was not superstitious, so she didn't view the loss as an omen of any kind at all. Only an inconvenience. The ring was probably insured and so could be replaced, though she knew better than to say that now. No, Angelica wanted everything to be perfect on this day of days, and the disappearance of the ring was interfering with that vision of perfection. Best to humor her.

"Where was it last?" Betsy asked as they all entered the room.

"Right there." Angelica pointed to the dresser, where a zippered leather case, still filled with the rest of her jewelry, sat open. Lenore walked over to get a better look. She recognized the locket Angelica wore all the time. And the charm bracelet, once hers, that she had given to her granddaughter.

Then she glanced around the room. What was she looking for? She didn't know, but it would come to her. And then quite effortlessly it did.

"Angelica, did you make the bed this morning?" Lenore asked.

"The bed? No. I had so much to do, and besides, Mom asks the maids to do it." She turned to her mother. "Didn't you say that neither of them were up here?"

"Well, I didn't think they were," Betsy began.

"You didn't think, but you didn't know for sure, did you?" Angelica looked at Lenore. "Thank you, Grandma; you're quite the cunning little sleuth. It's pretty clear that at least *one* of them was in here today, if only to make the bed."

"That's a serious accusation," Betsy said. "I think we

should explore all the options before we're so quick to condemn anyone."

"Who's condemning?" Angelica said. She sat down on the bed. "But could it hurt to ask a few questions?"

"Was anyone else up here?" Lenore asked.

Betsy, no longer so confident, looked down. "I don't know," she said.

"Justine was here," Angelica said. "I ran into her earlier. She seemed surprised to see me."

"Justine was in here?" Betsy asked. Angelica nodded. "We should ask her if she saw the ring."

"Definitely," Angelica said. And then: "Ohad was in here. Things were hectic at the hotel, and he came over to have a rest."

So Ohad naps too, thought Lenore, obscurely pleased by this information; she herself often felt the need to take naps these days. But she only said, "Let's ask everyone to join us. Ohad, Justine, the maids. It would be good to talk to everyone."

"That's a very smart idea," said Betsy. To Lenore she suddenly looked drained, as if all the color had been sucked from her face.

"It is," agreed Angelica. She put her arm around Lenore's shoulder and gave her a little squeeze. "I'm sorry if I snapped at you," she added. "I'm just a nervous wreck."

"Of course you are, darling." Lenore forgave her granddaughter in an instant. How could she hold a grudge against the girl—so brilliant, so beautiful, so filled with energy, purpose, and drive? And it was her wedding day; she was entitled to her wedding-day jitters. "You're getting married today, and getting married is a very big deal." She inhaled that scent again, the one she had noticed yesterday. She would ask Angelica what it was and where she could get a bottle. Only she would not ask right now.

Betsy and Angelica left the room, in search of the two maids, whose names Lenore could not remember, Ohad, and Justine. Lenore supposed she ought to stay, though she really did want to have a little chat with Caleb if she could find him. He had been out by the pool earlier, but she had not seen him since. Now, that was odd, because he usually sought her out at family gatherings. She sank down on a slipper chair covered in a tasteful paisley but realized she was not inclined to sit still—*schpilkes*, as her own mother would have said. *Ants in the pants.*

Lenore rose and surveyed the room once more. Betsy had had it redone recently, and so everything in here was new to Lenore. On the walls hung three Japanese prints in thin bamboo frames; over the dresser was a large mirror flanked by a pair of sconces with frosted glass. She looked down at the leather case, where the ring had been and now was not. Lenore picked up the charm bracelet; she remembered receiving it from her father when she was about fifteen years old. "For my *shaine maydele*," he'd said and fastened the clasp around her slim wrist. Lenore had moved her hand this way and that, liking the tinkling sounds the charms made when she shook them. She set the bracelet back down again.

There was a pair of double doors leading onto a small

balcony, and Lenore opened them to step outside. The view from here was especially nice: a glimpse of the roses, the lawn, the pool, and the tent, whose flaps and pennants waved in the breeze that must have just started up. Lenore's eyes were quite good for a woman her age; she wore glasses to drive, read, or watch television, but otherwise she could rely on her unaided vision. So she was quick to notice a figure bent down and scrabbling furiously in the grass as if searching for something. Who was it? Lenore stepped closer to the railing to see.

Justine, that was who. Did she know that Angelica and Betsy were looking for her? And was her frantic search connected to the missing ring? Lenore stepped back. Should she alert Betsy? Angelica? But a decision was rendered unnecessary when she heard Betsy calling Justine, who jumped up from her knees and ran in the direction of the house, ignoring the path and cutting directly across the lawn. Much to Betsy's annoyance, she was forever doing that.

Moments later they all trooped in: Betsy and the two maids—one was called Carmelita, Lenore remembered, pleased with herself—Angelica, Ohad, and Justine bringing up the rear.

"I think you all know what this is about," Angelica began. She clasped her hands earnestly to her chest. "Today I've lost something that is really precious to me, and I'm hoping one of you can help me find it." She took a deep breath. "I've lost my engagement ring. The beautiful, *irreplaceable* ring that Ohad gave to me."

"That's terrible!" Justine said. "Who would do a thing like that?"

Lenore studied the girl. Why did she sound so, well, theatrical? So insincere?

"Oh yes," Angelica said. "And that's why I'm hoping that one of you might know something—anything—that will help me to find it."

"Of course we'll help you, Angelica," Justine said. "You know we will." Lenore saw Betsy nodding and the two maids looking terrified, as if they expected to be handcuffed and hauled off any second. Ohad just crossed his magnificent arms over his chest and said nothing. Clearly no one else had noticed how false Justine sounded. Or, if they had, they were not mentioning it.

"Carmelita, you were in here making the bed, right?" said Betsy. But her voice was kind, not accusing.

"Si, *señora*," Carmelita said softly. "But I no see ring. I don't know it here. I never touch."

"I know you don't, Carmelita," said Betsy. Then she turned to the other maid. "What about you, Esperanza?"

"I no in here, *señora*," Esperanza said. "I no do this room today."

Betsy turned to everyone else in the room. "Carmelita has been with me for years. If she wanted to, she could have helped herself to what was in my jewelry box a hundred times over. But she never has. I don't think we can assume she has anything to do with this. The same is true for Esperanza."

"I know that," Angelica said impatiently. "But I just thought since Carmelita was in here, she might know *something*, might have seen *something*."

"I sorry," Carmelita said, raising her large brown eyes to Angelica in a supplicating look. "I wish I help."

"You know, there's someone else who was up here," Justine said. Everyone turned away from Carmelita, who must surely, Lenore thought, have been grateful for the shift in focus.

"Who was that?" Betsy asked.

"Bobby," said Justine. Suddenly an invisible but distinct change came over the assembled group.

"Bobby," breathed Angelica.

"Who is Bobby?" Ohad asked.

"Caleb's boyfriend. None of us had met him before," Angelica said. "This is the first time."

"Oh, that's right," Ohad said. "He got here late last night, didn't he?"

Angelica nodded. "Well, can we bring him here? Talk to him?" she said.

"Do we really want to accuse your brother's new boyfriend of theft?" Betsy asked.

"Mom, I do not understand why you are so timid! *Someone* had to have taken that ring—it was right there." Angelica gestured to the dresser. "And now it's not."

"Let me see what I can do," Betsy said. "But I want to be . . . tactful, all right?"

"I think the time for tact has passed!" Angelica said sharply. "Someone needs to talk to him. And if you won't do it, I will." She turned and marched out of the room. Lenore was puzzled. Something was not right here, though she could not say what it was. She did not like this Bobby person, not one bit. But somehow she had a hard time believing he had slipped into this room and stolen that ring. Call it an old woman's intuition, but she simply did not think he was guilty. Justine, on the other hand, was hiding something. What it was Lenore did not know, but she aimed to find out. Everyone else had started filing out too.

"Justine," she called to her great-granddaughter, but the girl had already skipped ahead of everyone else and was flitting down the stairs. She did not turn.

Lenore watched her go, yet said nothing. What she had just heard did not correlate at all with what she had seen: Justine pawing the grass, looking so frantic. Justine insinuating that Bobby could have been the culprit. Bobby, Lenore decided, did *not* take that ring. Lenore was as sure of that as she was sure that Monty had loved her or that she would continue to miss him until the day she died. So the story was clearly a *bubbemeisser*, but the question was why. Why did Justine lie? Did she take the ring? Then why would she be looking for it in the grass? If that was what she had been looking for. There was a meaning to this, an order that had yet to be revealed. And until that order had made itself clear, Lenore did not want to say anything to anyone else in the family about what she had seen.

These were the thoughts that occupied her as she walked out of Angelica's room and down the hall to her own. Round and round they circled like a pair of puppies nipping at each other's tails. She stopped, her attention arrested by a sound. It was a small yip. No, it was more like a whimper. Betsy's odious little dog clamoring for attention—

again. But hadn't Lenore left it in her room with the door closed? Maybe Betsy found it and brought it back to her own room. Had she seen the stain on the rug yet? Lenore had forgotten to mention it.

The sound continued, and Lenore realized that it was not coming from the room that was Betsy and Don's. No, it was much closer than that; it was coming from behind the door where she now stood, the door to Caleb's room. And it was not canine but human. With a sick feeling Lenore realized she was listening to Caleb, who was crying, crying as if his tender boychick's heart were breaking right in two.

Ten

The motel was every bit as grim and dispiriting as Lincoln had anticipated: the torn window shade, the lumpy mattress, the collar of rust encircling the toilet's base, the rhythmic drip, drip, drip of the bathroom faucet were familiar and predictable, all features common to this breed of forlorn roadside establishment.

But the painkiller had blunted the throbbing, and he was grateful, even buoyant, for the reprieve. He immediately hung up the rented tux, sparing it from further travel-related indignities, and he unpacked the rest of his things, placing them neatly in the drawers, two of which were of course broken. He showered, glad he had thought to pack a pair of flip-flops; the shower floor was no doubt teeming with fungal spores and God knew what else; he didn't want his bare skin to touch anything in this place. He shaved too and trimmed the damn hairs that poked out from both his ears and nostrils; he neatly combed what remained of the hair on his head.

Then, still wearing his flip-flops and robe, he stretched out on the unforgiving mattress for a nap. Though jittery and uncomfortable, he nonetheless fell into a deep, dreamless sleep. The sound of his phone—the opening chords of Beethoven's Fifth—so startled him that he jumped up in the bed, knocking his head against the reading lamp that was attached to the wall above it.

"Hello?" he fairly shouted into the thing. "Hello?"

"Dad, it's me, Caleb. You don't have to yell—I'm not on Mars."

"Caleb." Just saying the name slowed and soothed the erratic pounding of his easily jolted heart. "What's up, big guy?" *Big guy* had been his nickname for Caleb when he was a boy; considering what a pip-squeak he'd been throughout most of his childhood, it had been a running gag between them.

"Dad, can I see you?" His voice sounded clotted; had he been crying?

"Sure—your mother asked me to be at the house around five for pictures."

"I can't wait that long. I need to see you now."

"Okay, okay," Lincoln said, rubbing the sore spot on his head. Now he knew that Caleb had been crying. "But let's not meet here," he added, eyes roaming the room with its bald carpet, its cheap and misaligned prints of sailboats and lighthouses.

"Well, I don't want to meet *here*," Caleb said. "Is there somewhere else?" Lincoln had not a clue. He hadn't been to this part of Long Island in more than a decade, and even then Great Neck was not a town he knew well. Too rich for his blood back then. And way too rich for it now.

"Tell you what," he said. "Come pick me up here, and we'll drive somewhere. I'll have all my stuff ready, and after we've talked for a while, we can head back to your mother's together."

"Be there in twenty minutes," Caleb said.

Lincoln looked forward to spending some time alone with him, the boy he loved best. Angelica had and would always come first in his heart, but then came Caleb. Gretchen and Teddy vied for third place, their respective ascendancy shifting and changing as they grew. Gretchen's dogged and often principled gravity had been engaging when she was a child, but as an adult, it was quite frankly a drag. Whereas Teddy's childish bellicosity had turned him into a driven, high-octane guy with his own successful Web-marketing firm; Lincoln, never more than a company drone, admired his elder son's initiative and finely honed sense of attack. Teddy was, as his grandmother Lenore would have said, a *macher*. But Caleb—well, Caleb had a quiet, self-contained sweetness to him, a sweetness that sometimes split Lincoln's heart but to which he was also perpetually drawn.

He got up and dressed with exceptional care. If he was going to be seeing Betsy, he wanted to look good. So he put on a fresh pair of pants and his best polo shirt—black with thin gray stripes, no guy on horseback galloping across his nipple. Then he shined his shoes with the doll-sized sponge provided by the motel, one of the few amenities he'd seen here so far. Okay, he was ready. Caleb would be here any minute. Just a last stop in the motel room's cramped bathroom, where he lifted the seat and a moment later flushed.

The foul water in the bowl rose so quickly that Lincoln didn't even have time to step back. Up and over the rim it rushed, splashing his pants, wetting his shoes. Damn. The water kept coming, gradually turning darker and more malodorous. He had to turn it off; wasn't there usually a spigot on the floor behind the toilet? But he didn't want to kneel down to locate it.

Lincoln grabbed the flimsy towel from its perch atop the tank and used it to staunch the flow. It might as well have been a tissue. As he looked wildly around for another towel, there was a knock on the door. Caleb!

"Just a minute," Lincoln called. Spying another towel on a slightly rusted rod, he reached to pull it down. He must have yanked too hard, because the rod—cheaply made and light as a chopstick—pulled right out of the wall and fell to the floor in a grayish flurry of plaster dust. "Jesus Christ!" he said. The knocking at the door continued. Lincoln heard Caleb call, "Dad? You okay in there?"

"Coming," said Lincoln. The water continued to pool on the bathroom floor; it had begun to saturate the room's carpeting, rendering the ugly burnt-orange color even uglier.

"I was out there for about five minutes," Caleb said. "Didn't you hear me?" Before Lincoln could answer, he added, "This place really is a dive. You sure you don't want to stay at Mom's?" He sniffed, a critical, what's-that-smell kind of sniff. "And it stinks too."

"I heard you," Lincoln answered. "But I was in the midst of a crisis. Actually I'm still in the midst of it." He turned and looked toward the bathroom.

"Jesus, Dad, I know it's a dump, but did you have to trash the place?"

"Trash the place!" said Lincoln. "*I* didn't *trash* the place! But I've got to get all this cleaned up, or Christ only knows what they're going to charge me for the mess."

"But if it's not your fault . . ." Caleb said.

"In a place like this, you're guilty until proven innocent."

"That's ridiculous, Dad. We'll just call the front desk and they'll send someone to deal with it."

"No!" Lincoln said. "Please don't do that." How to convey the sense of humiliation he was feeling? The panic? He didn't want to call the front desk or to face the inevitable arguments about whether he had stuffed something in the toilet that had caused the overflow or should be held accountable for pulling the towel rack out of the wall. No, he just wanted to deal with it himself as expediently as possible. "I don't want to call anyone, okay? I can handle it." He looked at Caleb, with his custom-tailored shirt, his blindingly white Keds, and hated the words that were about to come out of his mouth. "If you'll help me, that is."

"All right," said Caleb, surveying the damage. "We'd better turn this off—now." And without showing any concern for his pants, he dropped to his knees, located the spigot, and gave it an authoritative twist. The water stopped flowing, though the bathroom and carpet were still a soaked, smelly mess. "Now wait here."

"Where are you going?" Lincoln asked.

"I'll be back in five," Caleb said, ignoring the question.

So Lincoln sat on the bed, his legs pulled up and nowhere near the floor. He was ashamed of needing help from his son but grateful to have it nonetheless. When Caleb returned, he was lugging two bags; one bulged with towels. He was also dragging a vacuum cleaner.

"Where did you get all that stuff?" Lincoln asked.

"Some of it was in the trunk of my car," Caleb said. "I like to be prepared." He dropped the bag with a thud. "The vacuum and the towels came from the motel maid I ran into on the way to the parking lot. She was happy to make an extra twenty bucks." Caleb began yanking towels out of the bag. "Let's get to work."

Together Caleb and Lincoln laid towels over the carpet and bathroom floor, and walked back and forth across them a few times. They each washed their hands in the hottest water they could stand, and while waiting for the towels to do their work of absorbing, they opened the window wide and sat across from each other on the bed.

"Thanks, Caleb," said Lincoln. "I really appreciate your doing this."

"It's okay," Caleb said. "I've got some baking soda in the bag. As soon as the rug is a little less wet, you can sprinkle that all over; it should help with the smell. Then you can vacuum it up later."

"Good idea," Lincoln said. He was resourceful, this son of his. No doubt about that.

"And I've got some tools in there too," he said. "I can probably manage to get the towel rack up again."

"You're a boy wonder," said Lincoln. "A regular boy wonder."

"*De nada,*" Caleb said, and his face twisted, a semaphore of pain.

Suddenly Lincoln remembered the urgency in Caleb's earlier request to talk. "You said you needed to see me. What's going on?"

Caleb stretched out on the bed and folded his hands very carefully behind his head, as if he didn't want to muss his hair. "My life is ruined," he said.

"Ruined how?" Lincoln asked. Caleb always had been dramatic.

"Remember you were asking me about work today? And I said everything was fine?" Lincoln nodded. "Well, that wasn't true. Everything isn't fine. And it hasn't been fine for a while. I hate retail. I hate folding and refolding the same goddamned sweater all day long. Straightening the tie racks, buttoning suits, sucking up to customers who treat you like shit."

"Sounds pretty mind-numbing," said Lincoln.

"Soul numbing would be a better way to describe it. And then, as if that weren't bad enough, I got passed up for a promotion. Twice. Both times I really thought I was going to get it, you know? All pumped up, strutting around the floor, waiting for the word from the man. Only when the word came, it was no. And I was back to stacking dress shirts and swiping gold cards."

"You can get out," Lincoln said. "Get out now while you still can. While you're young."

"That's what I'm planning to do. I decided to go to cooking school. To become a pastry chef." He rolled over onto his side. "The school's in France. Mom said she would pay for it." Caleb looked at his father as if expecting his disapproval or, worse, his scorn.

"That's great. Just great. She's got the money. Why not use it for a good cause? And you're one of the best, okay? The very best. And don't you forget it."

"Thanks, Dad," Caleb said wanly.

"So why is your life ruined? Sounds to me like you've got things pretty well figured out."

"It's Bobby." Caleb dropped the name as if it were a brick.

"What about Bobby?"

"I thought he was the one, Dad. The one I'd been waiting for, the one I'd dreamed about. We were so good together. So damn good."

"Were?" asked Lincoln, seizing on the past tense.

"We were having a great time. I introduced him to Mom and everyone; they all loved him, I could tell. He seemed to really fit in; he told me how much he was looking forward to the wedding. I even used my discount at the store to buy him a new suit, new tie, new shoes, new everything. But this morning after we went swimming, I found him making out with some half-naked guy on Mom's payroll."

He took a deep, melancholy breath. "Gretchen was with me. She saw him too."

"Son of a bitch," Lincoln said, heart constricting like a fist when he thought of what it must have felt like to have seen that. "Son of a bitch." To his surprise Caleb actually smiled.

"Yeah," he echoed. "Son of a goddamned bitch."

"Throws a monkey wrench in your plans, huh?"

"Totally. I wanted him to come to France with me."

"Fuck him," Lincoln snapped. He got off the bed and began padding around the towel-covered floor. "You go to France yourself. You go to France, and you become the best damn pastry chef in the country. Hell, on the planet, okay? You've got what it takes. Remember the scones? The *tarte tatin?*" He mangled the last name, the French one, but so what. Caleb knew what he meant.

Caleb swung his long legs off the bed and went into the bathroom with his tools. Lincoln followed, waiting for him to say something. But Caleb was silent, immersed in the job of screwing the shoddy thing back into the wall while Lincoln swept up the debris and deposited it in the trash.

"What am I going to do?" Caleb asked, finally breaking the silence. "I've got to face him tonight. We're seated at the same table."

"Let's talk about that when we're on our way to your mother's," Lincoln said. "I've had about enough of this motel from hell for right now." He changed back into the pants he had worn on the plane, but he didn't have another pair of shoes; he hoped the ones he was wearing didn't smell too bad.

When they got into the car, Lincoln laid the rented tuxedo out across the backseat. When he turned around again, he saw Caleb sitting, not moving, with his hands clasped at the top of the steering wheel. Lincoln waited a beat; Caleb lowered his head until it touched the top of the wheel.

"I know your heart is breaking," Lincoln began.

"Not breaking. Broken." Caleb's words, though slightly muffled, were still discernible.

"Broken, then. Broken." Lincoln paused, not entirely sure how much of the past he wanted to dredge up. "And I know how you feel, buddy. Believe me, I know."

"You mean—Mom?" Caleb turned his head slightly so that he was no longer speaking into his hands.

"Big-time," Lincoln said.

"So how did you get over it?" Caleb asked.

"I didn't," Lincoln said, finding a strange relief in coming clean. He'd never talked to his kids about the residual mess of feelings he had for Betsy; there had never been a reason to before.

"You didn't? Even after all these years?" Caleb sat up now; his hands, though still on the wheel, were no longer gripping it so tightly.

"Even after all these years."

"I didn't know," Caleb said.

"Why would you? I never wanted to bring it up with you kids; it didn't seem right."

"You mean you still love her?"

"Still," Lincoln said. "Still and always."

"Jesus, Dad," Caleb said. He looked at his hands like he

expected to find some answer in them. "Is it going to be tough for you to see her today?"

"What do you think?" Lincoln countered. "It fairly kills me that she's happier now. So much happier than when we were together. She really loves this guy. Even if the reason why beats the hell out of me."

Caleb didn't answer, but his fine, sensitive mouth twisted into a smirk.

"Oh, you think she loves his wallet, right? That it's all about the money? I told myself that," Lincoln said as much to himself as to Caleb. "I told myself that for a long time, because it was easier and because it let me off the hook. But you know what? I don't think that anymore. And you kids shouldn't either."

"So why are you doing it?" Caleb asked. "Why are you here?"

"Why am I here?" Lincoln felt his agitation spreading like a rash. "Why am I here? Because Angelica is getting married, that's why. And I wasn't going to let anything— even my own goddamned broken heart—keep me from seeing it." Sensing he might sound too rough, Lincoln began again. "It hurts like hell, but you can get through this, big guy," he said softly. "I know you can."

"Do you really think so?" Caleb put his head down again; his words were directed to the floor pad beneath his feet.

"I know so," said Lincoln. "I'm positive, in fact."

"I can't face him. Not tonight, not with everyone there."

"You bet you can." When Caleb didn't answer, he went

on. "Look, what are your options? You want to kick him out now, fine. I get that. But if you do, most likely there will be a scene—a big one too. So you'll be making a scene on the day of Angelica's wedding. Which will hurt her, no matter how you slice it."

"I have a reason. A good reason."

"Sure you do. But will Angelica see it that way? And when you look back on this day, will you?"

Caleb remained silent. Lincoln looked past him, out of the window. Did the sky look a little less sunny, a shade more gray? He directed his gaze upwards. Definitely some cloud action going on up there. Was it going to rain? Jesus, he hoped not.

"Look, Dad, I appreciate what you're trying to do here." Caleb lifted his head from the steering wheel. "But it's not going to work."

"Why not?"

"Because it's different. You had time to process everything with Mom before tonight. Plenty of time. For me it's all brand-new."

"I know that, big guy, but—" said Lincoln.

"And could you please stop calling me *big guy?*" Caleb said. "It's getting a little old."

"Okay," Lincoln said, more hurt than he would let on. "Okay." There was a long, uncomfortable silence, in which Lincoln wished, in that idle way that recovered drunks could still wish, for a drink. He remembered achingly the way the late-afternoon light hit his whisky glass with its merry cargo of ice cubes as the sun turned the brownish liquid to shimmering gold; the anticipatory, almost tingling chill of the green beer bottle when first pulled from the fridge. *Just one*, he thought. *Just one* . . .

"Sorry." Caleb interrupted his fantasy. "I didn't mean it to come out like that. I'm just upset, that's all. No, more than upset. I'm furious, heartbroken, and slightly out of my mind. There's my mental state, twenty-five words or less."

"Look, I *know* what you're going through." Lincoln stopped himself just in time from saying *big guy*. It was going to take him a little while to reprogram. "And I want to help." He was almost afraid to ask the next question, but he asked it anyway. "So what *are* you going to do tonight?"

"I don't know," Caleb said, slipping the key into the ignition. "I can't promise anything."

"You'll have to deal with Angelica," Lincoln said. "And remember—crossing her is no picnic."

"Angelica!" Caleb said. "What a prima donna! You'd think no one else in the world ever got married before."

"That's Angelica, all right," Lincoln said.

"Dad, you sound like you *admire* her!"

"You're damn straight I do," Lincoln said. "In fact, more than admire her, I *love* her for being such a royal pain in the ass. That girl"—and here his heart swelled with a crazy, convoluted sort of pride—"knows how to get what she wants out of life." Caleb laughed, even though it came out as more of a snort than anything. He started up the car, and off they went.

But wait—what had Caleb said earlier? That Lincoln favored Angelica? Christ. Lincoln wished fervently that he could take the words he'd just uttered and stuff them right back in his mouth. "Caleb, did you mean what you said to me before?" he asked. "About my loving Angelica more than the rest of you?"

"Of course," said Caleb, eyes on the road. "Why would I have said it if I didn't mean it?"

"I'm sorry you feel that way," Lincoln said. This, more than anything else, made him feel like a failure.

"Don't worry about it, Dad," said Caleb, still looking straight ahead. "I know you love me and the rest of us. We all know. But we also know how Angelica kind of casts a spell over everyone. Guys especially. Teddy calls her the sorceress. No one is immune—not even you."

Not even me, Lincoln thought sadly. This whole interlude had turned out to be a major bust: the toilet, the towel rack, being rescued by his son instead of the other way around. He hadn't been able to help Caleb deal with Bobby, that cheating little turd, either. And to cap it off, hearing that his preference for Angelica was just common knowledge among his kids, one more annoying trait of his that they had to contend with. Lincoln let his eyes linger on the passing scenery. The spreading trees and verdant lawns of Great Neck sped by, taunting apparitions of wealth and privilege that he would never, ever come even close to having.

Well, he had tried, hadn't he? Tried to be the caring, supportive dad that all his years on the sauce had kept him from being. But it looked like he was a bit late. He had no idea what would go down tonight; all Lincoln could do was stick close to Caleb and try to contain the damage. Right now there was the more immediate hurdle of facing Betsy and the Bozo. Once again the siren song of a drink, *just one, just one*, started to hum in his waiting ear.

"Did you know that Ennis showed up?" Caleb asked after a few minutes.

"I heard," Lincoln said but did not volunteer how he had obtained this information. "How is Gretchen taking it?" He had not forgotten his promise to Angelica either; he would talk to Gretchen just as soon as he could.

"All right. I guess."

"No shit." Lincoln was skeptical. Nasty business with his ex-son-in-law: the girl, the pregnancy, and the suicide attempt that yanked Gretchen into her sorry-ass orbit. Did that girl have her baby yet? Did his granddaughters know? Jesus, what did guys these days want? Gretchen could not hold a candle to Angelica—no one could—but she was a damn fine-looking woman. Smart too. Okay, so she was a bit humorless. A bit lost at times. But she was a devoted wife, a caring mother. She'd loved that kilt-wearing guy of hers— yes, she did. He could tell. So why had Ennis let his dick do his thinking? Thrown away a good woman, a nice house, a couple of kids, all for a roll in the hay with a schoolgirl? A schoolgirl he'd gone and knocked up. Jeez. Lincoln, whose own transgressions had been legion, understood the enormity of what Ennis had done. And he took a useless satisfaction in knowing that despite everything, he hadn't cheated on Betsy. No matter how damn drunk he'd been.

"You don't believe me?"

"How would I know?" Lincoln said. "I haven't seen

her or talked to her yet." He wanted to, though, and not just because he had told Angelica he would. He wanted to see them all. Immediately. He willed himself not to ask, *Are we there yet?*

Instead he turned his attention to the sky once more. Crap. Those looked like rain clouds; they sure as hell did. "Do you think it's going to rain?" he asked Caleb. But he suddenly lost interest in the answer, because Caleb had just pulled into the grand, curving driveway that led to Betsy's house.

Lincoln stared. He'd never actually been here before; he'd seen pictures sent by the kids and heard their descriptions, dripping with detail. But hearing and seeing were two decidedly different things. It was even bigger than he expected, and its two massive, elaborately carved wooden doors were flanked by stone urns that spilled magenta flowers. Betsy had always wanted flowers by the front door, hadn't she? Well, now she had them.

While Caleb parked, Lincoln attempted to check his breath discreetly, using the palm of his hand. But, hell, why bother? That's what mints were for, right? He popped one in his mouth and held out the roll to Caleb. Caleb shook his head. "No, thanks," he said, and the casual coldness in his voice was another snub. Then he got out of the car and closed the door with a small, articulate slam, leaving Lincoln to face his ex-wife all on his own.

Eleven

❧ · ❧

"There you are!" Gretchen said to Caleb when she found him out on the lawn, near the dolphin statue. "I've been looking everywhere!" The sky above had grown gray and heavy with clouds; it looked like it was about to pour any second.

"I went to get Dad," he said. "Sorry if I worried you." But he didn't sound sorry, not a bit.

"You could have told me that's where you were going," Gretchen said. "I wanted to talk to you." Was that ominous sound she heard a rumble of distant thunder?

"Well, you found me; what do you want to say?" He stopped and put his hands on his hips, a truculent stance better suited to a five-year-old.

"Caleb, would you stop being such a little shit? I know you're upset, but—"

"*You* think you know! *Dad* thinks he knows! But what do *any* of you know? Nothing! Not a thing."

"All right, then," she said. "If you're not interested in

being consoled, fine. Have your little tantrum." Leaving him in that rigid, unyielding posture, she turned to go back to the house. It was only when she could no longer see him that she heard behind her the sound of his weeping.

Gretchen paused. Should she go back and risk being rebuffed again? Or should she let him tough it out on his own? Compassion won, and she turned. She approached quickly and sank down to the grass where he now sat curled like a shrimp with his face in his hands.

"I'm sorry," she said. "So very sorry."

Caleb continued to cry quietly.

"And no matter what you think, I do know how you feel. I lived it too, remember?"

"I guess you did," Caleb said, lifting his wet face to look at her. His nose was running, and Gretchen handed him a tissue from the packet in her jeans pocket.

"Only I didn't actually catch them in the act the way you did," she continued. "But then there was the little matter of the pregnancy and the botched suicide attempt. That kind of evens things out."

"Okay, okay," Caleb said. "So you're in the club too." He blew his nose loudly.

"Club?"

"The Duped and Dumped Club."

"The Duped and Dumped Club," said Gretchen. "I like it. It has a nice ring. But it's not exactly accurate, you know. I mean, we were both duped, but in my case, I did the dumping. And in yours, the outcome remains to be seen, right?" When Caleb didn't answer, Gretchen added, "What *are* you going to do, anyway? I assume you're going to talk to him."

"Dad said he thought I should wait," Caleb said.

"Wait?" said Gretchen. "Why would you do that? I don't think waiting is a useful strategy."

"Well, what do you expect from Dad? His emotional range extends from about one glass of scotch to the next."

"That's mean," Gretchen said. "And, besides, that's not even true anymore." Her father *had* spent a good portion of their childhood drinking, but he'd been sober a long time, and Caleb's assessment seemed a bit harsh. Anyway, where was her father? Why hadn't he come to say hello? "Is Dad here now? I didn't see him."

"He went inside to say hello to Mom and Angelica."

Well, no surprise there. The other women in the family came first for her father. Gretchen was, as ever, the afterthought. She was surprised that this information—hardly new—hurt as much as it did; a film of unshed tears momentarily blurred her vision. But she blinked them away and all she said to her brother was, "Why did Dad think you should wait before talking to Bobby?"

"Because of the wedding, of course! The all-important, everything-must-be-perfect-for wedding. He was worried I might make a scene. Well, I just might."

"Ah, the wedding," Gretchen said. There was another rumble of thunder; this one sounded closer. "The wedding that may very well take place in the rain."

"There's a tent," Caleb said. "No, there are two. It's beginning to look like Disney World around here."

"Angelica is *not* going to be happy if it rains," Gretchen said. "Tents or no tents."

"Tough luck," Caleb said. "She may order Mom, Don, and all their minions around, but she doesn't have any clout with the weather." He wadded up his used tissue and flicked it across the lawn. "Not a bit."

"You're littering! On Mom's property!" Gretchen said in mock admonition. "That's a serious transgression. Much worse than using an upstairs towel at the pool."

"Big deal," Caleb said. "She's got someone to clean up, remember? We've seen him. He's no doubt good at . . . so many things."

"Don't I know it," Gretchen said.

"What?" He turned to scrutinize her. "Don't tell me he was doing you too."

"Only in my dreams," Gretchen said. "He is a piece, you know. And he struck up a conversation with me, that's all. How did I know he liked boys?"

"Well, maybe not all boys. But he liked Bobby just fine."

"So where exactly is Bobby-boy-toy at the moment?" asked Gretchen.

"Damned if I know. Or care," said Caleb. But this remark was clearly just bravado.

Before Gretchen could reply, the rain started coming down, delicately at first and then quickly turning to big, fat drops that splashed their knees and shoulders, hands and faces.

"Come on, we'd better go inside," Gretchen said, jumping to her feet.

"It's raining!" Caleb cried. "Raining! Angelica is going to have a fit."

"A major fit," Gretchen said as they hurried toward the house. "A fit to end all fits." The rain was drenching; her T-shirt was already soaked.

"I just can't believe it's going to rain on Angelica's wedding."

"Caleb, you actually sound happy about this."

"Me? Happy? Oh no, no, no, big sis! I'm not happy it's going to screw up Angelica's wedding. But I am happy about the rain." They had reached the kitchen door. "Very happy."

"Why?" Water was streaming down her hair and into her eyes. Drenched and shimmying, Caleb broke into a more than passable imitation of the Temptations singing their 1967 hit. "Oh, I wish it would rain," he crooned into an imaginary microphone.

"You're nuts!" Gretchen said, but she was laughing, and he was laughing too. It was good to see him laugh. Still giggling, they went inside and upstairs together.

"What are you going to do now?" she asked when they reached the door to her room.

"I'm going to find him," Caleb said, serious again. "I think I should do that before tonight. Otherwise God only knows what I'll do when I see him at the wedding. There's going to be a lot of breakables floating around, and I'm not sure I trust myself; things could get ugly. To say nothing of loud."

Trying to decide whether he meant it, Gretchen studied his face. Finally she said, "I'll check in with you later, okay?"

"Later," he said. "Got it." He leaned over to give her a quick peck on the cheek, and on impulse she pulled him to her in a tight hug. Uh-oh. He might feel patronized and push her away. But, no, he not only submitted to the embrace; he actually returned it.

"Caleb," she said when he had released her. "Caleb, I have to ask you something." She was still clammy, and chilled too, but she didn't want to let the moment slip away; it might not come again.

"Go ahead."

"Do you think Angelica is Dad's favorite?" The hug gave her the permission to ask.

"You're almost forty, and you don't know the answer to that?" He gently tugged the wet band of his shorts away from his waist.

"I always thought so when we were kids. But I hoped it would have changed by now. That giving up the booze would have opened his eyes a little more. Let him see that we were there too."

"Dad is Dad," Caleb said. "He loves us. He really does. But he loves her most of all."

To her surprise—and apparently to Caleb's—Gretchen's own eyes filled up with tears, which spilled neatly, in a pair of lines, down the center of each cheek.

"Hey," he said, gathering her once more in his embrace. "Hey, don't take it so hard. He can't help it, okay? No one can. You love who you love."

You love whom *you love*, the editor in Gretchen wanted to correct. But did not. She looked searchingly into her brother's face. But she wasn't seeing him, not at all. Instead she had a vision of her two daughters—wrinkled, wet, and just minutes old—clutched tightly in Ennis's arms.

Caleb turned away, headed toward his room, and Gretchen was about to go into hers when Teddy appeared— also soaked, still wearing the god-awful flowered trunks— and stopped her. He had one of the yellow-and-turquoise towels wrapped around his head, like a pasha, and another wrapped around his shoulders. Was it also considered a transgression to bring the pool towels up here to the second floor?

"So what's the deal with Caleb?" he asked. "You can tell me now; Marti's in our room, changing."

"I like her," Gretchen said, wanting to deflect the question.

"That's great; me too. But you haven't answered."

"Why don't you ask him?" Gretchen said. "Wouldn't that be the best thing?"

Teddy didn't say anything but reached up to steady the makeshift turban; it looked in danger of coming loose. "Caleb doesn't really confide in me," he said finally.

"Has that ever bothered you before?" Gretchen crossed her arms over her chest.

"No," Teddy said in what felt like a rare moment of candor. "It hasn't."

"So then why do you expect him to now? And why do you even care?"

"I don't know," Teddy said. "Maybe it has to do with the wedding. Or Marti. Or both." Gretchen was interested; this line of conversation was so *not* like Teddy, and she wanted to hear more. "Caleb's always been so . . . emotional. Easily upset, you know? I just couldn't relate."

"But you think you can now?"

"Marti's been after me," Teddy said. The turban sprung loose from its tentative moorings, unfurling as it collapsed. "She thinks I shouldn't *alienate my family*. And she wants me to be more open, *more in touch with my feelings*." He sounded mocking.

"Which you are not interested in doing."

"Feelings!" Teddy exclaimed. "Why is everyone always bitching and moaning about feelings? You do it too, Gretch." Gretch (it had a most unfortunate resemblance to *retch*) was a childhood nickname she loathed now every bit as much as she had loathed it then; just hearing it made her want to terminate this conversation immediately. But something told her to stay, to wait it out. Teddy wasn't using it to rile her; he'd really seemed to slip back into some earlier, more approachable incarnation of himself. "What good are feelings?" he continued. "What matters is what you do, how you act."

"And you don't see that there just might be a connection

between the two? That how you act just *might* be predicated on how you feel."

"I know that, Ms. Amateur Psychologist."

"Good," she said. "So now put your knowledge into action."

"Meaning?"

"Go and talk to Caleb yourself. If you understand how he's feeling, maybe you'll have a clue as to why he's acting this way."

"You coddle him," Teddy said. "But, then, you coddle everyone, Gretch." Had she actually thought mere moments ago that she had detected a chink in his frat-boy armor?

"Asking your brother what's wrong is hardly coddling," Gretchen said. "I'd call it decency. Or compassion."

"We'll just have to agree to disagree on this one, Gretch," said Teddy. And, picking up the towel, he ambled off.

Twelve

❧ • ❧

Betsy stood quietly in her bedroom and stared out the window at the rain. In her arms she held the whimpering dog—nervous even at the best of times, the poor thing went nearly berserk from the thunder. Contrary to the expectations of her family, she did not cry or carry on. With her lips drawn together, as if she did not want to let even a word of complaint escape them, she just looked at the water dripping down the windowpanes in sinuous rivulets.

How could it rain today of all days? How? She had not even seen Angelica since the skies had opened up; she had wanted to compose herself first. The dog, still shivering, pressed its small, furry head against her clavicle and looked up at her adoringly.

"You don't like the rain either, do you?" asked Betsy. The dog's plumelike tail stirred.

Betsy knew she had to get a grip. The rain was not all that was upsetting her. The rain was an annoyance, to be sure. But she was prepared for the rain, as she was prepared for most things. Of course the cocktail hour, which was to have been held in the rose garden, would have to be moved to the dinner tent instead, but the waitstaff had already been alerted to the possibility, and they knew what to do. It would be a pity, because the garden was particularly beautiful this year, with a dense profusion of blossoms dripping from the latticework top of the octagonal pergola to create a most fanciful bower; Betsy had already arranged for photos of the bride and groom to be taken inside it. Although she had not planted any of the roses—arrayed in a deepening spectrum from purest white to darkest crimson—herself, she loved the garden and spent hours with the gardener, Clyde, overseeing every aspect of its care.

No. She had to admit that she was also upset by Pippa and the inexplicable hold she seemed to have over Angelica. Angelica, whose affection had always seemed to Betsy just the slightest bit out of reach: tantalizing, elusive, and never quite fully hers.

Didn't the kids always complain that Angelica was Lincoln's favorite? Well, it worked both ways; Lincoln—perpetually plastered, irresponsible, impossible Lincoln—had been Angelica's favorite. No matter how soused, how sloppy, how rip-roaring drunk he got, Angelica's devotion did not waiver; she was the compass needle to his North Star.

It had galled Betsy quietly for years, and it was galling her less quietly today. How could this daughter she had done so much for—the countless miles clocked ferrying her to this practice and that study session, the extra job Betsy had taken to pay for the fancy camps, the tennis and riding lessons, the weekends devoted to inspecting all those colleges—have preferred Lincoln? There was no sense in this and no justice either. But, then, when had sense or justice ever been governing forces in the inexplicable workings of a family?

The bedroom door opened, and Betsy turned. "You okay?" Don said. He was a big man, a bit bearish, but Betsy thought he carried himself well.

"No," she said. "I'm not."

He crossed the room in what seemed like two long strides. "Come on, tell Papa all about it," he said. He put his massive arm around Betsy, and she let herself melt into the embrace. Even when the dog—as jealous as she was high-strung—growled at him, he didn't get rattled, but delivered an affectionate swat to her snout. "That's enough out of *you*, midget," he said. The dog seemed startled, and her growling stopped at least for the moment.

"It's just everything," she said. "The rain, the kids, Ennis, Lincoln—"

"Did he do something that upset you?" Don interrupted.

"No, it's not that. But seeing him brings up the past. And of course his being here affects the kids."

"Aren't they glad to see him? He's their father after all." Don didn't have children of his own, but had embraced Betsy's fully and without reservation.

"Yes, but it brings up all the old tensions. The drinking, the fighting—they remember all that. Remember it and resent it. You know how it is . . ." She was babbling, leaving a trail of partially accurate emotional breadcrumbs to divert him from the real issue, which was that she, Betsy Kalb Silverstein Grofsky, mother, grandmother, and sixty-four years old in April, was so jealous of Pippa Morganstern that she fantasized about pushing her smug, overly made-up face straight into the multitiered, elaborately decorated wedding cake.

"Weddings always bring up the old, unfinished business in families," Don said. "That's why we decided to skip having one, remember?" It was true. One glorious September weekend half a dozen years ago, Betsy and Don had driven up to New England, where they had risen early, canoed in a pond, walked in the woods, snapped pictures of the changing leaves. And at the end of it, they had become man and wife, courtesy of a justice of the peace (an elderly man with gold-rimmed spectacles—really! truly!) they found in Dorset, Vermont, who had been happy to marry them on the spot. Betsy's kids had groused of course, but she suspected that secretly they were relieved they had not had to witness her marrying the man who had replaced their father in her heart.

"I remember," she said. "But Angelica wanted a wedding, and I said I would make her one."

"And you've been doing a helluva job too," Don said. "As for what's out there"—he pointed to the rain-streaked windows—"it's beyond your control, and it's not going to matter anyway. You've got the tents, the umbrellas, the runners—everything. And whatever you didn't remember, that wedding planner person, Poppy what's-her-face—"

"It's Pippa," Betsy said, failing to suppress the humiliating little sob from escaping her throat. "Pippa Morganstern, and I've never in my life hated anyone quite as much as I hate her!"

"So fire her," Don said calmly. "Right away." When she didn't answer, he added, "I'll do it for you. Just say the word." Don ran a good-sized company with a hand both fair and firm. He treated his employees well, but when someone had to go, they were gone; he didn't waste any time, because that just made things worse. Swift, clean, and a decent severance package, he always said. That was the best way to handle it.

"Angelica would be furious," Betsy said. Her glance went back to the window, still dripping with rain. Who knew what state her daughter would be in at this moment anyway?

"Who's paying Pippa Morganstern's fee?"

"We are," Betsy said.

"Then do it," said Don. "Now."

The idea bloomed easily in Betsy's mind: confronting Pippa, thanking her for her time, and escorting her out. She experienced an anticipatory frisson as she imagined the astonished look on Pippa's face, the satisfying slam of the front door. "You really think I should?" she asked.

"I know you should," said Don. "Don't let her spoil the day."

"It's Angelica's day," Betsy felt compelled to point out.

"That we have bought and paid for." He gave her a gentle little shove in the direction of the door.

But Betsy stopped, thinking again of the rose garden.

Although the décor in both tents had been confined to a so-phisticated palette of white, silver, and gray, Betsy had suggested a warmer color for the napkins and carpet runners (those old bricks that made up the paths were charming, but uneven and slick with moss in places) in the garden. "What about pink?" she had said. Pink was so feminine, so pretty; pink would set off the colors of the roses nicely.

"Pink is so obvious," Pippa had said disdainfully. "What about lilac? Or a very subtle periwinkle blue?"

"Yes!" Angelica said, clearly delighted. "Periwinkle is the exact color of a drawing room I saw in Moscow; I thought it was the most exquisite space I had ever seen."

"Oh yes, it's a real Muscovite color," Pippa said, and Betsy had to keep her mouth from falling open in stupefied disbelief. *Muscovite color?* How on earth would she know? Then again, how would Betsy know that it wasn't? She had never been to Moscow. So Betsy said nothing, and the carpet runners and napkins had been ordered in periwinkle, a color she privately found both anemic and uninspired. Recalling all that, she seethed afresh. She looked down at the dog, whose head remained snuggled against her chest. "You wait here," she instructed, depositing the animal on the bed. Then, shoulders squared and head erect, she marched down the stairs and straight into the lion's den.

Thirteen

꧁ · ꧂

As soon as Gretchen opened the door to her room, she yanked her wet shirt up and over her head. The powerful central air-conditioning was making her shiver. Once she had dry clothes on, she'd feel more comfortable. And then maybe, just *maybe* she would go off in search of her father, who had to be skulking somewhere around here.

Gretchen had just started to unbutton her jeans when she realized that she was not alone. Ennis sat quietly in the flowered (what else?) armchair that was tucked into one corner of the room. At least he hadn't had the gall to sit on her bed.

"What are you doing in here?" she said, scooping the wet, discarded shirt from the floor and using it to cover her midsection. Of course—*of course*—she was wearing her oldest, rattiest bra; had Lenore seen the disgraceful thing, she would have disowned Gretchen.

"I told you: I wanted to talk to you. You've been avoiding me all day."

"No, I haven't," she said. But it was a lie. She had most

certainly been avoiding him, and she would like to continue avoiding him, only it was difficult when he barged uninvited into her room. "And, anyway, you could have waited instead of sneaking up on me like this."

"No, I couldn't," he said. "I wanted to do it before the wedding. It's important."

"Well at least let me change," she said testily. She dug through her suitcase, disappeared into the bathroom, and shut the door tightly behind her. The wet jeans were difficult to pull off; they stuck to her skin and seemed to take forever to remove. Which wasn't so bad, because it gave her time to prepare herself for talking to him.

Even when she was finally free of the jeans and attired in a moderately rumpled but still passable-looking skirt and gingham blouse, she took her time, combing out the wet tangle of her hair and dabbing a little blush on her face. She had wanted to present herself to Ennis wrapped and ready: a new dress, a new attitude, a new Gretchen. She didn't like being caught off guard; it was unsettling and unfair. Glancing at the lace-bedecked window, she briefly entertained the viability of climbing out, but the long drop down to the stone-covered driveway below stopped her. That and the realization that she would need to face Ennis at some point this evening; she might was well get it over with now.

"So," she said, finally emerging from the bathroom. "We meet again."

"It's good to see you," Ennis said quietly, ignoring her wan attempt at wit.

Gretchen didn't know what to say to that; it was not

good to see him, but it seemed gratuitously rude to say so. Instead she perched tensely on the end of the bed, which had been expertly made in her absence.

As soon as she sat down, Ennis popped up as if responding to some internal cue. She noticed then that he'd lost weight—not that he needed to—and appeared a bit gaunt. Maybe life on his own wasn't so terrific; well, it served him right. She lifted her chin and sucked in her stomach. Some people lost interest in eating when they were in turmoil, but Gretchen, alas, had never been one of them.

"What was it you needed to tell me that couldn't wait?" she said finally.

"It's about Eve," he said.

Just the name uttered here in this room felt like a slap. Gretchen could see the girl's pale, miserable face after she had appeared at their house and told Gretchen she had only minutes before swallowed thirty Ambien tablets, a month's supply; she proffered the empty bottle as proof. She said she had decided to do it when Ennis was teaching, because she hadn't been able to face him. But she'd had no problem facing Gretchen, had she? And what about the girls? Had she thought of what it might be like for them if they found her in their home in that condition? So Gretchen had dialed 911 and done her best to soothe Eve until the ambulance arrived. And then, because she really was so pitiful and seemed to have no one to lean on at all, Gretchen rode with her to the hospital and waited outside the emergency room until she was sure Eve was all right.

"What makes you think I want to hear that name ever

again?" said Gretchen. But she did want to know whether Eve had had her baby yet and whether Ennis was as smitten with it as he had been with Justine and Portia. The twins did not yet know they were going to have a half sibling. They had reacted so poorly—Justine in particular—to the separation that Gretchen had not wanted to tell them immediately.

"They'll hate you for keeping it from them," Ennis had pointed out during the tense phone call they'd agreed upon to discuss the subject.

"I don't care!" she'd said hotly. "It's just too much to handle right now, and I want you to back me up."

"It doesn't seem right," he had said. "You're coercing me into keeping a secret that I don't want to keep."

"Ennis," she said, "if you tell them now, I'll keep you from seeing them."

"No judge would go along with that," he said. But he didn't sound so sure.

"Oh? How about when the whole sordid story of how you knocked up your *student* comes out? Maybe a judge would view you as a less-than-fit sort of parent."

Ennis was silent. "All right," he'd said sullenly. "You win."

Her eyes had filled with sudden, hot tears; she was grateful he could not see them. "Ennis, you lied to me, cheated on me, and someone *else* is having your baby. How can you say I've *won*?" And then she'd gotten off the phone.

Ennis stared at her now. "But I have to talk about it," he said. "You'll see why when I tell you."

"All right," Gretchen said. She sat up as straight as she could, still sucking in her stomach. Damn, but this proper posture business was *work*. "Shoot."

"After I left," said Ennis.

"You mean, after I kicked you out," Gretchen said.

"After you kicked me out," he repeated, rubbing his fingers over the bridge of his nose, "I felt terrible. As if I'd ruined everything, thrown away everything that ever mattered to me."

"You did," Gretchen said. She had always loved Ennis's elegant, aquiline nose and was supremely gratified when it appeared, in a somewhat modified form, on the faces of their daughters.

"But I also felt this—this sense of responsibility to Eve. I'd done this monumentally stupid thing that affected her too. She was really and truly devastated by what had happened."

"Ennis," Gretchen said sharply. "Spare me these details. *I don't care* one iota about Eve's feelings! Do. Not. Care. Get it?"

"Would you let me finish?" he said. "Please?" But a knock on the door silenced him. Gretchen glanced in his direction before saying, "Come in."

"Mom, have you seen—Oh! Daddy! I didn't know you were in here," said Portia, looking from Gretchen to Ennis and back again.

"Sweetheart, hey," Ennis said. "I like the hair." Portia was sporting a newly shorn coif, which had the perhaps unintended but nevertheless fortuitous result of neutralizing— almost eradicating, in fact—the fuchsia streak in her hair.

"Do you? I do too. I wanted to show Justine, but I can't find her anywhere, so I thought I would check up here. Have either of you seen her?"

"I haven't," Gretchen said, and Ennis added, "Neither have I."

"Can you help me look?" Portia asked. Gretchen suppressed a sigh. She did not want to look for Justine at the moment; she was keenly aware that Justine had no desire to be found by her. And though she was reluctant to admit it, she wanted to finish the conversation with Ennis, wanted, despite everything, to hear whatever it was he thought was so essential to tell her.

"Not right now," Gretchen said. "Your father and I are . . . talking."

"Talking?" Portia was instantly suspicious. "I thought you two weren't talking. That was the whole point of Dad's moving out, wasn't it?"

"Just because I've moved out doesn't mean I don't talk to your mother," Ennis said with unexpected dignity.

"Well, okay. I'll look for her myself," said Portia, and she turned to go. But then she stopped. "Mom, do you like my hair? You didn't say." There was something shy, almost pleading in her tone.

Gretchen, not one of those mothers who cooed, *It's a masterpiece!* over every scribble her kids produced, looked hard at her daughter. "Come here," she said, and when Portia complied, Gretchen took her chin in her fingers, tilting it this way and that, to see how the haircut played off the various angles of Portia's face.

"It's very sophisticated," she said at last. "It makes you look older."

"Do you really think so?"

"Definitely."

That seemed to be the right answer, for Portia responded by grabbing each of her elbows and squeezing as if giving herself a hug. Then she was gone, closing the door behind her. Gretchen waited a moment and said to Ennis, "Go on."

He went and stood by the window. "I didn't feel I could just abandon her," he said, staring out at the rain. "She really had no one."

"I thought she was going back to Kansas or wherever it was that she came from," said Gretchen.

"Wisconsin, and, no, she didn't," he said.

"Why not?"

"She said she wanted to have the baby here."

"Why? Aren't her parents out there?" But Gretchen knew the answer. Eve must have thought that if she was nearby, Ennis would be more likely to soften, to change his mind. Maybe he wouldn't marry her. But she'd have the baby to draw him to her, and babies cast a powerful net. When Ennis didn't say anything, Gretchen added, "So she had the baby in New York?"

Ennis nodded. "April eighth."

Even though Gretchen had known about the pregnancy, the news of the birth still felt like an ambush, swift and sudden. So that meant Justine and Portia had a half sibling, who was now almost two months old. Clearly Ennis had kept his word and not told them. Oh God—how would they take it? Gretchen sat back down on the bed and resisted the urge to slide under the covers and pull them up to her chin—no, over her head. She was freezing; the air-conditioning was turned way up, and the room had a meat-locker chill.

"Well, congratulations," she said, barely able to get the words out. "I guess you're a dad—again." She stood, pulled on the sweatshirt she had pried from her suitcase, and sat back down.

Ennis ignored this and came over to the bed. He hesitated for a moment before sitting, and Gretchen toyed with the impulse to ask him to please get up. But the king-sized bed allowed him to keep his distance, so she let it go.

"I had seen her throughout the pregnancy," he continued. "Just to make sure she was getting to her doctor's appointments and that she had enough money. There was nothing else"—he paused for emphasis—"and I mean *nothing* else between us."

"Was that what she wanted? Or was it you?" As soon as she said these words, Gretchen wished she could take them back; she didn't want to let him know that it mattered to her one way or the other.

"It was my choice. What happened with her was a one-time thing. It was wrong, I was wrong, and even though I can't undo it, I didn't have to keep doing it either."

"All right," Gretchen said. "Keep going."

"So when she called me to say the baby had been born, I said I wanted to come see her in the hospital. It seemed like the right thing to do."

"And doing the right thing is clearly so important to you," she said, unable to contain herself. "So deeply, truly important." He had the effrontery to look hurt. "What?" she asked. "You deserved that, you know."

"I suppose I did," he said, looking down at his hands. Gretchen had loved his hands too—strong, firm, and well shaped. She had loved so many things about him, hadn't she? Well, she'd just have to get over them, every last one. "Anyway, she didn't want me to come to the hospital. She kept saying that it wasn't necessary, she'd get along just fine, she knew I wasn't planning on being a father to this baby, so there was no point in my getting to know him."

"So it was a boy."

"A boy. Yes." He continued studying his hands. "This was kind of strange, hey? All during the pregnancy she had been so eager to see me. She talked about the baby and said that even though I didn't want to get married, she hoped I could have some role in its life. So her reluctance to see me was a switch. Something new. Something I didn't expect."

Gretchen had nothing to say; she buried her own hands in the kangaroo-like front pocket of the sweatshirt and waited for him to continue.

"I decided to go to the hospital. I checked the visiting hours; I bought flowers and a couple of things for the baby. One of those little outfits with a hood, hey? A teddy bear. And I planned to give her some money too. I figured she would need it." He stopped, and the only sound in the room was the rain, which continued to patter heavily against the panes.

"Was she glad to see you?" Gretchen found herself increasingly drawn—despite her resistance, despite her quiet fury—into this narrative.

"Was she glad? No, I wouldn't say glad exactly. Surprised was more like it. Even alarmed."

"Alarmed? I don't get it. You *are* the father. Even if you're not going to *function* as the father."

"That's what I thought too. So then I asked to see the baby. He had been taken for some test or shot, and they were just about to bring him back. I said I would wait. She didn't want me to, though. She thanked me for everything but told me not to bother staying, just to go. Practically begging me, in fact. Stranger and stranger, hey? She was almost pushing me out the door. But I didn't go. No, I sat and I waited. She looked more and more uncomfortable. Nearly jumping out of her skin. And when they brought him in, I understood."

"What do you mean? Was there something wrong with him?" This was going from bad to worse. Not only a half sibling but a half sibling with *issues*.

"Wrong? No, nothing was wrong with him. He was beautiful. Perfect. A perfectly beautiful, beautifully perfect baby boy."

"So what was the problem?" Why was he drawing this out? Did he enjoy hurting her?

"Gretchen, the baby was black."

"Black!" Here was a piece of information lobbed in from left field. Gretchen felt as if she had been physically hit by it, squarely, right between the eyes.

"Well, part black anyway."

"So that means . . ."

"That means that he isn't mine. He never was. And whatever happened with Eve, he was not the result." Ennis exhaled mightily.

"What a story." *What a stroke of luck.* Gretchen's first thought was relief. There was not going to be a half sibling added to the family equation after all. No long and undoubtedly teary discussion with Justine and Portia—that whole scenario had just been eradicated. And then there was Gretchen's own reaction. Even though she and Ennis were separated, it would have hurt her to know he had fathered a child with someone else. She may have exiled Ennis from her life, but she was not ready to give him over to anyone else.

"What a story," he agreed. "I held the baby for a few minutes. He was a cute little guy. I gave her the gifts, the money. And then I walked out of that hospital feeling so— free! So wonderfully, marvelously free, hey? You can't imagine what a weight it was, thinking about that baby and what I was and wasn't going to be to him. And now it's all just gone, vanished, just like that."

"Well, I wouldn't say that it's all gone," Gretchen said

carefully. "It's not like the whole thing never happened. You did sleep with her, and she did pull that stunt with the pills. What if the girls had been there when she showed up? I haven't said a word to them about her, you know. Not a peep."

"I appreciate that," Ennis said. "It's very kind of you."

"I didn't do it for *you*," she said. "I was trying to protect *them*."

"Well, whatever your motive, I'm grateful for it. I don't want them to despise their old man, hey?"

"They don't despise you," Gretchen said. "So you can stop worrying."

"What about you? Do you despise me?"

Gretchen inched away as far she could from him on the bed; if she moved any more, she'd be on the floor. "I don't know how I feel," she said finally. "You hurt me, Ennis. You hurt me more than I knew I was capable of being hurt."

"I know I did. And I'll regret it for the rest of my life. But I thought if you knew about Eve, it would change things."

"How? Why?"

"Because you'd understand that I really am done with all that. Finished."

"Well, that's all very well and good for you. But I still don't see how it affects me. You still betrayed me. Betrayed all of us. And as for the baby not being yours, that was just luck, Ennis. Pure dumb luck."

"Isn't everything?"

"No," she said. "Some things are the result of rigorously

delayed gratification, meticulous planning, relentless hard work, and obsessive attention to the smallest detail." She stood and stretched; sitting so tightly wound in the room's unrelenting chill had made her stiff. And she'd heard enough anyway. Time to get moving.

"That's it?" Ennis said when he saw he was being dismissed. "That's all you have to say to me?"

"What were you expecting?" She was still reeling from his news. So the conversation with Justine and Portia about a new baby brother would never—thank you, God—have to take place. But how could Ennis show up here and think that revelation would wipe away all the hurt of these past months? There was something so cavalier about the expectation, so clueless, selfish, and entitled. She looked at her estranged husband, and she realized she was even angrier than she'd been before he had made his grand confession. *The nerve of him*, she thought, adopting an expression that had tumbled so effortlessly from Lenore's lips throughout her childhood. *The nerve.*

Fourteen

Lenore was torn. She simply had to find out what had made Caleb cry like that—with such abandon, such sorrow. He sounded devastated, her sweet boy. She had a strong hunch his tears had to do with that Bobby person, though until she spoke to her grandson, she could not be sure. But she also wanted to talk to Justine, whose puzzling behavior earlier this afternoon continued to prick the edges of Lenore's consciousness. Something was not right with that girl, and Lenore was determined to find out what it was.

What to do? Justine, then Caleb? Or Caleb and then Justine? And could she hope to talk to both grandson and great-granddaughter and still have time to have her hair blown out before the wedding? This too was important; she was intent on looking her best.

Since Caleb's room was on this floor, she decided to check on him first. She passed one of the maids—Esperanza, yes, that was it!—in the broad hallway and smiled at the girl. See, her mind was still sharp. Today she remembered the names of *both* maids all by herself with no help from anyone.

Still smiling, Lenore stopped in front of the door to Caleb's room. She raised her fist to knock but was startled by a knock from the other side. No, not a knock. More like a thud. Something had been thrown against the door, and the impact caused it to vibrate slightly in its frame.

"I saw you." That was Caleb's voice; Lenore was sure of it. His words, icy and furious, were perfectly distinct; he must have been standing directly in front of the closed door. "I saw the two of you, okay? So don't try to bullshit your way out of it." There was an answering murmur from within the room, but Lenore couldn't make out the words. *Sorry* was one of them; that much she could glean. The rest was indistinct. The speaker—Bobby?—was not so conveniently situated for eavesdropping.

Lenore stepped back. *Eavesdropping* was just a fancy word for *spying*. And as badly as she wanted to find out what her boychick had seen and if in fact it was connected to the sobbing she had heard earlier, she was not going to spy on him to find out. No, she would wait for Caleb to tell her; she had supreme faith that he would. And when he did, she wouldn't say, *I told you so; I knew he was phony-baloney from the minute I laid eyes on him.* No, she would say nothing of the kind. She would just listen and offer the soothing words she prayed would ease the hurt.

Lenore turned resolutely from the door and descended the stairs. Rain was pelting the big windows with gleeful abandon. Lenore knew that Angelica and Betsy would no doubt view this as a tragedy, but Lenore had lived long enough to know that rain, even on a wedding day, wasn't a tragedy; it was barely even a blip. After all, Betsy had planned every last detail perfectly. There were elaborate enclosed tents, which would keep the rain from blowing in on the wedding party and the guests. There were dozens of compact, white folding umbrellas, each trimmed with a discreet border of gray, to hand out, and there were pairs upon pairs of clear plastic sandals—small, medium, and large—so that no one's shoes would get ruined. The wedding would proceed as planned. Angelica, flanked by her handsome groom, would be the most radiant of brides. The music would play, champagne corks would pop, and Lenore, dressed to the nines, would be there to see it all. Somewhere in the vast house Betsy's little dog gave a single, exclamatory yip, as if to punctuate Lenore's musings.

Where was Betsy? Kitchen? Den, where the hair and makeup girls had been stationed and were now attending to a couple of the bridesmaids? Lenore did not see or hear her anywhere, but when she poked her head into the laundry room behind the kitchen, she ran smack into Lincoln, her former son-in-law, just as he was walking out. What was he doing in there, anyway? A load of whites? He looked to be in a big hurry, but stopped when he came face-to-face with her.

"Lincoln," she said. Should she hug him? She wasn't sure and didn't especially want to, so she extended her hand.

"Lenore," he said. "It's been a long time." He took her hand and gave it a squeeze.

"How have you been, Lincoln?" Lenore had known all

about the drinking, of course; everyone had. Was he still drinking now? She'd heard not, but you never knew with these things.

"I've been fine. Great, in fact. Because today is a great day. A great day. If only this damn rain would let up, it would be absolutely perfect." He glanced over at the small laundry room window.

"The rain won't spoil a thing," Lenore said. "You wait and see."

He looked as if he was trying to decide whether she was making fun of him. "Maybe you're right," he said finally. "Maybe you are."

"Have you seen Angelica yet?" Lenore asked.

Lincoln shook his head. "I just saw Gretchen, though. And Portia."

"Not Justine?"

"No one seems to be able to find Justine," said Lincoln. Lenore was quiet as she thought of her great-granddaughter scrabbling urgently in the grass. "Gretchen, Ennis, and Portia were all wondering where she was," he added.

"Ennis is here too?" Lenore was surprised. She had been told Ennis had declined the invitation—good thing too. What had changed? And why had no one told her?

"I guess it was kind of a last-minute decision. Gretchen is pissed as all get-out."

"She said that?" Lenore decided to overlook his vulgarity; he could be crude, but he did care for his children.

"No. But I could tell. She had that look."

"What look?" asked Lenore.

"You know," Lincoln said. "That *verbissen pisk*. It could curdle milk."

Lenore had to smile. *Verbissen pisk*—a sour, angry face—was an expression her own mother had frequently used; Lenore had not heard anyone say it in a long while. But she didn't want to be disloyal to Gretchen. "Can you blame her?" she asked. "The way that man behaved."

"Of course, of course," Lincoln hastened to agree. "I can understand how she feels."

"We all can," Lenore said. She had not planned on Ennis. How would he figure into her scheme for introducing Gretchen to Mitch? Would they all be at the same table? She sincerely hoped not. Suddenly she felt she could not spare another minute to chat with Lincoln. She had so much to do before tonight. She needed to hurry.

"Well," she said brightly. "Kiss the bride when you see her. I'm sure she'll be thrilled you're here." And she marched off resolutely, leaving Lincoln standing in the doorway just where she had found him.

Caleb would have to wait, Lenore decided; her great-granddaughter's disappearance was a clear sign of something, though she did not know what. What she did know was that Justine needed her—needed all of them really—and so she set out to locate her. She went back upstairs and began a methodical search of all the rooms up there; Justine was not in any of them. Nor was she in any of the downstairs rooms, not even the basement lair where she and Portia had slept last night.

Without saying anything to Betsy—who was marching about the kitchen issuing orders and clutching that absurd little dog as if it were a security blanket—Lenore took one of the white umbrellas earmarked for the guests and stepped outside. Even though it was pouring, there was plenty of activity out here, what with people making sure the tent poles were secured and rolling down the flaps, and the handsome, bare-chested, heavily tattooed gardener—Lenore hoped he would be dressed by the time the guests descended—going back and forth repositioning the potted plants. She ignored them all. Her instinct told her that Justine was also shunning the flurry and bustle; she wanted to be someplace where everyone wasn't. Someplace that was hers alone.

Lenore set out on the path leading to the swimming pool and gave only the merest acknowledgment to the dense plantings of pale pink and white heirloom roses whose petals were beaded with raindrops. These were not the only roses on the property; directly behind the house was a formal rose garden. Lenore had not even seen the garden since she'd arrived, but if the rain ever let up, she would see it later at the cocktail reception.

As she walked, Lenore remained on the lookout for anyplace—shed, cabana—where Justine might have been hiding. But Justine was not to be found, and so she kept going. Lenore had never been to this part of Don's property before; when she visited her daughter, they tended to remain indoors. If they did go out, it was only to sit by the pool or in the rose garden. Sometimes they drove into town and had lunch at one of the nice little places on Middle Neck Road, or to the posh stores at Americana Manhasset, where Betsy would insist on buying a present—a scarf from Hermès, a Gucci bag—for Lenore. So this was all new to her.

She was vaguely aware from Betsy's explanations of how far the property extended—beyond the well-manicured privet hedges on either side of the house were tall pines, and beyond those, dense wooded areas that spread out in either direction. Don had deliberately left them wild and over-grown, though there were some serpentine paths that wound through them. The girls had liked to play here when they were younger, and Lenore had a feeling that Justine might have come this way today.

Lenore kept walking, not sure if she was still on the property. She did not see any paths out here. She must have been nearing Long Island Sound, which was about a mile from the house. The ground showed streaks of sand, and the shrubbery was wild and unkempt. Even though she could not see the water, she could smell it, and the moist salt air clung to her cheeks, her lips. Under the white um-brella, Lenore felt pleasantly cocooned. It was a beautiful rain, really—lush and warm and not at all threatening. It was good luck to get married on such a day; she'd tell An-gelica that when she got back.

Getting back. Lenore realized she had better start thinking about that. She was not wearing a watch, so she did not know the time. But surely it was getting late, and she was having no luck finding Justine. She was annoyed by her failure; failure had always irked her. Yet there wasn't much more she could do. Justine could be anywhere out here or not here at all. Lenore still wanted to try to speak to Caleb, and there was the matter of both doing her hair and getting dressed; Betsy had planned for some prewedding photographs. Plus Lenore realized that she was a bit winded from her walk, and she might actually need to take a teeny tiny nap before the evening's festivities.

The dense trees had thinned out, and the wind was stronger, yanking on the little umbrella and turning it inside out. Lenore fought with it valiantly, but the wind was stronger than she was; a rude gust snatched the thing up and sent it skittering, broken and useless, beyond her reach.

Impatiently she turned back in the direction of the house. Only where exactly *was* the house? She could no longer see it from where she stood. But it couldn't be too far away; she hadn't walked for all that long. Should she go right or left?

The wind whipped around her as she tried to decide. The filmy leopard-print blouse that seemed so perfect when she had put in on earlier was now wet and sticking to her skin. Ordinarily she would have put on a raincoat—she had brought a canary yellow one with white piping along the pockets and collar—but she had been in such a hurry that she had not bothered to go back upstairs to get it. She now regretted her haste.

It seemed better to start going in one direction, even a direction that might be wrong, than to stand here getting wetter and more chilled by the minute. So she started off again, walking as briskly as she could given the slippery ground and her own not-entirely-confident footing. She was tired, she really was; though she tried to ignore and suppress the fact, it was there nonetheless, dogging her along with the rain.

None of this scenery looked familiar, not a bit of it. Of course, she had not been paying strict attention to her sur-roundings; she had been preoccupied. But it was unsettling that nothing stood out as a landmark. A flash of lightning suddenly split the sky and then was gone. Lenore was pant-ing now, panting like a small, alarmed animal. Rain dripped from the end of her nose and off her chin; she swiped at her face angrily. She was going to have to sit down pretty soon, even if meant sitting here out in the open.

But wait. What about over there? There were some scraggly bushes that might offer a little protection. A little protection was better than none. She summoned whatever strength she had left and set off for the bushes. And then her foot in its dainty, slick-soled sandal slipped on the wet grass, and down she went in an unceremonious heap.

"Ooh!" she cried, but softly, as if she did not want to waste any of her precious energy. And she was not hurt any-way, not really. Just flustered. When she tried to get up, though, she discovered that she must have turned her ankle in the fall; even putting a little weight on it sent a slice of pain that coursed as swiftly as that flash of lightning right through her. "Ooh," she said again more loudly as she sank back down.

She could not get up; she absolutely could not. Her ankle, she saw, was starting to swell. There was no way she could walk on it. What to do? Sit and wait to be rescued? Who would know that she was here, and how long would it take for anyone to come looking? What with all the excitement over the wedding, it might be some time—a long time, in fact—before anyone missed her.

Lenore scanned the horizon and tried to formulate a plan. She was good with plans, she reminded herself. Excellent, in fact. Her eyes drifted once more toward the knot of bushes. That was it. She had to get to them. But how? She could not walk. She could crawl, couldn't she? So she got down on all fours and set out. Her swollen ankle was not only useless; it was an impediment; she had to drag it along behind her, and it slowed her progress through the soaked grass, mud, and sand.

After about ten minutes, she finally reached her destination. Burrowing as far under the bushes as she could, she was at least able to keep her face and upper body out of the rain. Wrapping her arms around her knees, she saw through her torn slacks that they were scraped and bleeding. Gingerly she lifted her wounded ankle and positioned it on a rock she spied nearby; maybe elevating it would relieve the throbbing. Weary and wet, she ached all over—knees, ankle, chest, and hands. But worst of all was the slow-dawning ache inside: if no one came for her soon, she would miss Angelica's wedding.

Fifteen

❧ · ❧

Lincoln stood watching as the waitstaff began assembling the bar. How many times had he walked up to a table just like this one, swathed in a white cloth, open and expansive as a snow-covered field? How many times had he eyed the bottles, weighed the options, and asked for a martini or a scotch on the rocks, a gin and tonic or a Bloody Mary? All the glasses of sangria, the crisp whites, the full-bodied reds he had consumed. The ales, pale and dark, the beers, tequila, bourbon, whisky, rye, gin—you name it, Lincoln drank it. Or used to.

They worked expertly and swiftly; soon the full-fledged bar, a living, glittering entity, was ready. The glasses sparkled; the silver buckets with their diamond-bright chunks of ice gleamed. The colors of the bottles—amber, blue, green— stood out against the white of the tablecloth. Next to them crystal dishes filled with roasted almonds and wedges of thinly sliced citrus fruit provided yet more bursts of color.

Lincoln gazed longingly at the bar. It seemed so unfair that he would have to spend the rest of his life exiled from the glorious, golden kingdom of liquor, abstemiously sipping his ginger ale or iced tea while the rest of the world was downing champagne. And at Angelica's wedding, no less. It was intolerable; that's what it was. He seethed quietly until he realized that the staff did not know him here; were he to walk up to the table and ask for a drink—early, before any of the wedding guests had arrived—he would no doubt be handed one. No one would think anything of it.

Of course he'd have to make sure Betsy or his kids didn't catch him. They knew his past and would view a misstep, even a small one, as a major calamity. But they were so busy. Who would even notice if Lincoln had a drink, just one single, solitary drink? He thought fleetingly of all the years of sobriety, how hard it had been to drag himself up and out of the drinking life. It had been such a long time, though. He wasn't that person anymore. And one drink wasn't going to put him back there. *One*, he thought; the number sang softly in his ear. *One. Just one.* How could a single drink consumed in honor of his daughter's wedding hurt? God knew he needed it. No, he decided. He *deserved* it. His broken tooth throbbed again as if to add its insistent voice to the chorus inside him, the chorus that chanted, *One, one, one.*

Lincoln moved toward the bar as if drawn by a gravitational pull. Two young men in black jackets, white shirts, and black ties were stationed near the phalanx of wine and liquor bottles. The champagne bottles were behind them, nestled in outsized tubs of galvanized metal that been filled with shaved ice; from a distance it looked like foam. But the rest of the liquor was right there, close enough to reach out and touch. He saw the men look briefly at him, then back at each other, immersed in some conversation of their own. They didn't care whether he had a drink or not. It was nothing to them. Nothing. His heart started beating very rapidly, and he felt his lungs tighten with anxiety. And the tooth—the tooth was getting worse. All the more reason for a drink, damn it.

"I'll have—" Lincoln began but then stopped, suddenly overwhelmed and unsure of what to ask for in this feared, longed-for moment. The choices fanned out before him and made him slightly dizzy with possibility. Wine? Beer? A mixed drink maybe? God, how he had loved the cool, citrus-laced tang of a gin and tonic, the perfect way to usher in a June evening. But, no, he should go with something less potent. How about that Chardonnay, its bottle sweating gently and leaving a patch of wetness on the white cloth? Or a beer? A beer was perfect. Beer was a simple, honest drink, a *man's* drink, all right. He'd ask for a beer, just one, and then he'd be through, never touch the stuff again.

"Dad?" a voice behind him said. "Dad, what are you *doing*?" Lincoln spun around to see Gretchen. Her expression—a mix of surprise, disbelief, and, he had to acknowledge, contempt—was not a pretty thing to behold. "You're not having a *drink*, are you?" She fairly spat the words. "God, of all times to fall off the wagon!"

"I did not *fall off the wagon*," Lincoln said, stepping back from the table. And he hadn't, had he? His killjoy daughter had made sure of that.

"Weren't you just going to ask for a drink?" When he

didn't reply, she said, "Well, it's a good thing I caught you before you did anything stupid." Lincoln continued to remain silent, excruciatingly aware that the two bartenders had lost interest in whatever it was that had been so compelling a few minutes earlier and were watching this exchange as if it were a hotly contested tennis match.

"I don't know what you're getting so excited about," he finally said, keeping his voice as low and even as he could. "I am not having a drink, am I? Do you see a drink in my hand?" He wiggled his empty fingers.

"Then why are you here?"

"Here? What do you mean, *here*?" Lincoln looked around as if his present surroundings were an utter mystery to him. "And, anyway, I'm not *here* anymore." He marched off, leaving the two jackasses behind the bar to wonder about how the last act of this ugly little family drama was going to play out. Jesus, he hadn't even said hello to Gretchen before she had started ragging on him. Well, she had always been a little goody-goody, hadn't she?

The rain continued to come down, and a strong breeze shook the sides of the tent. The cool air felt good on Lincoln's face; the exchange with Gretchen had made him sweat even more than the bottle of Chardonnay. If he wasn't going to get a drink, maybe he could find something to eat around here. He realized that he'd barely had anything all day, and he was suddenly starved.

"Dad." That would be Gretchen again. "Dad, don't run off. I've been looking for you." He turned to his eldest daughter. Her tone was gentle; she was no longer in her avenging-angel mode. "I came over to say hello. I've hardly even seen you since you got here."

"Hello," he said sullenly, looking at her more closely now. She had gained some weight, but he actually thought the extra few pounds had filled out her face in an appealing sort of way. She looked soft, dewy even.

"Hi," she said and walked closer to where he stood. "Where are you going?"

"What, are you keeping tabs on me? Do think I've got a flask in my pocket and I'm sneaking off to the john to take a hit?" His annoyance flared again.

"No, that's not it. I know how hard you worked to get sober and to stay sober, and I admit I got scared when I saw you near the bar. I'm sorry if I overreacted, though. It's only because I love you."

Lincoln grunted. He was touched by her concern but not entirely ready to give up his grievance. Who wanted to be lectured by one of their kids, even if that kid happened to be right? He decided to change the subject. "Do you think I can find anything to eat around here? I'm so hungry, I could start chewing on one of your mother's Louis-whatever armchairs."

"There's going to be so much food at the wedding; are you sure you don't want to wait?"

"Wait for what?" Lincoln asked. "I need to eat now."

"The food prep station is going to be insane," she warned. "But maybe we can find you something in the house."

Together they walked into the kitchen, where a team of florists was scurrying back and forth carrying vast armloads of white roses, white lilacs, and white lilies veined with deep pink. The photographer was there too, along with Betsy, who pounced on Lincoln as soon as their eyes met.

"Have you seen my mother?" She looked rattled, a state of mind that Lincoln from long experience knew was not typical for her.

"Why? Is she missing?" Gretchen asked.

Betsy nodded. "The door to her room was open, and her outfit for tonight was all laid out on her bed. But she wasn't there, and I haven't been able to find her anywhere in the house."

"I saw her a little while ago," Lincoln said, remembering their brief exchange in the laundry room. "I think she was going out."

"Out! In the rain!" Betsy said. "Why would she do that?"

"I don't know," said Lincoln. "But she was carrying an umbrella. It was white, I think," he added uselessly.

"The umbrellas I bought for the guests," Betsy said. She turned to Gretchen. "When did you see her last?"

"We went out for breakfast this morning," Gretchen said. "I didn't pay too much attention about where she went after that. And now I was actually looking for Justine. No one has seen her either."

"Justine is missing too?" Betsy said.

Gretchen nodded. "Ennis and I were going to try to find her, but if you want me to stay and help you look for Grandma, I can send Ennis by himself."

"She was here when we were talking about the ring," Betsy said, and when she saw that Gretchen looked confused, she added, "Angelica's diamond engagement ring is missing. We were up in her room trying to figure out where it could be. That wasn't all that long ago."

"So, where would she be going in the rain?" Gretchen asked. "Do you think she went looking for Justine?"

"Maybe," Betsy said. "But in any case we should find her. It's nasty out there." She looked over at the photographer, who had been standing there patiently with her camera bag settled at her feet like a cat. "Amber, I am so sorry for making you wait. It seems we have a couple of missing family members to deal with here, but I'll be with you in two minutes." Amber, an intricately pierced and braided little person, nodded. Then the florists, all three of them, came in, their arms emptied at last, and they too seemed to be waiting for further directions from Betsy. *Wasn't there supposed to be someone helping Betsy out with all of this?* Lincoln wondered. *An expensive wedding planner that everyone in the family kept talking about?*

"Mom, I'll go look for Grandma; Ennis can go looking for Justine," offered Gretchen.

"Justine has been located." This last remark was delivered by Betsy's husband, Don, who had just lumbered into the room. Lincoln hadn't seen the guy since he'd arrived, but he'd been preparing for the moment when he'd have to face him. Well, the moment was here. He looked even larger than Lincoln remembered. Or maybe it was the oversized shirt he wore along with the baggy, knee-length madras plaid shorts. There were some people who should never even go near madras; Don was one of them.

"Why not? Is she here?" Gretchen asked. Her hands went to her hair, pushed it up and out of her face. The curls immediately sprang back to where they had been seconds before.

Don shook his head and slipped his iPhone back into his pocket in a seamless, decisive gesture. "Let's all step into my office for a few minutes, okay?" He looked at Amber and the florists. "Family crisis. We need to have a powwow." Lincoln cringed. *Powwow?* Where had this guy learned his vocabulary? From a comic book? "Can you find something to do until we're through?" And to Betsy: "Where's Pippa when you actually need her, anyway?" No one had an answer for that, but Lincoln, Gretchen, Betsy, and Don went down a short hall and into Don's study.

A two-foot-long fish—Lincoln had no idea what kind—had been gruesomely preserved and mounted on the wall; its glazed and unseeing eye presided over a room filled with golfing trophies, a forty-two-inch flat-screen television, and a sofa covered in a plaid even more raucous than the one on Don's shorts. Betsy sank into the sofa immediately, and Gretchen sat down next to her, reaching—almost reflexively, it seemed—for her mother's hand. Since Don remained standing, Lincoln felt that he too had to stand, though really he wished he could have sat down and joined hands with his ex-wife and daughter.

"That was Garry Mulligan on the phone," Don said. Since the name clearly did not mean anything to anyone in the room, he went on. "He's the chief of police and a good friend of mine. Helluva nice guy."

"I'm sure he is," Betsy said. Her voice held the hint of exasperation that Lincoln remembered quite well. "But what does that have to do with Justine? Does he know where she is?"

Don nodded his great head, and in the gesture Lincoln saw a rhino lowering its face to the watering hole. "It seems she was picked up by two officers in a patrol car not far from here, and when Garry found out where she was staying and who she was, he called me himself."

"Picked her up! Whatever for?" said Gretchen. She looked wild, and Lincoln's heart constricted for her.

"Apparently she borrowed one of the cars from the garage and decided to take a little ride," said Don. "They found her about two miles down from the house, heading towards town. Garry said she was weaving all over the road; at first they thought she was drunk."

"She must have taken the keys from me!" Gretchen burst out. "Mom gave me a set yesterday."

"It's not your fault," Lincoln said. "How the hell would you know she would take them and go out for a spin?"

"She wasn't drunk, was she?" asked Gretchen, as if Lincoln had not spoken.

"No, no, she wasn't drunk. But to be behind the wheel of a car sober at that age . . ." Don didn't have to finish. There was a tentative knock on the door. "Yes?" Even in the slightly imperious way Don said that single syllable, Lincoln could see the CEO in the guy; it was bred in the bone somehow.

The door opened, and Ennis poked his head into the room. "I was looking for Gretchen. . . ." He trailed off.

"Ennis! Perfect timing," Gretchen said. "Don was just telling us that Justine was picked up by the police. She took Mom's car and went out for a joyride."

"She did?" Ennis came into the room slowly as if it were alien territory. "What did she do that for?" Gretchen just shook her head. "Well, we've got to go get her, then, don't we?"

"Yes," Gretchen said. "We do. Right now."

"Ennis, you and Gretchen can take my car," Don said. "I'll call Garry back and tell him you're on the way."

"Where is she?" Ennis asked.

When Don said, "At the police station," Gretchen emitted a little moan.

"Go ahead, go now—as soon as you can. I'll go out and look for Lenore. You"—he looked at Betsy—"try to find Pippa and see if you can get some help around here. God knows we're paying her enough."

Lincoln watched and marveled. *Look at how smoothly Don took charge of everyone and everything.* Jeez, some guys just had it, didn't they? That I'm-the-one-running-the-show gene. Why had it skipped him? And if it hadn't, would he be the one standing here in his Great Neck manse giving the orders?

"No, wait," said Lincoln, stepping into the limelight. "Why don't you stay here to help Betsy? I'll go and look for Lenore. I'm the one who saw her last." Lincoln knew this last comment was irrelevant, but he was grasping at straws here, desperate to find some emotional purchase, some basis for his newly assumed authority.

"Would you?" Betsy said, bringing her clasped hands under her chin like a little girl. "That would be such a help."

"Good plan, Dad," Gretchen added. "Do you have your cell phone? In case you need to call us?"

Lincoln tapped the breast pocket of his shirt. His tooth hurt like a bitch, but he made a command decision to simply ignore the pain. "I could use a raincoat, though. And an umbrella." It was still pouring and showed no signs of letting up. He thought briefly of his shoes, which were apt to get ruined slogging through the wet grass, mud, and sand. He'd have to navigate the wedding in ruined shoes. But what the hell? Everyone would be looking at Angelica, not at his feet.

A few minutes later, draped in the XXL yellow rain slicker that Don had graciously loaned him, Lincoln opened the kitchen door and stood there for a moment. Rain pelted him from all sides, and the wind yanked at the umbrella in his hand. He had not a clue as to where to begin or what direction to take. But, then, hadn't that been the story of his life? Armed with that dubiously useful insight and one of the dainty white umbrellas earmarked for the guests, Lincoln set off into the storm.

Sixteen

"This is all my fault," Gretchen kept saying as they drove the few miles to the police station. "Totally, completely my fault."

"Stop saying that," said Ennis, who was driving. "Stop thinking that."

"But it's true," Gretchen said. "And if it's true, why shouldn't I think it? Or say it?"

"Because it isn't." Rain streamed down the windows and made the road a blur; he drove slowly, hunched over the wheel, peering intently ahead.

"How would you know?" Gretchen said bitterly. "Though you're right: it doesn't really matter. All that matters is that we get to her. That we help her."

"You make it sound like she's in serious trouble," said Ennis.

"She is!" Gretchen stared at him. "She is in trouble. I just haven't told you."

"Why not?" Ennis said, turning his eyes briefly from

the road to look at her. "You should have, hey? It was my right to know." He sounded accusatory.

"I didn't tell you because I didn't know it. No, that's not true. Because I wouldn't let myself know it. Until now." She slumped against the rain-glazed window.

"What's been going on?" Ennis asked. Even though he kept his eyes on the road, she could feel his empathy, his concern. "Can you tell me?" So Gretchen told him everything, all the bits and pieces she had been gathering and saving. Justine's fits of inconsolable weeping, for one thing. Or the way she would totally freeze Gretchen out as if she neither saw nor heard her. Her near-fanatic obsession about her grades. "She got an A-minus on a history paper, and when I told her I thought it was a terrific grade, she was so furious that she threw a mug of hot cocoa against the kitchen wall. I made her clean it up, of course. But I didn't really get into how much it scared me."

"She's always been intense, hasn't she?" said Ennis.

"That's what I tried to tell myself," Gretchen said. "But this is more than intense. This is serious; this is bordering on dangerous. Until now I was hiding from what I knew. I can't do that anymore." She hesitated before adding, "I mean, *we* can't." Because it was *we*—like it or not, she wanted Ennis's involvement. More than wanted—needed it. No matter what else happened—or did not happen—between them, she had to enlist his help with Justine. She saw that very clearly now.

"What do you want me to do?" said Ennis quietly. "Just tell me. I'll do it. I'll do anything."

How about turning back time so that you never touched that girl? Gretchen wanted to say. Instead she said, "I don't know, Ennis, but when I do, I'll tell you."

She turned her face away, and they rode in silence for a few minutes. Finally Gretchen felt compelled to ask, "Shouldn't we be there already? Don said it wasn't far."

"Just about there," Ennis said. The car's GPS had directed them along Kings Point Road; they had passed Tideway Street and then Lighthouse; Stepping Stone Lane, their destination, should have been right up ahead.

"Wait—why are you stopping?" Gretchen asked as the Mercedes slowed and then came to a halt.

"Look," said Ennis. "Just look."

Gretchen had to open the window to see anything. Ahead of them was a dip in the road; a rush of water, maybe five feet wide and who knew how deep, was pouring across the depression, making it impossible for a car to pass. On the other side of the gushing stream stood a cluster of men in bright orange rain gear. Then she saw the squad car. Police. One of the cops was speaking loudly into a cell phone. The others were talking, pointing, and, from the looks of it, arguing.

"Hey," called Ennis, sticking his head out of his window. "Is there an alternate route?"

"We're working on it," one of the orange-clad officers called back. "But the road we usually use is washed out too. It's really coming down." Ennis pulled his head back inside the car. Mist from the rain had filled the small space, and Gretchen could feel it moistening her cheeks and forehead.

She glanced anxiously at the clock on the dashboard. Three fifty-nine. How long would they have to sit here? Behind them a line of cars had already formed and begun to sound a chorus of blaring honks and angry beeps. Ennis took his hands from the wheel, a gesture of surrender that affected Gretchen like a jolt from a cattle prod.

"What are we going to do?" she said. She knew she sounded shrill, but she didn't care. "Justine is at the police station. She's waiting for us."

"There's nothing much we can do," Ennis said. "You heard him. Both roads are washed out." He put his hands back on the wheel as if he didn't know what else to do with them.

"The word is not *oot*," she said angrily. "It's out. *OWT*," she repeated for emphasis. "You've been living in the United States for more than two decades. Enough time to get it right."

"Fuck off!" said Ennis. "Attacking my accent is juvenile. Juvenile and not worthy of you."

"So I'm juvenile. Deal with it. I'm mad too. Furious, in fact."

"I know you are. But don't take it out on me. None of this is my fault. I'm not responsible for the rain, the washed-out road, or Justine's latest little attention-getting ploy." He emphasized the syllable—*oot*—in what seemed like a burst of spite.

"Is *that* what you think this is?" she shot back. "A ploy? Have you been listening to anything I've said?"

"Yes, I heard you. She's angry, she's moody, she's in trouble. Well, maybe what she needs is a firm hand. Maybe both the girls do. Which you, clearly, have not been able to provide."

"What are you talking about?" Gretchen could not stand how self-righteous he was.

"Those awful piercings Justine has! Portia's crazy hair color! How could you let them do that?" he demanded.

"It seemed very important to them," Gretchen said quietly. "And it wasn't important to me at all."

"Maybe it should have been. It's important to *me*." He sounded sincere; she had to give him that.

"You're free to voice your opinion. And your disapproval," Gretchen said.

"How? You won't let me."

"Who's stopping you? I haven't kept the girls from you." And she hadn't. Or had she?

"You have!" He smacked his hands on the wheel for emphasis. "You've kept me from both of them. Why was it a given that they both got to live with you? Justine could have lived with me, hey."

"Where? In that frat house you call home? Or with that underage tart who wrecked our marriage?"

"She is not underage, and she did not wreck our marriage!" he shouted.

"Well, excuse me!" Gretchen was taken aback. Ennis rarely raised his voice.

"We both wrecked our marriage," he said more quietly.

"You're implicating me in this? What are you talking about?" Didn't this have a name? Blaming the victim?

"You withdrew. Not physically. But emotionally. You were somewhere else. Distracted. Preoccupied. You stopped wanting to have sex—"

"We had plenty of sex!" she interrupted.

"We did. But I always had to initiate it. *Always.*" It was true. Gretchen said nothing. "I hated that, hey? Made me feel you never wanted it; you were just doing it to accommodate me. Sex was something you submitted to because you felt obligated. Or because you pitied me."

"I never pitied you," she said. "Never. That wasn't it at all."

"Then what?" His voice got softer, more coaxing. "What was it? Because even though what happened with Eve was not the way to deal with it, there was something wrong between us. There was—you know it too."

"Okay," she said. "Okay, so something was off. But did that mean you had to go and screw a student?"

"I don't want to talk about *that*. We've already talked that one into the ground. I want to talk about *us*." He paused. "What happened to *us*, that's what I want to know. Can you tell me?"

You want to know what happened? Gretchen thought. *Life happened. You had kids, and raising them completely took you over. One of them was in trouble, and you didn't really want to face it, but somewhere deep down you knew. You had known for a long time. And you never really figured out what it was you wanted to do with yourself, did you? That made you feel like a stranger to yourself and to everyone else too.* But all she said was, "I don't know."

"I don't believe you," Ennis said. "You're just not telling."

"If you felt I wasn't emotionally available, wouldn't it have been better to talk to me about it? Instead of screwing her?"

"I tried," Ennis said. "You know I did."

Gretchen was quiet. It was true. There was the time he'd made all the arrangements for a weekend away, just the two of them. She refused to leave the girls. He'd make reservations at a restaurant, and she would claim she was too tired to go out. She stayed up late, long after he'd gone to sleep, so she wouldn't have to talk to him, at least not about anything of substance. She still loved him; she loved being married; but she so often felt ground down to the nub by the wheels of her own life; there was just no energy left for him anymore.

"At least we're talking now," Ennis said. "We're talking, and talking is good. That baby"—he was so excited he couldn't seem to get the words out fast enough—"that baby was a sign, Gretchen."

"A sign of what?" she said, suspicious.

"A sign that we could try again."

"A sign to you maybe. Not to me." Gretchen glared at him and then out the window. The rain continued to splatter the windows, and the road ahead was still impassible. This conversation was keeping them from their true mission, which was to get to Justine as soon as they could. "I don't know why you keep harping on that baby anyway. I'm glad it wasn't yours, especially for the girls' sake. But it doesn't change a thing between us, Ennis."

"Doesn't it?" He leaned over to cup her cheek with his palm.

"No." She let herself feel the warmth of his hand for a second before she drew back.

"Don't push me away," he said softly. He reached for her again, this time for her hair, not her face. "I love you, Gretchen. I love you, and I'm sorry I hurt you. That's why I came here this weekend. To tell you that."

"I thought it was to tell me about . . . Eve." The name still stuck in her throat. "Eve and the baby who was not yours."

"That was only a prelude to what I really wanted to say. I want to come back, Gretchen. To you. To the girls." He swallowed. "Give me another chance."

For a few seconds all Gretchen could do was stare. Then she yanked off her seat belt and got out of the car. "You want another chance?" she said. "Here it is."

"What are you doing?"

"Going to get Justine. You can come with me if you want."

"But the road," he said, gesturing in front of him. "The road's not passable, hey."

"Not by car. But I can wade across. Or swim if I have to."

"Gretchen! Are you daft?"

Daft. It had been a long time since she had heard Ennis

use that word, and it still affected her in a soft, private place she didn't want to have exposed, not even to herself.

"It can't be that deep," she said. "And it's obviously not all that wide. I'll get across, and then I can walk the rest of the way to the police station. It's close; you even said so yourself." She threw down the words like a gauntlet.

Ennis scrambled out of the car and slammed the door shut. "You *are* daft," he said with a great exhalation of breath. "Totally, thoroughly, and completely daft."

"Whatever. I'm going to get Justine. You can do what you like." Gretchen called to the policemen on the other side, "I'm coming over, okay?"

"You're doing what?" one of them yelled back.

Gretchen didn't bother to reply. She could feel Ennis watching as she boldly stepped down and into the water. It was cold but not as deep as she had feared, and she was able to wade rather than swim. She was almost across when she felt one of her shoes—a black ballet flat—come loose from her foot and get carried away by the current. Damn! But there was no time to go looking for it now. She continued on until she had reached the other side. Once there she shook herself off like a retriever and turned to the cluster of incredulous men who had been watching her. "Where's the police station?" she asked.

"Wait!" cried Ennis from the other side. "Wait for me." Gretchen looked to see him scramble down toward the water and then plunge in. As she watched him, she felt something rise and bubble inside her. It was not as strong or as sweet as happiness. But it was something.

"What the—?" the officer said as he watched Ennis slogging through the water. "Is he going to the police station too?" Gretchen nodded. "Well, I guess I can give you both a lift. It's not very far from here."

Gretchen got into the passenger's seat, while Ennis got in back. "Sorry about your car," she said as the water pooled from her clothes and hair onto the floor.

"Don't even worry about it," said the officer. He looked at her and then in the rearview mirror at Ennis. "You folks are in a big hurry to get there, huh?"

"Our daughter is waiting for us," was all Gretchen said. He nodded and didn't ask anything else, for which Gretchen was grateful. In minutes they pulled up to the police station, a sprawling complex made of bleached-looking stone.

"It looks like a bunker," Gretchen murmured to Ennis when the officer had deposited them in the parking lot. "Do you think there's a jail in there?"

"Even if there is, Justine is not in it," he said firmly. He started walking.

"How do you know?" she asked, scurrying to keep up with him. Her wet, bare foot was like a magnet for every pebble, stone, and leaf it encountered. He didn't answer and didn't speak again until they were inside the doors and dripping onto the floor.

"You look like a wreck," he observed. "But I'm sorry for what I said before. About the hair and the eyebrow and all. You've done a good job. And I don't just mean right now either. It can't have been easy dealing with them all by yourself, hey?"

"I've done my best," Gretchen said, oddly mollified by his acknowledgment. Now that they had finally arrived, she felt paralyzed. Her earlier fury at Ennis had dissipated, washed away by the rain and the rushing stream of water she had crossed to get here. "Ennis, I can't even begin to imagine what I am going to say to her. Can you?"

"Come on," he said, taking her by the hand. "We'll figure it out." *Oot.* Gretchen did not answer but squeezed his hand in return. Then, squelching their way toward the front desk, they went in search of their girl.

Seventeen

❧ · ❧

Justine sat mutely in a hallway of the Kings Point police station, her head tilted back against the wall, her eyes closed. But even with her eyes shut, the events of the past hour and a half played out with relentless clarity; nothing could obliterate them from the merciless exactitude of her memory.

"Your parents are coming to get you. They're on their way." Justine recognized the voice of the officer who had pulled her over on the road earlier. She nodded, not opening her eyes. "You'll have to fill out some paperwork, but everything will be all right." Still she said nothing. "Do you want a glass of water?" She ignored this question as she had ignored most of the other remarks he had addressed to her. He waited; she could feel his presence, which was *so* annoying, even without seeing him.

Eventually he must have gotten tired of standing there, because he left. Good. The less she had to say to him—to anyone in this place—the better. At least he hadn't asked the female office to search her. If he had, the officer would have discovered the diamond ring—Justine had found it deep in the recesses of the terry robe, where it had slipped through a hole in the pocket and lodged between the lining and the outer layer—and which she *still* had not managed to find a way to return. So then she would have been branded as a thief in addition to everything else. The fact that she actually *was* a thief did not make this any less humiliating a prospect.

As soon as she sensed the officer had gone, she opened her eyes. She was seated on a bench in a hallway; at least no one had thought to put her in a jail cell, not once they found out where she was staying and with whom. Apparently Grandma Betsy's husband—and his big bucks—had some serious influence around here. Well, that was no surprise, was it? *Money doesn't talk, it swears.* Bob Dylan said that. Though Justine had to concede that spending time in a jail cell might have had some cachet with her friends when she was recounting the story later on. Not that she had any friends anymore. Not really. And she knew Portia wouldn't have been impressed. There was no bullshitting Portia, not now, not ever. She would ignore the part about the jail cell entirely and go right to the deep, dark heart of things. *What made you go for the car, you idiot?* she was likely to say. *Don't you know you could have been maimed or killed, totally taken out in, like, a minute? And if you're dead, you're definitely not getting into Yale. Death disqualifies you. Like, immediately.*

Of course Justine had a very good reason to have taken

the car, even in the rain, even though she was underage. But it was not a reason she wanted to tell anyone—ever. And now it looked like everyone was going to find out, whether she told them or not. Shame seeped through her like an indelible dye. This was reason enough to close her eyes again, so she did.

But here were the images, the ones she wanted to escape, playing over and over in her mind, a repetitive, relentless loop. Everyone turning to look at her as she stood in Angelica's bedroom and uttered Bobby's name. *That* was a truly inspired move. Bobby and Caleb had been having a fight of some kind—she'd heard their raised voices behind the door—and it seemed so easy, so plausible, to direct the blame toward him. They all believed her too. All except Grandma Lenore, who had looked at Justine as if she'd known Justine had taken the ring and that her story about Bobby was a pure fabrication. But whatever Lenore thought or knew, she had not said a word.

Angelica had been the first to leave the room. Then Grandma Betsy had consulted her watch—again. Everyone was moving toward the door, and Justine had gone right along with them. The two maids were practically crying with relief; clearly they had thought the blame for the lost ring was about to be pinned on one of them. Justine was glad to have helped them out, even if that had not been her exact intention.

Then she heard her great-grandmother calling her name; now, that was one conversation she had *not* wanted to have. Ignoring the summons, she fled down the stairs and into the media room, where she changed out of her bathing suit and waited for a little while. Then she quietly crept up again. There was no sign of Grandma Lenore or Grandma Betsy. Good. Maybe she could finally put the ring back; Angelica would find it later on. And then, as if she had summoned him, there was Ohad. He smiled at her; his teeth were a shining flash of white in his dark face.

"Hi," she had said, her panic mounting. She'd better not fuck things up this time. She had to get those pictures; she *had* to. The ceremony was soon, and she was not going to get another chance.

"I'll be going back to the hotel soon to get my mother," he said. "Do you want to come along for the ride?"

"Sure," she said, surprised by how easy he had just made her task. *Alone in a car together,* she thought. *Perfect.* She discreetly patted her phone, which was now tucked safely in the pocket of her shorts. They started down the hall toward the stairs.

"So, how old did you say you were?" he had asked.

"Almost sixteen," Justine said. "My birthday is coming up soon."

"You'll have to meet my nephew Gidon," Ohad said. He stopped and knelt to tie the laces on one of his sneakers. "He's almost eighteen. I think you'll like him. You can meet him when we drive over." He pulled up on the shoelace, and it snapped. "Damn," he said, straightening up.

"Almost eighteen," said Justine. "Is he done with high school, then?"

Ohad shook his head. "Not quite. In September he'll

start his last year." Somehow they had not resumed walking again but remained where they were.

"And then he'll go into the army?" Justine asked. The word was rank, offensive in her mouth.

"Every eighteen-year-old in Israel goes into the army," Ohad replied. He smiled, but the smile did not include his eyes. His eyes looked sober, even grave.

"Why?" she blurted out. "Why does everyone go? What if instead everyone said, *No, we won't; you can't make us?* Swords into ploughshares and all that."

"Then our enemies would drive us into the sea," Ohad said calmly. "And the tiny, besieged state of Israel would cease to exist."

"Maybe that wouldn't be such a bad thing," Justine said. "Maybe it would be better."

"Not for us."

"Yes, for you too. Because what's happening in Israel now is so wrong, so evil, it's turned all of *you* evil. You've become the oppressors. You're as bad as any terrorist blowing up a bus or sending rockets into a settlement. Maybe even worse because you're so self-righteous."

"That's what you think?" Ohad had said. "That I'm evil? Self-righteous?" He pressed his fingers to the back of his neck as if he were rubbing a sore spot. "I'm sorry you feel that way," he added. "Because it isn't true." He continued to rub. "What my country is doing is painful to me. Deeply painful. But I love it just the same. Love it and am prepared to defend it."

The motion of his hand, the fingers gently kneading the flesh triggered something in Justine. It had been building for the past couple of hours, she knew, but the clamor of it—no, the roar—was unmistakable now. It grew louder and louder in her head so that she could no longer think straight. The confused tangle of her emotions, the way Ohad's fingers were rubbing, palpating, kneading. That unfamiliar smell of his: sharp, tangy even. She felt giddy, crazed. Like she was on something, though in fact she was not. It was like being overtaken, overpowered by the tumult inside of her. Needing some form of release, she abruptly thrust herself against Ohad's chest, tilting her face up and pressing his lips with her own.

So many sensations. The sudden shock of contact with his body. His lips—full but taut, and not soft. The aching in her boobs. Her nipples two hot points of light beaming into his chest. Her mouth opened involuntarily, and her tongue tried to find his. But Ohad did not open his mouth, did not return her embrace. Still she couldn't stop. *The phone*, she thought feebly. *I need to take a picture with the phone.*

"Hey," Ohad had said, breaking the spell. "Easy now." He stepped back and grasped her upper arms. Justine could not look at him; his face would scorch her. She stood there in his grip, breathing hard and staring at the thick pile of the carpeting until her vision blurred. Finally she forced herself to look up.

"You okay?" Ohad looked neither angry nor alarmed.

If she had been the wild thing, he was all calm, stasis, and control. He acted as if it were nothing to have a fifteen-year-old girl grab him and try to thrust her tongue into his mouth; *no big deal,* his look seemed to say.

"I'm fine," she croaked. And then she took off, not toward the stairs but in the other direction. The first door she opened was the door to her mother's room. Luckily Gretchen was not in it, but the keys to the car were tossed casually on a nightstand, and Justine grabbed them and went back out into the hallway. Ohad was gone—yes!—so she could make her escape: down the stairs, streaking through the house, and into the garage.

It was still pouring, but who the fuck cared about that now? Her hand trembled as she tried one car and then another; the keys started the third car like a charm, and she was behind the wheel in seconds, revving up the engine and ready to go. Ennis had taught both her and Portia the rudiments of driving already; even without a permit, she could *do* this. She knew she could.

She'd eased the car awkwardly out of the garage and down the driveway, fumbling until she found the windshield wipers. No one even noticed. Then she was miraculously on the road, creeping along, trying to keep her hands steady as the rain sluiced down the windshield and made seeing, much less driving, a nearly impossible task.

Still she kept at it, driving away from the big, ugly house, the pool, the locus (oh, she was good, really good, with her SAT vocab, wasn't she?) of her unending humiliation.

Fuck the wedding, fuck Angelica, fuck Ohad—oh God, how she had wanted that very thing! But she had to stop thinking of that now. There were other things to focus on. She'd find the train station, leave the car parked somewhere, and head back to Brooklyn. She had a key to the house; she could let herself in. She would find comfort in her room, her books, her bed, and in their ancient cat, Rani, who was being fed by a neighbor this weekend. Rani! How Justine longed to bury her face in the tabby's soft fur, gaze into her round green eyes. She knew there would be no judgment in them. No judgment, no expectation, and no blame.

Almost there, she told herself, hands still trembling but remaining on the wheel. She forced herself to maintain her grip despite the tremors. *Almost there.* And then the terrifying blare of the siren, the cop car alongside her, and the mortifying exchange with the pair of officers who picked her up and brought her here to the station on Stepping Stone Lane.

What a stupid name anyway. It didn't sound real at all; it sounded made-up, like something in a lame kids' story. Maybe it was; maybe this was all made-up, a crazy, convoluted dream she was having. Maybe she'd wake up, and this day would start anew: she'd find herself back in the vast media room at her Grandma Betsy's, glaring at the monster-sized electronic equipment or twitching with impatience as Portia snored.

But then the officer came back into the room with a step so silent that it took her by surprise. This time she couldn't close her eyes and blot him out; he'd already seen her looking at him, and it was too late to pretend she hadn't. "Your parents are here," he said. Justine blinked, momentarily crushed by the knowledge that this was no dream, and that there was no do-over button in the real life—*her* real life—that was unspooling right now, this minute, as she sat here and waited for whatever was coming next.

Eighteen

⮞⮞ · ⮜⮜

B y the time Lincoln had reached the second tent, he'd set
the umbrella down. It was useless anyway, and the effort of hanging on to it in the wind was more trouble than it
was worth. He pulled up the hood on the slicker over the
back of his head. The tent seemed firmly set in place, but
Lincoln still held out hope that the rain would stop. Angelica should not have to get married in a downpour.

He kept walking, picking up his pace when he neared
the bar. He didn't want to be tempted again even for a minute. That had been a close call. Too close for comfort. And
even though at the time he'd been pissed as hell that Gretch-
en's appearance had stopped him, right now he was extremely grateful that she had. Because for him there was no
such thing as one drink. Never had been, never would be.
No, if he'd let himself slip, one drink would have been two,
and two, three; before he knew it, he'd be on a pull-out-all-
the-stops bender. He cringed, imagining the scene he might
have made: insulting Donny boy, growing weepy over the

bride, lamenting his loss of Betsy, punching Bobby, pow, right in the kisser—on and on. Lincoln knew he'd been a loud, messy, exuberant drunk, and no doubt he would be one still. Angelica would have been so disappointed, so hurt, and Gretchen—finger-wagging, naysaying Gretchen—had saved him from the whole sorry mess of it.

He was in such a hurry that he didn't notice there was someone else on the path until they had nearly collided. "Ohad," he said, surprised. "What are you doing here?" Lincoln had met his future son-in-law only once, a couple of years ago, before he and Angelica had become engaged. They had flown out to LA for a quick visit, staying in a garden cottage at the Chateau Marmont and sparing Lincoln the embarrassment of hosting them at his modest studio near MacArthur Park. He'd liked the guy, but he was also a little intimidated by him; Ohad was so fucking macho, it hurt. It wasn't just the looks; it was the whole damn package.

"I was looking for Justine," Ohad said now. He wore a navy Windbreaker, and droplets of water shone on his black hair. No hood for *him*.

"They've found her already; Gretchen and Ennis went to get her at the police station."

"Police station?" Ohad looked alarmed. "What happened?"

"She took one of Betsy's cars; the police picked her up a few miles from the house."

"Oh," said Ohad. "I didn't know." A few drops of water slid down his face, and he quickly brushed them away.

"How would you?" Lincoln said. "You weren't there

when Don got the call." Then he added, "Why were you looking for her anyway?"

"It's complicated. Something happened between us," Ohad said. When he saw Lincoln's skeptical expression, he added, "I can't say what it was. Not right now, anyway."

Lincoln said nothing. He didn't like the sound of that. What the hell could have happened? He hadn't put the moves on her, had he? The thought made Lincoln feel sick. And then murderous.

"I think Justine would rather I didn't broadcast it," Ohad said gently. He looked at Lincoln engulfed by the yellow slicker. "What are you doing out here, anyway? The wedding's going to start soon."

"I'm looking for Lenore," Lincoln said. He didn't know what to think about Ohad and Justine, but he couldn't focus on it now. As Ohad had pointed out, the wedding would be starting very soon. And Lincoln had to find Lenore before it did.

"I'll tell Angelica," Ohad said. Lincoln watched as his about-to-be son-in-law continued walking toward the house. Gretchen and Ennis should have gotten to the police station by now; he hoped they could sort things out quickly. He decided he wouldn't say anything about his exchange with Ohad—not yet. First he wanted to see Justine for himself. Talk to her. Then he could decide what to say and do.

Lincoln kept going, passing a privet hedge and then coming to a stand of tall pines. Could Lenore be out here somewhere? He had a hunch she was. No particular reason why. Just a hunch. But a hunch was better than nothing. He looked right and he looked left. Nothing jumped out at him. He was a lefty, so he'd try going left first. See where that took him.

As he walked, he tried to be methodical in his search, looking in both directions as well as up and down. He called her name at regular intervals and then stopped to listen for a possible reply. He'd been walking for about fifteen minutes when the thought came to him that he'd been wrong; maybe he should turn around and go in the other direction after all. His hunch had not panned out. But then a flash of color snagged his attention; he could see something a slight distance off in the grass.

He hurried over to inspect. It turned out to be a scrap of brilliant, flame-colored material. The finished edges and perfect square suggested it was not a scrap but a scarf. Just the sort of scarf that Lenore, with her crazy colors, her flounces and ruffles and bows, might have worn—and dropped—on her walk. Wet and muddy as it was, he stuffed it into his pocket and picked up his pace. "Lenore!" he yelled into the wind. "Lenore, are you there?" Nothing. Still Lincoln kept going, calling, calling, calling until his voice was hoarse. His tooth continued to hurt, the pain a steady counterpoint to everything else. She was out here, damn it. He could feel it. He just had to zero in on where.

"Lenore!" he fairly shrieked. "Lenore!" And, thank the living God, this time there was a reply. He couldn't quite make it out, but he began to trot in the direction of the sound. The impact of his steps intensified the throbbing of the tooth; with each footfall, pain drove through his head with a fresh, lacerating twist. "Lenore, I'm coming!" he called. "Where are you?"

"Over here," the voice called faintly. "I'm in the bushes." He kept going in the direction of the sound. Trees, grass, sand, mud, and, everywhere he looked, rain. But over there, wasn't that a clump of bushes? He was wheezing with exertion and anxiety when he found her, a crumpled little heap of person, sopping wet and hunkered down under the meager protection offered by the foliage.

"Lincoln!" she cried weakly.

"Are you all right?" He thought she looked strange and then realized it was her hair, which hung straight down, plastered to the sides of her head as if with glue. The familiar poofs and waves had given her volume; without them she seemed to have shrunk several inches.

Lenore nodded. "I'm all right. I fell and hurt my ankle. But I don't think it's serious, just a sprain." She gestured to her foot, perched on a rock. "What time is it?"

He checked his watch. "A little after five."

"Thank God! I haven't missed the wedding."

"No," he said, and he smiled. "You haven't missed a thing." Then he looked at her knees. "You're bleeding. We should get those scrapes cleaned up. Can you walk?"

"I don't think so."

"Okay," he said. "Okay." He wished he had thought to bring a blanket for her, but, then again, it only would have gotten soaked. Betsy. Betsy could bring a blanket. Or ask someone else to. He pulled out his phone and punched in the numbers.

"I found her," he said when his ex-wife answered. "I found her, and she's fine."

"Oh, Lincoln," Betsy said. He could hear the relief flooding her voice. "You're my hero."

Lincoln puffed at her praise. "She hurt her ankle, and she's a little banged up, but I'll get her back to the house as soon as I can. Have Caleb come and meet me. Tell him to go out the kitchen door, past the pool to the edge of the property and turn left. I'll be coming back the way I came, so he can keep in touch via cell. Oh, and, Betsy—" He looked down again at the old, frail woman on the ground. "Have him bring a blanket too. A thick, warm one."

Lincoln lifted her easily; she was like a child in his arms. But though she was not at all heavy, the act of carrying her made him deeply uncomfortable. She had never liked him, never thought he would amount to much, and she was right: he hadn't. And, sensing her disapproval, he had not liked her either. Yet here they were, the rescued and the rescuer, engaged in their unexpectedly intimate dance.

"Lincoln," she said. "Lincoln, I cannot tell you how grateful I am that you found me. How grateful and how overjoyed. If I had missed the wedding . . ."

"I know, Lenore," he said. "That would have been terrible. For all of us." And he meant it. Lenore had lived long enough to see this wedding, and she cared so much about it. She deserved to be there.

"I misjudged you, Lincoln," she said as if he had not spoken. "I misjudged you, and I'm sorry."

"What do you mean?" he said, though of course he

knew; he'd known for decades. The tooth, which had miraculously calmed down for a few minutes, had once again started unfurling its insidious tendrils of pain.

"I thought there was something weak about you. Something vague and not quite one hundred percent. But I was wrong. You are one hundred and ten percent. You are"—she paused, and her head (it was so small, really) touched his chest—"magnificent."

"Thank you, Lenore," he said quietly. "That's very nice of you to say." At that moment his cell phone buzzed, and he fumbled around in his pocket to get to it. Caleb. "Where are you?" he asked and then listened to his son's coordinates. "Okay. I'm coming along that way. Five minutes, seven max, and you'll see me. You have the blanket? And a big umbrella? Good." He clicked off.

"Caleb is coming to meet us," Lincoln said.

"I'm so glad. I was worried about him. That boy he brought with him—no good. I knew it from the start."

"You're right about that," Lincoln said. To his amazement the rain seemed to be tapering off; it had become more of a drizzle now.

"But I was even more worried about Justine," Lenore continued. "That's why I went to find her first."

"Why were you worried about Justine?" Lincoln asked. He debated whether he ought to tell Lenore about the car, the police, and what Ohad had said. Then he decided it could wait until she was safely back at the house.

"Justine told a lie today. And I caught her in it. But I didn't let on. Though I think she knows that I know."

"And what lie was that?"

"Maybe I'd better wait to tell you," she said. "Not"—and she lifted her head to look into his eyes—"because I don't trust you. But out of respect for her."

Lincoln nodded, wondering whether what Lenore was referring to had anything to do with whatever it was that had happened with Ohad. Well, Gretchen and Ennis ought to be back at the house by the time he got there; he'd find out more then. He rounded a corner and there was Caleb, carrying a golf umbrella that must have been three feet in diameter, and a puffy down quilt.

"Grandma!" cried Caleb when he saw them. "Grandma, I'm so glad you're all right!" He rushed up, dropped the umbrella, and then fumbled to retrieve it. "When Mom told me you'd gone missing, I was so worried about you."

"You're a sweetheart," Lenore said. "But I'm a tough old bird. You don't have to worry about me. Your father"—she beamed up at Lincoln—"is bringing me home to get cleaned up. And then it will be time for the wedding! I can't wait."

But apparently this scenario did not sit so well with Caleb, whose face contorted into a mask of sorrow as the tears, copious as the afternoon's rain, began to flow. He handed both quilt and umbrella to Lincoln.

"What happened now?" Lincoln asked. Caleb just put a hand to his eyes and continued to cry.

"Can you answer your father?" Lenore said from her nest in Lincoln's arms.

"It's Bobby," Caleb said from behind the screen of his fingers. "He's gone. He called a taxi to the train station and went back to the city."

"Well, good riddance!" Lincoln said. And Lenore added, "It's for the best. You'll see."

"No, it's not!" Caleb said, lifting his tear-glazed face to look at them. "It's not, because now it's really, truly over!"

"It's been over for some time," Lincoln said, ostensibly to Caleb but really to himself. "You just weren't able to read the signals."

Caleb opened his mouth as if to say something. Then he closed it and walked over to where Lincoln stood holding Lenore. There was a sound, and they all turned to look. Teddy was approaching.

"Mom told me where to find you," he explained. "I thought you might need some help getting back."

"Thank you, Teddy, sweetheart," Lenore said.

"Good going," Lincoln added. Teddy's appearance was a nice surprise. His elder son could be a little self-involved; it was not like to him to extend himself for anyone else.

Teddy and Caleb made a seat with their four arms for Lenore; Lincoln laid the blanket over her and held the big umbrella over the group. They didn't really need it anymore, but somehow it seemed right. Then they carefully transported Lenore back to the house. On the way Lincoln saw Teddy observing Caleb, on whose face the vestiges of recent tears were still evident.

"You okay?" Teddy asked his brother in a quiet voice. Caleb actually stopped, and Teddy, clearly unprepared, lurched a bit; Lenore swayed in their arms. "Whoa!" she said softly, and the frail arm wrapped around Caleb's shoulder tightened.

"Yeah," Caleb said, clearly suspicious.

"I'm just asking," Teddy said mildly. "No offense or anything."

"No offense," repeated Caleb.

Lincoln listened to this small, seemingly inconsequential exchange intently. Teddy was making some kind of move toward Caleb. An overture. And Caleb had not exactly rebuffed him. Now, who would have figured on that? And who could say where it might go?

When they walked in the door, Lincoln was given what amounted to a hero's welcome: cheers, hugs, kisses, back-slapping, and vigorous hand-pumping from many sides. But he couldn't linger in the moment; he had to extricate himself and left Caleb with Teddy while he went off to get cleaned up. He needed to shower again, of course. And even though his rented tuxedo awaited him, Don insisted that he take a quick look through the ample supply of jackets, slacks, shirts, ties, and shoes he kept on hand for the weekend guests who wanted to dine at the country club or one of the tonier restaurants in town and had brought only sweats and polo shirts.

From this generous stash Lincoln had scored a white Armani shirt, a black Ralph Lauren belt, black patent leather Ferragamo slip-ons, and, most amazing of all, a tuxedo that fit better than the one he had rented back in LA. His fingers smoothed the matte satin lapels; he examined the expert tailoring of the pants. While he hated like hell taking anything from Don, he hated the idea of appearing like a schlep at Angelica's wedding even more. "You look sharp," Don said when he saw him.

"Thanks for the loan," Lincoln replied. "I appreciate it."

"It's not a loan. You might as well keep all that stuff. I sure as hell don't need it, and it looks good on you."

"Thanks," Lincoln said. "Thanks a lot."

"It's nothing," Don said, smoothing his own finely tucked shirt down over his sizable gut. "Anyway I'm the one who should be thanking you. You really came through, buddy. Saved the day."

Lincoln, who did not expect this, looked away, trying to determine whether he felt humiliated or flattered. Neither, he decided. It was what it was. "I'm just glad I found her," he said.

"Damn straight," Don said and smacked him heartily on the back. Lincoln winced slightly from the impact; his tooth sent a silent howl of protest to his brain.

Lincoln surveyed himself in the full-length mirror in Don's dressing room. "I do look good, don't I?" he said. And without waiting for Don's reply, he left the room, ready for the family, the friends, the old, the new—ready for the about-to-unfold pageant: Angelica's wedding.

Nineteen

❦ · ❦

Although Lenore resisted mightily, Betsy insisted that she submit to an examination by Betsy's friend Azar, who was willing to come right over. Azar—plump, dimpled, motherly—had been a cardiologist back in Iran; her husband, Farid, was an anesthesiologist at North Shore University Hospital. Of course they did have two doctors already in the house, but, needless to say, both were highly distracted. And given Lenore's age and chronic heart condition—she'd had bypass surgery a few years back—Betsy thought it wise for her to be seen by Azar.

Azar and her husband symbolized the transformation of Great Neck: no longer the exclusive enclave of the affluent Ashkenazi, the town was now home to a significant influx of equally affluent Iranian Jews who prized its tree-lined roads and streets, excellent school system, and superior housing stock. Many of Betsy's Great Neck friends deplored the arrival of the newcomers, but Betsy was not in their number.

"She's fine," Azar said, straightening up and putting

the cover on the tube of Neosporin she'd used to anoint Lenore's scraped knees. "In fact she's in wonderful shape for a woman her age." They were upstairs in Lenore's bedroom, where Lenore herself had been bundled into a large terry cloth robe and fluffy slippers and given a mug of steaming tea.

"You see?" Lenore turned triumphantly to her daughter. "All this bother about nothing. I told you I was fine." She drained the last of the tea from the mug and set it down.

"And the ankle isn't broken?" Betsy asked yet again.

"Not broken, just sprained. She can use those crutches"—Azar had presciently thought to bring a pair with her—"to get around tonight."

"I don't think I need them; it doesn't hurt that much." To prove her point she stood up and put some—though not all—of her weight on her foot.

"Ma!" cried Betsy. "Would you please be careful?" She hovered anxiously, ready to catch Lenore if she toppled.

"I'm all right," declared Lenore, sitting down again. "Perfectly all right. And now I am going to take a bath and get dressed. But I do need some panty hose. Nude, beige—anything like that would be fine. Your little dog ruined mine." She waved in the direction of the shredded pair on the bed. "And I need the hairdresser; would you ask her to please come up?" Lenore's hair, which she had combed, still hung straight down around her ears.

"I'll send the hairdresser up as soon as you've finished your bath," said Betsy. "And Pippa will get you the panty hose." The woman had been conspicuously absent for the past hour; maybe she could actually make herself useful now. Betsy's earlier decision to terminate her employment had lost its urgency in the face of the twin emergencies of her mother and her granddaughter. Well, one fire had been put out; now there was only Justine with whom to contend.

"Dr. Rachlin," Lenore said, looking at Azar. "Thank you for coming. I know it helped to put Betsy's mind at ease."

As if this were all a whim of mine! Betsy silently fumed. But she had no time to wrangle with her mother now.

"Leave the door to your bathroom partially open," she said to Lenore. "And the door to your room too. I'll help you get in and out of the bath."

"All right," Lenore said petulantly. "But Dr. Rachlin *said* I was fine. More than fine—'in wonderful shape' were your exact words, weren't they?" she asked. Azar nodded as she walked toward the hallway.

"Thanks so much for coming," Betsy said, giving her friend a hug.

"Just humor her," Azar whispered in Betsy's ear. "You'll save yourself a lot of grief."

After Azar left, Betsy went back to Lenore's room and hesitated outside the partially open door. "Ma?" she called.

"Do you have my panty hose?" Lenore, still wearing the robe, appeared in the doorway.

"Not yet," Betsy said.

"I *need* them. We want to do those pictures soon."

"You'll get your panty hose. But I wanted to ask you

something important. You said you had gone out to look for Justine. Why? You never told me that."

Lenore sighed, an expansive sound that seemed to emanate from deep within. "I haven't wanted to say this until I talked to her myself first. But I suppose it will all come out in the end."

"What will come out in the end?"

"Right before you called everyone up to Angelica's room, I saw Justine out by the pool digging around in the grass for something. She looked—well, she looked *frantic*."

"And why is that so strange? Maybe she dropped something, and she was looking for it," Betsy said, puzzled.

"I thought maybe she was looking for the ring; that's what she was so desperate to find out there."

"How would the ring—if it *was* the ring—have gotten over by the pool?" asked Betsy. Lenore was laying out the pieces like a series of tarot cards, but Betsy could not decipher their meaning. "And how would Justine have known to look for it there?"

"That's what I wanted to find out," Lenore said. "And so that's why I went looking for her."

"Oh," Betsy said. "I think I see. . . ."

"And there was something else—I didn't think Bobby had taken the ring; that seemed like something Justine invented to deflect the blame. But of course now that Bobby's upped and left, it's possible he might have done it after all. Right from the start I didn't trust him. Did you ever manage to talk to him about it? Or did Angelica?"

Before Betsy could answer, the doorbell rang, and the

dog began her frenzy of high-pitched yapping. "Let me see who that is," she said, hurrying downstairs.

There was a small crowd gathered at the door: Gretchen, Ennis, and Justine, as well as the musicians—all eleven of them—had arrived. Angelica and Ohad hired a classical group to play before and during the wedding and a jazz band to play afterward. They had shown up, improbably, together—the classical contingent having come on the eastbound Long Island Rail Road train and the jazz band in a beat-up minivan with red and black swirls spray-painted across its sides. They had been told to use the service entrance to the property, but they must have forgotten, because here they were right at the front door. Betsy squelched the urge to mention it.

Instead she dispatched them to various places in the house or outside to set up; at least the rain had stopped. Then she turned her attention to her family, still assembled like life-sized chess pieces on the massive black and white squares of the foyer's marble floor.

"Justine!" She tried to gather the unyielding girl into her arms. "We were so worried when we heard about what you'd done. You could have been hurt or even killed!"

"Well, I'm not hurt, and obviously I'm not dead," Justine said flatly.

"You're being rude," Gretchen admonished. Justine did not apologize but simply stood there rigid until Betsy let her arms drop to her sides.

"They let her off with only a warning," Ennis said. "They're not going to press charges or anything."

"It's because of Don," Gretchen added. "We have to thank him. We really do." Betsy looked from her daughter to her estranged son-in-law. Something had happened between those two in the past hour. But what? Something that was going to knit the rift between them? Or drive them further apart? She couldn't tell.

"Your father found Grandma," Betsy said. She turned to Justine. "She was out looking for you, you know. That's how worried she was."

Justine remained silent, but Gretchen said, "What a relief! Where is she now?"

"Upstairs getting ready," Betsy said. "Which is what everyone here should be doing too; the guests are going to be arriving soon."

"I'm not going to be at the wedding, Grandma B.," Justine said. "So I don't have to get ready."

"What?" Gretchen and Ennis said practically in unison. "You didn't say anything about not attending the wedding."

"I didn't say anything at all," Justine said. "Remember? I kept my mouth shut the whole drive back."

"Justine, why don't you want to go to the wedding?" Betsy said. In the background, she heard the sounds of the various musicians tuning up—a violin, a cello, a trumpet, a saxophone—along with the dog, who had not stopped barking.

"I don't want to talk about it. And no one can make me."

A reply was forming on Betsy's lips when Pippa strutted into the foyer. "So there you are!" she said, as if Betsy had been the one who had disappeared.

"I've been here all along," Betsy said. "Where were *you*?"

"With Angelica of course," was the smug reply.

Betsy felt yet another small pinch of rejection but decided to let it pass. "Well, I'm glad you're here now, because there's something I need you to do. Lenore, my mother, needs new panty hose. Can you drive into town and pick her up a pair? Size extra small; any neutral shade will be fine."

"I really don't think Angelica can spare me right now," Pippa said. "The photographer is set up for the pictures, and I really should be here to oversee the shooting." She looked around the room. "Shouldn't you all be *ready* by now?"

"Well, I would have been ready if I hadn't had to handle every single thing by myself for the last two hours!" Betsy said, boiling over. "Where have you *been*? What have we been *paying* you for, anyway?"

"I really don't appreciate being spoken to in that tone of voice," Pippa said, her nostrils quivering rabbitlike with indignation.

"What tone of voice?" said Don, who was wearing a tuxedo and gleaming white shirt anchored by a black satin bow tie and a pair of heavy gold cuff links. He looked at Pippa. "Why are you still here? I thought Betsy had given you your marching order hours ago."

"I have never been spoken to this way before. Never," said Pippa. "I would leave right now except that would be a totally unprofessional thing to do. And I *am* a professional," she added, her chin trembling slightly.

Betsy felt no sympathy at all; now that she had started, she didn't want to stop. "Well, if you're such a professional, please get into the car, drive into town, and get Lenore her panty hose. Immediately." Gretchen, who had the keys in her pocket, held them out to Pippa.

As Pippa took the keys, her phone started buzzing; she whipped it out and stepped closer to the door to conduct her conversation. Betsy couldn't believe she wasn't moving in the direction of the garage *now*, but before she could interrupt, she was literally faced with Lincoln, who had just come in and was now standing inches away from her. "Do you know what's going on between Justine and your future son-in-law?" He spoke quietly, but there was an intensity to his words that put Betsy instantly on the alert.

"What are you talking about?" she asked. Had he been drinking? She scanned his face for the signs but did not see any. In fact he was looking very pulled together and spiffy; that was *definitely* not a rental tux.

"Ohad told me something happened between them. But he wouldn't say what. Do you know?"

"I don't," Betsy said, immediately imagining several possible scenarios; she didn't like any of them. She turned to look at Justine, whose arm was being held—rather tightly in Betsy's view—by Ennis.

Gretchen must have thought so too. "You're going to hurt her," she said to Ennis.

"No, she's fine—" Ennis began. He let her go, but the rest of his sentence remained unspoken because he, like

everyone else, was suddenly distracted by a voice that emanated from the top of the stairs.

"What is *wrong* with everyone?"

They looked up. There was Angelica, resplendently
garbed in her wedding gown, reproaching them all with her
beautiful, furious gaze.

Twenty

❧ • ☙

Gretchen heard her father's small intake of breath at the sight of her sister, and she could understand why. Angelica was less adorned—but even more exquisite—than Gretchen would have expected: the dress, a gleaming yet simple undulation of heavy white satin, the glossy black hair pulled up and back revealing the crisply articulated point of her widow's peak, the ebullient froth of the net veil spilling over her shoulders. She was, as Lenore would have put it, a vision.

"Mom, you're not even dressed yet!" Angelica cried.

"I'm about to go up right now," Betsy said. "I was just asking Pippa to *please* drive into town to buy your grandmother a pair of panty hose."

Angelica looked at Pippa, who was finally off the phone. "Could you?" she said. "For me?" Pippa nodded, mouth tight, and, clutching the keys, she walked out without another word.

As soon as Pippa left, Esperanza, the maid, walked in,

carrying Betsy's wretched little dog in her arms. It was wheezing pathetically, and even Gretchen, no friend to high-strung, sleep-decimating creatures, could see that something was terribly wrong.

"Excuse me, *señora*," said Esperanza. "The dog. She no good. Look."

"Oh my God," Betsy said. "Her tongue is blue!" She grabbed the gasping dog and ran off to the kitchen with Esperanza hurrying behind her. Seconds later they heard the rush of water and Betsy's voice loud and clear above it. "Ice, please, someone get me some ice!"

"What's going on?" Gretchen asked.

"I have no idea!" Angelica snapped. "All I know is that my wedding is about to start, and Mom is in the kitchen with her dog! I cannot believe it." She moved along the marble floor. The long dress swirled around her ankles and made sibilant whispers as she passed. "At least *you're* dressed, Daddy!" she said to Lincoln. "But what about the rest of you?"

"I'm not getting dressed, because I'm not going to be there," Justine announced. She clenched her fists slightly as if for resolve. Gretchen stared at her. Was nothing about this day going to go smoothly? Was it going to be a battle every damned step of the way? That phone call from the police, the ride with Ennis, sloshing through the rising water, the humiliation of reclaiming her child from the station—and now this out-and-out refusal to attend the wedding.

"What are you talking about?" Angelica stopped in

front of her niece. "How could I even think of getting married without you there?"

"I'm sorry," Justine said. "But I'm not going. Don't you see? I *can't* go."

"Why not, sweetheart?" Angelica's tone had softened, and she placed her hands on Justine's shoulders. Galvanized by Angelica's touch, Justine reared back and attempted to bolt. Ennis caught her first and this time took both of her arms in his hands.

"Oh no," he said. "Not again."

"Let me go!" Justine wriggled in her father's grasp.

"Ennis!" Gretchen cried. "Stop being so rough!"

"I'm not hurting her," Ennis said. "I'm just setting some limits. She can't go running off again. This has got to stop, and it's stopping right now, hey."

"Why do you want to run away, sweetie?" Angelica said. She made no other move to touch Justine but stood very close to her with their faces mere inches apart.

"Ask Ohad! Ask that murderer you want to marry!" Justine wrenched her face away and pressed it to her father's chest. Then she began to cry. Gretchen was too stunned to approach her and stood there staring.

"What is going on here?" Betsy said. She and Esperanza had walked back into the room, still holding the dog, which was now soaked and trembling violently. The animal's abundant fur was tamped down, and she seemed diminished, small as a rodent.

"That's what I'd like to know!" Angelica whirled

around to face her mother. "Justine is calling Ohad terrible names and says she's not going to be at the wedding, and you run off into the kitchen with your damned dog—"

"My *damned dog* was minutes away from death," Betsy said. "This has happened before; she gets herself overwrought and goes into some kind of shock. I had to get her under cold water immediately to bring her body temperature down." She gave Esperanza a quick hug. "Thank you for letting me know so quickly," she said. "You saved her life."

"Mom, this is surreal," said Angelica. "All those years of not allowing so much as a canary to cross our threshold, and now you're catering and kowtowing to the most neurotic animal on the planet. And on my wedding day no less!"

"The goldfish . . ." Gretchen said. "She wouldn't even let me have a goldfish . . ." She was transported back to that rueful day when she'd had to surrender her shimmering orange prize.

"And you!" Angelica said, turning her wrath on her sister. "Why aren't you dressed? And why can't you control your own daughter?"

"This is not a matter of *control*, Angelica," flared Gretchen. That was so like Angelica, blaming everyone for everything. How was it that Angelica, so much younger, nevertheless had always managed to wield such power in the family? Gretchen had never been able to figure that out, and now, even on the cusp of forty, she was no closer to knowing her sister's secret. "Justine is suffering. Can't you see that? Is everything always about you?"

"Mom, stop talking about me like I'm not here!" Justine

said, lifting her face from Ennis's chest. "You're always do-ing that, and I hate it!" Gretchen felt something inside crumble; how wounding were your child's offhand and so casually hurled recriminations.

"You're jealous," Angelica said, ignoring Justine. "You've always been jealous of me. You want to ruin my wedding, don't you?"

"I was jealous of you in the past," Gretchen said. "And maybe I'm still jealous of you now. But accusing me of want-ing to ruin your wedding? That's a total distortion. Because I wouldn't do that—not to you, not to anyone. I wouldn't rob you of something so precious and important. But you can't say the same thing, can you?"

"I don't know what you're talking about," Angelica said. It was clear, though, that Gretchen's comment had in some way registered; her enviably white skin had turned ever so slightly pink, and she gripped the folds of her dress more tightly than necessary.

"Oh yes, you do," Gretchen said. She hadn't thought about the incident in years, though she remembered how dismayed she'd been at the time. Yet she'd said nothing to Angelica; even then her sister's armor had been proof against any question.

"It was that spring you graduated from college. After you'd walked off with about every honor there was—departmental, summa cum laude, Phi Beta Kappa. But there was one thing you didn't get. It was that fellowship to go off to . . . Sweden?"

"It was Copenhagen!" Angelica said, flustered. "It was

Copenhagen, and I was the one who should have been chosen; everyone thought so!"

"Not the committee who made the decision," Gretchen said. "They didn't think so. They picked someone else." She felt the air in the room subtly changing as this conversation was taking place and sensed how everyone—her parents, her daughter—was regarding Angelica as if they had not seen her, or at least not all of her, before now. "But you didn't like that, did you? More than not like it—you wouldn't stand for it. So you tipped off someone on the committee about the graduation party she was hosting, didn't you?"

"She invited all her druggie buddies to that party! The committee had a right to know. And I had an obligation to tell them." Angelica was so self-righteous, so odiously sure of herself.

"Wasn't your first obligation to her? She was your friend. Your *best* friend," said Gretchen quietly. "And, anyway, you're making it sound way more serious than it was. We're talking about pot, Angelica. Those kids were passing around a few joints, not mainlining heroin."

"Pot is illegal! It was then, and it is now! She was a lawbreaker. A lawbreaker engaged in a criminal activity." Angelica's voice had scaled up. "And she was a fool to have jeopardized that fellowship just to get high. She didn't deserve it."

"You had so much already," Gretchen said, ignoring her sister's last remark. "But you couldn't let her have that. You wanted it, so you took it from her. The way you take just about everything."

"How do you *know* all this?" Angelica burst out. "Who even *told* you?" Her voice had a desperate edge.

"She did," said Gretchen. "After it was all over, and you had flown off, she called me. She was miserable, disgraced within the department, afraid she wouldn't be allowed to graduate. She wanted to talk to someone who knew you as well as she did. Someone who could explain what it was that you had done. I guess she thought that would be me."

There was a deep and powerful silence that lasted several seconds. Gretchen was the one who broke it. "I spent years envying you," she said to her sister as if they were the only ones in the room. "At first it was because everyone doted on you, and later because you were so good at everything. But I'm not envious of you anymore." Was this even true? She didn't know, but she felt good saying it, felt good *acting as if*, so she continued. "I don't want your life, Angelica. Not the big splashy wedding, not the high-powered career—none of it. I'm different from you—and from Teddy and Caleb too. I don't want what the rest of you want, and that's always made me feel insufficient. Lacking. I spent so much time feeling that way that I couldn't figure out what it was I did want. That's going to change, though. In fact, I think it already has." Gretchen stopped talking. She felt everyone looking at her now, as if she was the one they had failed to see clearly.

"Well, I'm glad you're not envious," Angelica said frostily. She had regained command of herself again; the momentary crack in her composure was sealed over by the carapace of her personality. "Because I never intended to make you feel that way. And if you did, it wasn't my fault. But none of you are being particularly supportive," she said, looking around the foyer at the assembled group. "Caleb having histrionics over his boyfriend, Grandma disappearing, Justine taking the car. And someone"—her voice rose, the angry queen once more—"has gone and stolen my diamond ring! I just can't believe it. You all want to sabotage this day. It's clear to me now. Even you, Mom. You're trying to turn this into *your* day, *your* event. That's why I hired Pippa: I needed an ally in this family—even if I had to pay to get her."

"You think *I* was trying to *sabotage* you?" Betsy said; the shock made her voice sound, at least to Gretchen, unfamiliar. "And that Pippa—*Pippa!*—was your ally? Angelica, that is the worst thing you have ever said to me in your entire life." And, still clutching the dog, she began to cry. Betsy, Gretchen knew, never cried, and the effect on everyone was immediate.

A weird hush settled on the room; even Justine stopped her own crying to witness the spectacle of Betsy breaking down—the loud, wrenching sobs that contorted her mouth and caused red blotches to appear on her cheeks and neck. Swiftly Gretchen walked over to her mother and took both her and her wretched dog in her arms. Betsy let herself be enfolded by the embrace; her small shoulders trembled as she wept. The dog trembled in sympathy. Awkwardly Gretchen patted her mother's back. Her father looked stricken and useless; even Mr. Know-It-All Don was without a solution.

And then Teddy and Marti came into the foyer; he

wore his tuxedo, and she was in a crisp linen dress the color of toast, with several strands of ivory beads at her throat. Caleb, also tuxedo clad, walked in just behind them. "What's going on?" Teddy asked. "The photographer is all set up, and she wants all you guys over there."

"He's right," Don said, finally jolted into action. "Betsy, honey, please stop crying. You need to get a grip." But Betsy kept crying and didn't answer, and everyone else started talking at once.

"Everyone's trying to ruin my day! Ruin!"

"It's always about her; no one else even exists!"

"That was such an uncalled-for comment! So cruel!"

"He's a murderer!"

"She's so self-centered! Selfish!"

"Have you all gone crazy?"

"Someone has to take this child in hand!"

"I don't want Marti to have to see *any* of this!"

"I should have left with Bobby!"

"There's a thief in this house. A thief!"

Gretchen didn't know which voice to listen to, what to do next. What had she set in motion here? Was Angelica right in her accusations—that Gretchen was jealous and wanted to spoil things for her? But no. She realized as she listened to all the strident, angry voices around her that was not what she wanted—not at all. They had gathered here to see Angelica get married. And that's what they were going to do. Everything else could wait.

Putting two fingers up to her mouth, she let out a piercing whistle, something she had not done since she was a kid.

Amazingly she still knew how, because they all stopped; every single one of them shut up and stared. Even Betsy's sobs ceased, and the little dog's ears pricked, two perfect triangles on its small, wet head.

"Enough!" Gretchen cried, a stern schoolmarm addressing her unruly charges. "There's no time for this now. Yes, everyone's angry. Everyone has an agenda. But for the next few hours, we have to rein it in. For Angelica and for ourselves too. Because otherwise all those people who are about to arrive will think we're totally out of control and coming apart at the seams. And I don't know about the rest of you, but I don't believe that about us, and I don't want anyone else to believe it either." Gretchen could not remember when she'd had the attention of her entire family all at the same time. "So are you with me? Mom? Caleb? Please?"

Angelica stood with her open hands at her sides; the dress had indentations, subtle but still visible, where she had clutched it. "Thank you, Gretchen," she said. Her voice broke the spell that Gretchen's whistle had cast, and again everyone was speaking at once, thanking her and agreeing that, yes, they would all pull it together for the wedding. "I told you I won't go—" These words, uttered by Justine, were lost in the general buzz as the door opened, and there stood Ohad, surrounded by the dark, noisy members of his family, all chattering in Hebrew. When Justine saw him, she burrowed under Ennis's arm as if trying to hide.

"I'm going to get dressed now," Gretchen said. She looked at Justine, who did not return the look.

"So am I," added Betsy. "Lincoln, would you tell Amber that we won't be doing the family photographs before the wedding, but that if she could get some pictures of the two bands setting up, that would be wonderful."

"Yoo-hoo!" a quavery voice called from above. There at the top of the staircase was Lenore. She wore the shimmering green brocade dress, and her hair had been restored to its bouffant fullness, the dips and waves crowning her head like meringue. Adhesive gauze pads neatly covered both knees, and her ankle was tightly bound in an Ace bandage. Her small feet were bare. "Where are my panty hose?"

"Your panty hose!" cried Betsy, mounting the stairs quickly. "I forgot! Ma, just use a pair of mine—"

"No, I can't!" Lenore said. "They'll be too big, and the ankles will sag! And I cannot attend this wedding with saggy ankles."

"I have your panty hose!" Pippa, who had just come in, was elbowing her way through the throng of Israelis; she held the package up in the air like a banner. "I have them right here!"

"Why, thank you, Pippa," Lenore said. "Thank you so much." Then, calling down softly but clearly to her great-granddaughter, she added, "Justine, would you please be a love and bring them up to me?" And everyone moved out of the way as Justine, now holding the panty hose, quickly ascended the stairs. Gretchen let her go and then went up too. Her dress was laid out on her bed; it wouldn't take any time to get ready.

But before she reached her room, she was distracted by the sound of loud, angry voices. Or at least one loud, angry voice. Now what? Bobby had left, hadn't he? So it couldn't be coming from Caleb's room.

"I told you to stop ragging on me about this." Teddy. That was Teddy's voice. "I'll talk to him when I'm good and ready." Suddenly the door was yanked open and then slammed. Teddy stood in the hallway; his cheeks were pink above the white of his dress shirt.

"This seems to be the day for eruptions," Gretchen said. "You too?"

"She won't let up!" Teddy burst out.

"Let up about what?"

"Caleb. She wants me to talk to him. Well, I tried talking to him earlier. He was less than receptive. So when I told this to Marti, she said that's because I needed to *apologize* to him. Can you believe that?"

"Actually, Teddy, I can," Gretchen said. "It seems to me you could apologize to a few people in this family."

"For what?" he said. "For being myself? For having a little energy, a little direction, a little drive? For not being like our sad-sack lush of a dad or our crybaby little bro? *That's* what I should apologize for?"

"For being such an obtuse, insensitive prick, Teddy. That's what you should apologize for. You always have been, you know. But you can change. I wouldn't have thought so before, but I think so now."

"And why, oh wise one, do you think that?"

"Marti," said Gretchen, crossing her arms over her chest. "If she loves you, there must be something in there worth loving, even if you're not showing it to the rest of us.

But if you slam the door and storm out every time you have an argument, she just might not keep on loving you."

"She does love me," said Teddy as if reminding himself. "And I don't want to lose her." He looked at Gretchen, stricken.

"Why don't you go back in?" said Gretchen. And when he didn't move, she stepped closer and gave him a little nudge. "You see, you put your hand on the knob and then you turn it. . . ." With one last look in her direction, Teddy grabbed the knob and pulled hard.

Evening

Angelica and Ohad

June 2, 2012

7:00–8:00: *Cocktail Reception in the Rose Garden*

8:15: *Processional—Pachelbel's Canon in D*

8:30: *Wedding Ceremony in the Small Tent
Led by Rabbi Yossi Sayegh*

READINGS FROM THE SONG OF SONGS:

Ohad Oz

Angelica Elise Silverstein

9:00: *Recessional—Brahms's String Sextet No. 1 in B-flat*

9:15: *Dinner and Dancing in the Main Tent*

Twenty-one

❦ • ❦

Peple had already started arriving. Even though her window faced the back of the house, Lenore could hear the sounds of cars pulling up and car doors opening and slamming again. She could picture them too: the Jaguars and Mercedeses, BMWs and Lexuses. A Bentley or two, maybe an actual Rolls-Royce. After disgorging their passengers, the luxury cars would be parked elsewhere on the property by a cadre of young valets hired for the evening, leaving the well-dressed guests to make the short distance to the rose garden, where the cocktail reception was about to begin.

Soon, Lenore thought; she would go down there very soon. But she knew that her presence downstairs amid the arriving guests could wait. Right now she had to deal with Justine.

"Sit," she told the girl and indicated the bed, on which now rested only the brocade coat, the gloves, and the clutch purse. She had managed to get into the panty hose with no help from anyone, and though she wasn't too pleased with the lumpy white bumps created by the gauze on her knees, she supposed she could live with them. She had cleverly concealed the Ace bandage using one of her smaller silk scarves; she thought it made a nice accent to the rest of the look. Maybe she would even start a trend—silk scarves knotted around the ankle.

Justine sat rigidly; nothing in her face or posture suggested that she was at all willing to talk. Arms crossed over her chest, eyes downcast, mouth held in a tight, unyielding line. *Oh, this was going to take work*, thought Lenore. "So, I hear you don't want to attend the wedding," she began.

"That's right," said Justine. "And you can't make me."

"I wouldn't even try," Lenore said. She waited a beat, and then she too sat down, but on the nearby armchair, not the bed. "It wouldn't be right."

"What do you mean?" Justine asked. "Everyone else seems to think that I should go no matter how I feel."

"Well, you know by now that your grandma Lenore is hardly *everyone else*, is she?" Lenore was rewarded by a tiny smile from that tight-lipped mouth. "Anyway, I don't even want to talk about the wedding. I want to talk about the ring."

"The ring?" Justine looked distinctly uncomfortable.

"Right before your mother asked everyone to come upstairs, I saw you over by the pool searching in the grass for something. And I have a suspicion that something was the ring. Am I right?" She didn't look at Justine but instead focused intently on the charming needlepoint footstool Betsy had placed in front of the armchair; it showed a carefully stitched basket filled with yellow and white daisies.

"You saw me out there?" Justine was clearly stalling.

"I did, but I didn't want to tell anyone right away. I thought I would talk to you first." Here Lenore felt a pang, because she *had* mentioned what she had seen to Lincoln. But still. Lincoln had not told anyone else; she was quite sure of it.

"Thanks, Grandma L.," said Justine quietly. "That was . . . nice of you."

"So, am I right about what you were looking for? Was it the ring?" She looked up from the footstool at her great-granddaughter.

"It was," said Justine.

Lenore waited, and when she began to speak again, she made sure her voice was very soft and very low. "How did you know to look for the ring out there? Had you seen Angelica—or someone else—drop it?"

"No!" Justine burst out. "I took it—that's how I knew. I took it, but I don't know why—I really, really don't! I was just up there in her room, and I was looking around. I saw the ring, and it made me angry. So I took it."

"You took it," Lenore repeated. "And then what did you do with it?"

"I tried to give it back! Honestly, I did! Look," she wailed, "it's right here!" She dug her hand into her pocket and pulled it out.

"The ring," Lenore said, marveling. "So you had it all along."

"For a little while I thought it was missing. That's why I was looking in the grass. But it had slipped through a hole in the pocket of my robe, and it was stuck in the lining."

Lenore nodded. "And that business about Bobby—you made that up, right? He was never in that room, and you knew it."

Justine nodded miserably. "I didn't want those poor maids to get blamed; I figured he could deal with it."

"You got that right," Lenore said. But when Justine looked confused, she added, "Never mind."

"Aren't you going to take the ring, Grandma L.?" asked Justine, who was still clutching it. "I don't want it. It doesn't belong to me. And I despise diamonds."

"I think you need to give it back," Lenore said gently. "It belongs to Angelica and should be returned to Angelica."

"I know!" said Justine. "How could I forget? How could anyone? She talks about it all the time!"

"You sound so angry," Lenore said. "And earlier you said that you were angry. Angry at what?"

"I don't know, Grandma L.! I honestly don't know. I get into these moods—I can't explain them really; I just know they come over me, and when they do, I can't help myself. I call that mood the mean greens."

"The mean greens," Lenore mused softly. "What are they like?" She wondered whether Justine had been in the grip of one of her "moods" when she allowed someone to desecrate her face in that horrible manner: the metal things in her eyebrow and nostril, the series of piercings that went all the way up both of her ears, each hole filled by a stud, loop, or, in one case, safety pin.

"Terrible. Like I said: I get angry, and I want to hurt

someone or something. Not"—she looked alarmed—"not really hurt, you know? It's not like I want to hit anyone or cause pain or anything like that. But when I get into that mood, I want to— Oh, I don't know. Break something. Wreck something. Steal something."

"Something like Angelica's engagement ring?"

Justine nodded. "As soon as I did it, I was sorry, and I wanted to put it back. But then she came into the room. And every time I tried to put it back after that, there was some reason I couldn't. Someone was in the room, or I got distracted. You won't tell her, will you?" she pleaded.

"No," Lenore said. "But you should. Must."

"Why? After today she'll never want to speak to me again."

"Are you sure?" asked Lenore. The sounds of the cars from downstairs continued along with the accompanying sounds of greetings exchanged, muffled shrieks of recognition, of happiness.

"I mean, do *you* think she'll want to talk to me? After what I've said about Ohad? And what I've done?"

Before Lenore could answer, there was a knock on the door. "Ma?" said Betsy from the other side. "Ma, are you okay in there?" Lenore limped over to open it.

There stood Betsy, fully dressed and looking so mother-of-the-bride pretty in her shirred lilac silk dress, her amethyst earrings, her ivory pumps with the kitten heels. But the bra—the bra was all wrong! "I'm fine," Lenore said. "Justine and I are having a little talk. You can go ahead without me. I'll be down as soon as I can."

"Are you sure?" She seemed to want to come in, but Lenore was blocking the way.

"Yes." Then Lenore leaned in closer to her daughter. "Your bra, darling. It's not doing a thing for your profile. Don't you have something with a little more uplift? And smoother, definitely smoother! If you had told me, I could have brought you something from the shop. We just got in a new Wacoal, and it is a *dream*."

"Ma!" said Betsy. "There is *nothing* wrong with my bra." Though she did cast a swift glance downwards at her chest. "I'm going to join the guests now. Please ask Justine to walk you down as soon as you can." She huffed off, and Lenore closed the door behind her.

"You are really into bras, Grandma L.," said Justine, who was actually smiling full out.

"Yes," she said. "I am." Lenore took the opportunity to sit on the bed, though not too close. "You were asking me about Angelica. Whether I thought she would ever speak to you again."

"Oh yeah . . ." said Justine, and the smile shrank until it was gone.

"The ring isn't why you don't want to attend the wedding, is it?" Lenore coaxed. When Justine shook her head, Lenore continued. "Something else is bothering you. Can you tell me what it is?"

"Oh, Grandma L., I want to! I really do! But I don't know how to explain what happened. Not to you, not to anyone. Not even to myself."

"Just try," Lenore coaxed.

"It's Ohad!" Justine said with a wail. "I hate him! But I kind of love him too."

"Let's start with the hate," Lenore said, inching a little closer to Justine. "He seems like such a nice young man. Smart, handsome, brave. Why would you hate him?"

"Brave! Grandma L., he was a *pilot* in the Israeli *air force*. That means he bombed people. And not just troops, either. *Civilians*. Destroyed their homes, their farms, whatever. He *killed* them."

"How do you know?" Lenore countered. "How do you know what he did?" And when Justine didn't answer right away, she pressed on. "So he was in the air force. You don't know what he did and why he did it. Besides, he's not in the air force anymore. He's all done with that. Now he's part of an initiative that is going to bring better health care to Palestinians, especially Palestinian women. Improved childbirth procedures. Routine gynecological care, like Pap smears and mammograms. Education and preventive medicine too." Lenore ticked off items on the list that Angelica had shared with her. "That's how he and Angelica met, you know. They were at a conference together in Jerusalem."

"It doesn't matter," Justine said. "He still did what he did."

"The details of which you don't exactly know."

"But I can guess. And all that do-good stuff now doesn't change it."

"No, the present doesn't change the past, but it puts it into context. Ohad is a complex person. Like me. Like you. And Israel—Israel is a *complicated* nation. What's happening there now is a horror. But the problems won't be easily solved and certainly not by hating Ohad." Lenore took Justine's silence as permission to move a little closer. "Now tell me about the love," she said gently.

"That's the worst part," said Justine. "He's so hot! And he's so nice too. I mean, you can really talk to him. He listens, you know? And not too many people do that."

"No," Lenore agreed. "They don't."

"But you do, Grandma L. And he does too." The girl looked so wretched; why? Lenore was not following the snarled thread of her emotions.

"Is that a bad thing?" she ventured.

"I didn't just talk to him," said Justine. "I kissed him!"

"Oh," Lenore said. She was very glad she was sitting down, because this was not good news, not good at all. "Oh."

"It was like I told you before: I suddenly felt overcome by this—this—this mood. And so I just did it."

"The mean greens?" asked Lenore.

Justine shook her head. "No, it was something different. I hadn't really felt anything like it before."

"I see," Lenore said. "And what did Ohad do when you kissed him?"

"Nothing! He didn't even act like it was weird. He just said, 'Take it easy,' like he was calming a horse or something. I was *so* embarrassed. That's when I decided to leave, to go back to New York and skip the wedding."

"So you borrowed Grandma Betsy's car."

"Uh-huh. And then the police picked me up, and, well, you know the rest." Justine, who had been sitting up all this time, suddenly flopped back on the bed and pulled one of the big, soft down pillows over her face. "I wish I could stay here forever," she said, voice slightly muffled by the pillow.

Lenore was framing a reply when she was once again distracted by a sound at the door. It wasn't a knock though. So what was it? She hobbled over to find out. There in the hallway sat Betsy's little dog.

"What are you doing here?" said Lenore. "Haven't you caused enough trouble for one day?"

"Hasn't who caused enough trouble for one day?" Justine put the pillow aside and sat up. "Oh—that's Grandma Betsy's dog. She's such a pain."

"She certainly is." But the dog was not a bother at the moment; she was not even barking. She simply sat there, holding Lenore's gaze with her own. Her black eyes were steady and unblinking.

"I suppose you better come in," Lenore said, and she picked up the dog. The animal's fur—now dry, and as fluffy as Lenore's own hair—was very soft, and the heft of her small body was, Lenore had to admit, quite comforting. And when she put her head against Lenore's collarbone and looked up at her, some small, unseen gear in Lenore's heart shifted; she suddenly understood the thrall that this creature, irritating as she could be, held over Betsy. It was that quality of surrender, she decided, the trust that the animal so freely bestowed. "Who's a cute little doggy, hmm?" she said in a low, gurgling tone.

"Grandma Lenore!" said Justine. "You sound like Grandma Betsy!"

"Oh—there she is!" Gretchen appeared in the open

doorway. "Here, let me take her," she said, holding out her arms. "She must have slipped away. Mom asked me to find her."

"She seems much calmer," Lenore observed, handing over the dog. Her arms, she realized, felt momentarily bereft without their small burden.

"That's because she's been given a tranquilizer."

"Ah," said Lenore. She looked Gretchen up and down. "You look lovely, dear. That black dress is so becoming on you." She continued her scrutiny, adding, "And it looks like you're wearing the perfect bra! Is it a Lily of France? Or maybe a Maidenform?"

"I don't remember, Grandma. I'm lucky it's clean; that's about all I can aim for these days." She looked beyond Lenore to her daughter, sitting on the bed. "Hi, honey," she said tentatively.

"Don't ask me if I'm coming to the wedding!" Justine said, yanking the pillow back over her face. "Don't ask me anything!"

"I've got things under control up here," Lenore said. "You go on ahead."

Gretchen looked at Justine's pillow-covered face but directed her next words to her grandmother. "The guests are all arriving. I saw several of your friends. Celia. Claire, too. The Blooms just drove up. And the Steins."

"Celia is here? With her son?" Despite the *meshegas* of the day, she had not forgotten about Mitch.

"I guess so. I don't really know. Why?"

"Oh, it's not important now," Lenore said. "Go, give

them each a kiss for me. Tell them I'll be down as soon as I can." She looked at the dog. "Where are you taking her?"

"Back to Mom. At least she's quiet now. She wrecked my sleep this morning." Gretchen waited and then said, "Justine?" When there was no reply, she shook her head sadly. Lenore squeezed her shoulder, gave the dog a final pat on her silky head, and closed the door.

"I really should be getting downstairs," she said to Justine. "All my friends are here." Justine peeked out from behind the pillow. "You can walk me down and then come right back up. Stay here in my room if you like. You'll be very cozy. I have all these magazines—" She fanned out her copies of *Vogue*, *Harper's Bazaar*, and *Elle*. And look at this." She got up and made her way over to the armoire facing the bed. She slid the door open to reveal a television screen. "Voilà! You can watch a movie if you like. They have every channel known to man."

"I despise television," Justine said as she leaned back against the headboard. "Loathe, hate, and despise."

"I guess I don't need to give you the remote, then, do I?" Lenore smiled and then limped back over to the bed.

"No remote," said Justine. "But there is something you can do for me."

"What's that?" Lenore asked.

"Give the ring back to Angelica. And tell her I'm sorry." Justine extended her hand; in the center of her palm the ring continued its indifferent twinkling.

"I think we both know I'm not going to do that," Lenore said. "And we both know why too."

"I figured you'd say that," Justine said. Her fingers closed around the ring again.

"Just promise me this," Lenore said, moving closer so she could smooth the hair back from Justine's forehead. To her relief, the girl accepted her caress without flinching. "Don't run away again, all right? Please? This old ticker of mine can't take the stress. Whatever it is that's got you in its grip, well, we'll find a way to deal with it. We're your family, Justine. Your mixed-up, *meshugenah* family, but we love you, and we want to help you."

Justine jumped up, and Lenore's "ticker" throbbed; oh no, she had said the wrong thing, and the girl *was* going to go running off again. It would be her fault—

"I'll go," Justine said.

"Go?" repeated Lenore. "Where?"

"To the wedding, okay? And I'll even bring the ring with me. If you won't give it to Angelica, I guess I'd better do it."

"Justine!" An effervescent elixir of relief and joy coursed through Lenore's veins. She had done it. Not that she had solved Justine's problems; she knew that was well beyond her scope. Kissing the bridegroom, mean greens—*oy vey!* But at least Lenore had persuaded her to come down and be part of the gathering, to join the celebration. It was a start.

"I'd better change first," Justine was saying. "And I'll even let you do a bra check, Grandma L."

"Good girl!" Lenore beamed, and she linked her arm with Justine's. Justine did not pull away, and Lenore felt herself yielding to the support unwittingly offered by that young, strong limb. It was only when she accepted it that she realized how truly exhausted this day had rendered her. Still, she had made it through and accomplished at least one important task. There were others—Gretchen and Mitch, Caleb—that awaited. Turning her face to the window, she glanced out again.

"I'm so glad the rain finally stopped," she told Justine. Justine did not say anything but stood there alongside her, and together they looked out at the slowly brightening sky.

Twenty-two

❧ • ❧

The musicians were playing Mozart, the waitstaff were circulating Parmesan crisps topped with caramelized pears, and the grounds crew, under orders from Pippa, had done their best to shake the water from the dozens and dozens of fragrant roses that filled the garden. True, the lawn under the swaths of periwinkle carpeting—it really *did* look nice after all—was still spongy from the afternoon's downpour, but the sky had cleared, and the only droplets visible were those that hung suspended and glistening from the leaves of the surrounding trees.

Betsy surveyed the scene and permitted herself a small sigh of almost relief. After the Sturm und Drang of the day, the evening seemed to be unfolding in a particularly idyllic fashion. She mingled easily with the guests, a mosaic of young and old, light and dark, Ashkenazi and Sephardi. Looking at the members of Ohad's large family—three sisters, two brothers-in-law, assorted nieces and nephews as well as his mother, aunts, and uncle—Betsy thought how similar they seemed in appearance and in gestures to so many of the faces here.

"There you are!" said Azar, who was now wearing a crinkled black silk dress; the pointy toes of her black lace shoes peeked out from the floor-length hem. "How are you holding up?"

"Still in one piece," Betsy said. "Though, an hour ago, I wouldn't have said that."

"And your mother?" Looking for Lenore, Azar scanned the crowd. "Is she all right? Any residual issues from the fall?"

"Is she all right?" Betsy said. "Take a look at her; she's amazing!" She pointed to where Lenore stood presiding over a small crowd of her friends. A glass of white wine was in one hand; her gold clutch blazed in the other.

"No crutches," Azar observed.

"They didn't go with her dress," Betsy said and then felt herself whisked around by a first cousin who wanted a hug.

"I'll keep an eye on her," Azar said, moving off.

"Thank you, Azar!" Betsy called out. "I'll look for you later." She hugged her cousin Jimmy—when had she last seen him?—asked after his family, and then continued to circulate.

Betsy was actually able not only to participate in but to savor this long-awaited evening, largely thanks to Pippa's behind-the-scenes efforts to keep everything moving along smoothly. There had even been time for some prewedding family photos after all; Pippa had rounded everyone up and made sure the photographer could do her job quickly.

Pippa. What a total turnaround. Betsy had simply not understood it would take but a few sharp words to snap this woman into line. Her previous efforts to accommodate, placate, negotiate—useless. Instead Pippa reacted like a dog in a pack: once she understood that Betsy was dominant, she retreated into easy—and efficient—compliance.

Over at one corner of the garden, Betsy saw Justine talking to a tall, dark-haired boy. One of Ohad's nephews or cousins; she could not remember which. Her granddaughter looked very animated, gesturing with her hands and talking rapidly. She was drinking something too; what was it? Betsy hoped Pippa had remembered to speak to the bartenders about serving alcohol to the kids, although she did say that everyone could have a glass of champagne after the wedding. Maybe she'd better check with her again just to be sure. But really, on the whole, things were going extremely well.

The only thing that still abraded, still hurt like a stone in her shoe she could neither dislodge nor ignore, was Angelica's earlier comment that she, Betsy, had somehow wanted to sabotage this day. How could her daughter even have entertained such a belief? And as if that wasn't hurtful enough, how could she have said it out loud—such a casual, damning accusation—in front of everyone? Even knowing Angelica as Betsy did, this was a painful surprise and one from which she was still smarting.

There had been no chance to speak to Angelica; clad in the stunning dress that Betsy had not, up until that moment, been allowed to see, Angelica had disappeared upstairs again. Her door stayed closed when Betsy had knocked; she'd said only, "I'll be out soon, Mom." Betsy had stared at the impervious paneled wood surface and brass knob for several seconds before heading back downstairs. It was showtime, and no matter what, the show had to go on.

Back in the rose garden, the Parmesan crisps had been supplanted by thin slices of salmon tartare topped with pinprick-sized dots of wasabi; Betsy saw the trays being held aloft by the waiters in their black cutaway jackets. People looked happy and relaxed; there was no particular urgency about starting the ceremony.

Nevertheless she wandered over to the tent where the ceremony was to be held. There was the *chuppah*, just waiting for the bride and groom to sanctify it. Ohad was the one who had suggested it, and looking at the simple, open-sided structure, whose poles and top were entirely covered in white flowers and tendrils of variegated ivy, Betsy was so very glad that he had. Her family had never been religious, and she knew they were not about to start now. Still, there were moments in a life—birth, marriage, death—when ritual suddenly mattered; ritual was the patient, waiting vessel for all that feeling, all that love.

Love, yes. How much she loved Angelica, her beautiful baby, her winning and accomplished child. Loved her despite her bursts of offhand cruelty, her occasional disdain, her supreme aplomb, which had, even when Angelica was a child, made Betsy feel superfluous. She'd always known herself to be vital to the well-being of her other children, but with Angelica she often felt that she was simply being tolerated.

Of course Angelica had had that special bond with her father; it had been true from the start. Lincoln, who had always resisted the messy, tedious aspects of child care, had given himself over completely to Angelica: cheerfully bathing, burping, and changing her, patiently spooning the oatmeal into her rosebud of a mouth, and not complaining when she dipped her tiny fingers into the bowl and smeared his face with the gooey paste.

As if summoned by her internal meandering back into their shared past, Lincoln appeared in her line of vision; he was carrying a plate in one hand, a glass in the other. Instinctively she found herself hoping that it was soda, not liquor, in the glass. But then she halted that train of thought dead in its tracks. It was no longer her business what Lincoln did or did not drink. It had stopped being her business a long time ago.

"Betsy," he said when he'd reached her. "Betsy, we did it."

"Not yet," she said, looking meaningfully at the *chuppah*. "They're still not officially married; let's not jinx it!"

"Yeah, I guess I am kind of a jinx," Lincoln said somewhat ruefully. He was poking his tongue around in the back of his mouth between his words; why was he doing that? It was annoying and unattractive.

"No!" she said earnestly. "Don't say that. Not today of all days. I told you before: you were the hero. Are the hero."

"Better a hero than a jinx," he said. He'd stopped the

poking, much to Betsy's relief, only to start it up again seconds later. "Delicious salmon," he said, inclining his chin toward his plate. "I don't want to get too full though; I know
you've got quite a spread after the ceremony."

"There will be a lot of food," she said neutrally. She
leaned in—not too obviously, she hoped—to see whether she
could catch a whiff of his drink. A familiar sweetness rose to
her nostrils. Coca-Cola. Unless he'd laced it with something,
it was perfectly benign. *But why should you care?* she scolded
herself. And then she realized: of course she cared. She
would always care. Lincoln was a part of her and she of him.
It was as simple as that. "I'm glad you're here," she said.

"You are?" He sounded surprised.

She nodded. "You're her father. The one she loves
best."

"Everyone keeps saying that," Lincoln said, looking
uncomfortable.

"Because it's true," Betsy said. There he was—doing
that thing with his tongue again. "Lincoln, what is going on
inside your mouth? Do you have some food stuck in there or
something? Because I can get you a toothpick if you need one."

"Cracked a molar this morning," he said, raising a
hand to his jaw as if to shield it. "Hurts like a son of a bitch."

"Your poor thing!" she said. "Why didn't you say something sooner?"

"I didn't want to bother you," he said. "There was
enough going on here today already. . . ."

"Have you been taking anything for it?" She was genuinely concerned.

"Just some over-the-counter stuff that I had with me. And that I'm all out of now anyway."

"Well, I've got something that will tide you over until you see a dentist," she said. "You are going to see a dentist, right? You do have insurance and all that."

"Yes, Betsy, I have insurance *and all that*."

"Good." But Betsy did not believe him and was already thinking about making him an appointment with her own dentist—and picking up the tab—before he left. "Now wait here and I'll be right back." Betsy hurried into the house and sped up the stairs to her bathroom, where that bottle of pain-killers was, and back down again. On the way she checked on the dog—asleep on Betsy's bed, thanks to the tranquilizer—and the kitchen, where everything seemed to be under control. She was just about to head through the French doors and back out to where she'd left Lincoln when she ran into Angelica.

She slowed, not sure of what if anything to say. She did not want to start another argument. But it was going to be hard for her to take the kind of pleasure in this day that she had dreamed of and felt entitled to without saying something.

"The dress . . ." Betsy began. "Your dress. It's so beautiful."

Angelica looked down at the heavy folds of satin as if they were new to her as well. "Thank you," she said. A beat. And then, "Mom, I'm sorry about what I said before. I was just so upset, I lashed out."

Ordinarily Betsy would have said, *I know, I understand, of course you're tense; it's your wedding day*. But although she was grateful for the apology—it meant she would not have to go through this day with a heart like a lead weight—she didn't want to let her daughter off quite so easily, not this time.

"You hurt me," she said simply. "You hurt me, and I didn't deserve it."

"Mom!" Angelica's hands, pale and graceful as a pair of doves, flew to her lips. "You know I didn't mean it!"

"If you didn't mean it, you shouldn't have said it, darling," Betsy replied gently.

"I'm so, so sorry," Angelica said. "Say you me forgive, please!"

"Of course I forgive you," Betsy said. "I'll always forgive you. I'm your mother. But I'm not your doormat, okay? And, Angelica—" She stepped closer and enfolded her daughter in a hug so that her next words would be delivered with the love she intended. "Neither is your husband. I want you to remember that."

Angelica said nothing, only returned the embrace and then let go. Betsy stood watching her, the train of the white dress shimmering as she moved. Then Betsy looked down at the bottle of pills still in her hand. Lincoln. She hurried out. He was there where she had left him; he had not budged.

"Take these right now," she said, shaking two of the capsules into his hand.

"You think this is okay?" he asked, staring at them.

"Why not? Your tooth has been killing you all day, hasn't it?" She looked at him, puzzled. "Oh—you mean because of AA?"

He nodded. "Maybe I shouldn't take anything that strong."

"Even if you're in excruciating pain? Lincoln, I of all people know how much you struggled to give up drinking. And I admire you for your scrupulousness. But, honey—" She stepped close, reached up, and laid a hand on his face. "Honey, suffering is suffering. And it's okay to make it stop."

"I guess you're right," he said.

Honey. Without thinking she had called him *honey.* And she meant it too. Despite everything, she still had some feeling for him. Not that she intended—or even wanted—to do anything about it. But it was comforting—to her and she imagined to him too—to know that it was there. Betsy watched as Lincoln downed the pills with a swig of Coke and looked for a place to set down the now-empty glass. A waiter glided by with a gracious, "I'll take that, sir," and then there was Don, touching Betsy lightly on the elbow.

"Shall we?" he said with a glance that included Lincoln too. "They're just about ready to start."

Twenty-three

L incoln was quietly frantic. Angelica was supposed to meet him right here by the entrance to the tent. In a matter of minutes he was going to be walking her down the white-carpeted aisle, and even though he had not been able to make the rehearsal last night, he knew exactly where he was to be and what he needed to do. So where was she? His eyes anxiously scanned the assembled group as he searched for her, but she was nowhere in sight.

He stepped back and looked up. The tent was an elaborate structure with its own shiny, wood-like flooring and arched windows. Although it was enclosed, it felt permeable because it allowed the rain-rinsed air to circulate freely. Lincoln had never seen such a thing before and could only imagine what it must have cost. The deluxe white folding chairs (padded, faux silver trim) had been set up in neat rows. Garlands of white flowers were looped through the backs of those chairs, and the poles supporting the lofting canopy were also covered in flowers, all of them heavy with scent and white, white, white. The guests in their expensive

clothes and more expensive jewels were all seated and mur-
muring with subdued but evident anticipation.

The other tent, where the dinner would be held, was
even more ornate, with chandeliers and a polished dance
floor. Lincoln knew that Don had ponied up most of the
money; Angelica and Ohad had contributed the rest. Lincoln had given not a single penny, and his offer of a five-
hundred-dollar savings bond as a wedding gift had been
gently but firmly refused. "I'm not taking your money,
Daddy," Angelica had said. "I don't need it; you do." Lincoln
burned at the memory. She was right, of course. But her refusal left him feeling insufficient and ashamed. Wasn't the
father of the bride supposed to pay for the wedding? And yet
despite all his failings, financial and otherwise, she had put
his name on the invitation and asked him to give her away.
He preened inwardly at the honor. Only, where the hell
was she?

Lincoln paced in the small space allotted to him, ner-
vously smoothing back his hair and readjusting his tie. At
least he looked good; he had to thank Don for that. The
other members of the processional were all here: Ohad's
mother and his uncle, who would escort her down the aisle
since his father had been killed years earlier while fighting
in the never-ending conflict in Israel. Don, with his arm
locked around Betsy's waist. The twins; his own sons; a bevy
of bridesmaids in simple but lovely pale gray dresses; their
escorts, many of whom were Israeli; the flower girl, basket
brimming with petals as she hopped from one foot to the
other in her excitement. But still no Angelica.

Lincoln leaned over to ask Betsy just where the hell she could be, but right then the first strains of Pachelbel's Canon—predictable but still so right for the occasion—began, and there was no chance to say anything. The bridesmaids were taking their turns walking down the aisle, and then the twins. When they had all reached the *chuppah*, Ohad's mother—deeply tanned and even more deeply wrinkled—moved to join them with her brother by her side. She seemed so solemn with her small white bouquet; she did not look right or left but kept her gaze straight ahead as she walked. As soon she got there and turned around, Betsy and Don began their walk; they were followed by the flower girl, who was all by herself.

The child—the granddaughter of one of Betsy's first cousins—took her job very seriously and was intent on covering every inch of the white path with her petals. No one else seemed to mind, though Lincoln wished she would hurry up. About three-quarters of the way down, she realized her basket was empty. She froze, eyes darting anxiously around. Betsy smiled, gesturing for her to keep on walking. Still she did not move. The musicians grew silent; the girl looked ready to cry. But then Ohad appeared, his shining black shoes covering the petal-strewn path in just a few long strides. He reached the panicked flower girl and, taking her hand in his, walked toward the *chuppah*.

Good, at least *that* was over. The musicians began to play again, and then finally, *finally* there was Angelica arriving in a golf cart! A flower-decked golf cart, no less! Now, who would have thought of *that*? But Lincoln had to concede that it was actually a very clever idea: it protected her long white dress from grass stains and allowed her to make quite an entrance.

As she stepped out and came toward him, he wanted to ask her where the hell she had been, but was stopped— stunned really—by her appearance. What was she wearing over her face? Jesus, it was her *veil*. Her entire head was obscured by the elaborate cloud of white netting, rendering her mysterious, even alien. Hardly the baby with whom he'd been instantly smitten or the girl who'd continued to en- chant him. No, the veil created a vexing distance between her and everyone else; she was like an apparition, hovering just slightly apart and out of reach.

The golf cart pulled away, and for a few seconds Lin- coln felt intoxicated—though he'd had nothing alcoholic to drink—by his daughter's unfamiliar aspect. Angelica. His angel. Then he got hold of himself. Goddamn, but he had a job to do, and he was going to do it. "Ready?" he whispered, and when the white nimbus that was her head inclined slightly, he took her hand, and they began to walk.

Lincoln felt the stares of the assembled guests like so many glowing stars, so many bursts of heat. Not for him, of course—this was not about him. He was the conduit, no more. As they walked, he saw people from his old life with Betsy—the odious Kleiers (God, but the wife was a bitch!), the Sugarmans, the Driscolls. Phil Driscoll gave him a pleas- ant nod, as did Ned Sugarman. Ned Sugarman was not a bad guy. And Phil—he'd always liked Phil. He'd make a point of talking to him later. Then Lincoln spied Ennis sitting there with his head down. He did not look happy.

Lincoln's ruined tooth began to throb again even through the cocooning haze of Betsy's painkiller. Yet it was a subtle and almost welcome feeling, one that kept him teth-ered to this earth, this life. Slowly and proudly he led his daughter toward the flower-covered *chuppah* that awaited her, and when they arrived, he stepped gallantly aside.

Betsy briefly pressed both her palms together when Angelica reached the *chuppah*. Although she looked as though she was praying, she was in fact merely dispelling the tension she had felt during the flower girl's mini-meltdown. But all was well now. Lincoln had conducted himself with dignity and poise, and Angelica—enveloped by the white veil—had seemed to float rather than walk down the aisle.

The veil was a surprise, at once radical and retrograde. Angelica had mentioned that she planned to wear it in her hair, not that she was going to cover her entire face and head with it. Well, that was certainly in keeping with her daugh-ter's character. She had rarely turned to Betsy for advice, and even more rare were the times Angelica confided in her. That had never been her way, and yet Betsy mourned it afresh, as if it were a newly realized insight. Would married life change Angelica at all? Betsy doubted it. But maybe, just maybe, if and when Angelica had a baby, she would need Betsy in a way she had not needed her before. You needed your mother when you had a baby, Betsy thought, remembering her own early days of motherhood. And you appreciated her too.

The music had stopped, and the rabbi stood looking out at the expectant crowd. Betsy watched as he brought his hands together—this time the gesture really did suggest prayer—and began to speak. "What a joyful day," he began, "a happy day in the lives of this couple and all those who love them. . . ." She stopped listening. She was instead overcome by just how much she wanted her previously unarticulated wish to come true, the desire seizing her in a way that felt urgent, even physical. The tears—for the *third* time today—that rose in her eyes were the manifest proof of her desire, her hope that one day her beautiful, distant daughter would come back to her, would come home at last.

The rabbi—Where had he come from? Gretchen had missed his entrance somehow—stepped forward. He was dark skinned, dark eyed, and possessed of a serious unibrow; he looked like another member of Ohad's large family—clustered on one side of the aisle and many wearing yarmulkes on their blue-black hair—though Gretchen doubted this was the case.

It felt odd to be sitting here watching when her daughters, brothers, and parents were all up there by the *chuppah*. But Gretchen had declined her sister's offer to be her matron of honor; given the wreckage of her own marriage, she had been in no state to be a member of a wedding party when the invitation had been issued. Angelica said she understood, and asked one of her med-school friends, a haughty auburn-haired woman named Drew, instead. Gretchen had disliked her instantly and was sure the feeling was mutual. There was Drew now, elegant in her pearl-gray dress, carefully cradling Angelica's bouquet. Looking at her Gretchen felt shamed. She, not Drew, should have been up there today; maybe she *had* been self-centered and churlish in her refusal.

"Beloved family and friends, tonight we are here to celebrate the union of two very special people, Angelica Silverstein and Ohad Oz." He paused briefly to smile at the couple, but Ohad and Angelica were looking only at each other. "Marriage is a holy state," he began again. "A joyful, much wished-for, fervently sought-after, and deeply desired state. And it brings us all"—he spread his hands out to the expectant group of guests—"great happiness to watch Ohad and Angelica enter into it." He talked for a few minutes about marriage, what it was and wasn't, how it could grow stronger or weaker depending on the commitment of those involved.

Gretchen, aware of Ennis in the row behind her, could not help but feel that these remarks were addressed to her in particular. How committed had she been to her own marriage? Had she taken Ennis for granted, left herself slip away from him, if not physically, then emotionally? She shifted uncomfortably in her seat as if her thoughts had been made tangible, like something sharp poking her from behind. Ever since that awful day when Eve had shown up at their house, Gretchen had nurtured, even cherished the role of victim, the one who had been wounded, wronged, and betrayed. But what if she had ignored her own role in the sequence of events? What if she had pushed Ennis out and right into the arms of someone else, someone who would give him the warmth and tenderness that she lacked? Their conversation earlier today had raised some doubts; this ceremony was raising yet more.

She did not like thinking this way and tried instead to focus on her sister, wrapped in white and standing straight and slim as one of the lilies in the numerous floral arrangements. But even this image would not stay fixed in her mind. She saw instead Angelica as a baby, waving her little fists in the air when Gretchen came into the room, reaching eagerly with both arms for Gretchen to pick her up. It was a sweet memory; she had loved her baby sister, doll-like and dimple kneed, and had loved the way her infant helplessness had recast her own position in the family. Unlike Teddy and Caleb, who were both closer to her in age, Angelica was almost ten years younger, and her birth had allowed Gretchen to assume a new, quasi-adult status among the Silversteins. How important that had made her feel. How proud.

The rabbi was quiet now and looked expectantly at Angelica and Ohad. Gretchen looked at them too. What would their married life be like? Filled with delight or disappointment or more likely an ever-changing mixture of both? Again she felt the presence of Ennis behind her. Was he aware of her? Thinking of her? She was tempted to turn around, but, no, she would not give him the satisfaction.

Justine stood very still in her place amid the wedding party. Her calf itched, but she did not move to scratch it; she was almost afraid to move, afraid to jar the fragile equilibrium that allowed her to be here at all, so close to Ohad that she could once again smell him. Nestled in the bodice of her dress, just above the bra that Grandma L. had approved, was a small cloth bag—Grandma L. had provided that too—containing Angelica's diamond ring, the ring that Justine now needed to give back as badly as she had earlier needed to steal it.

She was grateful her sister was beside her now, and even more grateful that she did not have to say anything to her. Portia had cornered her before the wedding demanding to know where she had been, but Justine had been able to put her off—at least temporarily. She looked around. There were a lot of people here she didn't know—friends of Angelica's, she supposed. The bridesmaids were strangers to her. The matron of honor too; Justine thought she looked bratty. What had her mother been saying before about Angelica and her former best friend? She hadn't supplied too many details, but it sounded as though Angelica had betrayed her somehow. Justine was still struggling to realign her previous perception of her aunt with this new information.

And what about Ohad? Was he really a murderer? It was hard to believe, seeing how sweet he'd been with that little flower girl. Grandma L. had said she didn't know what he had done as a soldier and a pilot; she had not been there. And she had to admit that Grandma L. just might have had a point when she said Ohad was complex. Then again, wasn't everyone complex if you got right down to it? Even the most boring, vapid person on the face of the earth? Too bad. It was so much easier to think someone you didn't like was a dickwad; it was much harder to acknowledge that they too had some kind of inner life, one you would never have a clue about.

As Justine watched, Ohad leaned over to lift Angelica's veil from her face in a gesture so intimate and tender that Justine almost could not bear to witness it. She was hideously aware of the engagement ring pressing against her chest. God, she wished she could get rid of it now. She tried to banish the panic that was hovering over her like a pair of black wings spread and beating near—much too near—her face.

She was saved by Ohad, who had started to speak in Hebrew, the unfamiliar, jagged cadences yanking her out of whatever it was that had threatened to engulf her. She listened, rapt, and then he translated. *Thy lips, O my bride, drop honey—honey and milk are under thy tongue; and the smell of thy garments is like the smell of Lebanon.* That was from the *Song of Songs*; Justine had read the whole thing in her English lit class in a recent segment on love poetry. And she had liked it too, even if she thought it was a bit over-the-top. But, then, it was okay if love poetry was over-the-top: passionate, extravagant, and emotional. She had said as much in the class discussion, and her teacher, Ms. Drezner, had started nodding excitedly, yes, yes, the way she did when some student— often Justine—made exactly the point she was hoping to get across.

Then it was Angelica's turn, and she too began reciting

in Hebrew. How had she found the time to learn those words and to practice them until they sounded so familiar, so effortless? Angelica was and would always be amazing. She spoke again, this time in English. *I am a rose of Sharon, a lily of the valleys*. There was a little more talk from the rabbi and then the actual vows, do *you* take, do you *take*, hands extended, gold bands offered, exchanged and slipped on.

Then the rabbi raised his arm to show everyone the wineglass covered by a white napkin. Except that Portia had told her it was really a lightbulb, because it made a more satisfying sound. When he seemed satisfied that everyone had seen it, he placed it down on the grass and together, as if synchronized, Angelica and Ohad each lifted up a foot—his in black leather, hers in ivory silk—and crunched down on it hard. There was a muffled shatter and then a long kiss.

Justine was mesmerized as the bride and groom clung to each other, faces and bodies pressed in a seamless embrace. How perfectly they seemed to fit together; yet Justine had the sense that they could just as easily have let go—their being together was a choice, not an obligation or a need. When the kiss finally ended, the guests erupted into cheers.

Around her, people were crying: Ohad's mother, Grandma Betsy, Don, and Justine's grandpa. Grandma Lenore was mopping her face with a handkerchief; she blew her nose loudly, and everyone started to laugh. Justine did not cry but experienced a sort of tremulous relief that Grandma L. had talked her into coming. Oh, Justine saw through her: pretending not to care was a much craftier— and effective—ploy than outright pressure. And it had worked; she was here, just where her great-grandmother had wanted her to be all along.

But Justine forgave the manipulation, because everything she had imagined about this day had been revised and rewritten as she had lived it. The wedding wasn't tasteless, vulgar, or corny. It was gorgeous, it was sacred, and she felt grateful to have been a part of it. But even more than that, she was overcome with remorse—those horrible black wings again, beating furiously—to think that she had almost ruined the day and prevented the wedding from happening. This was the feeling she often had when she had stolen something, only this was worse, much worse. She pressed her face into her hands, and it was then that the tears—galling and hot—came. Portia turned to look at her. "Are you all right, Teeny?" she whispered.

"No," Justine said, unable to lift her face from the protection of her own palms, "I'm not."

Lenore, still standing near the *chuppah*, beamed as the bride and groom, smiling, laughing, and reaching out to touch the hands of their guests, walked back up the aisle. They came slowly as Angelica paused to look around at all the people who had assembled. Lenore saw her nod and smile, smile and nod. Every now and then she blew a small kiss to someone as she sailed serenely by.

A small sniff from somewhere nearby diverted Lenore's attention. She turned. Justine crying—again? Upstairs in Lenore's room, the girl had seemed all right, agreeing to attend the wedding without any real pressure; the hysterics and drama had mercifully passed. And she'd seemed fine in the rose garden too; Lenore had been watching. What could have set her off again?

But as Lenore continued to observe, Justine rallied, drying her eyes with her fingers—at least it wasn't the hem of her dress!—and scurrying around the back of the *chuppah*, along the outside of the tent, and up to the head of the aisle. She met Angelica midway down. Many people had already gotten up and, chattering and happy, were milling around near their seats. People were talking, smiling, laughing. No one except Lenore paid attention when Justine reached inside her dress and then pressed something into Angelica's palm. The ring. Although Lenore could not actually see it changing hands, she felt a palpable sense of relief that it had now been restored to its rightful owner. And because Angelica's back was to her, she could only imagine the fleeting trajectory of emotions crossing her lovely face: surprise, confusion, joy, all giving way to something sterner, something that seemed to expect—no, demand—an explanation. For several seconds Justine simply stared at her aunt before she stepped aside and let her resume her progress.

Lenore now saw that the little flower girl—Zoe was her name, and Lenore was delighted she had recalled it—was walking alongside the bridal couple. She skipped and pranced as she went, waving her empty basket gaily with one hand. With the other she held tightly to Ohad's broad palm.

Twenty-four

❦ • ❦

O n her way to the outlandish, fairy-tale tent where dinner was to be served, Gretchen ran smack into Ennis
and Portia. Portia, who had been holding her father's arm,
disengaged herself to lean her cropped head on Gretchen's
shoulder; for a few blessed seconds Gretchen savored the
weight and feel of her until Portia righted herself and trot-
ted off. Gretchen was then left standing with Ennis on the
wide swath of carpet that had been laid between the two
tents to keep the guests' heels from sinking into the wet
grass.

"That was a lovely ceremony," she said, just to say
something that did not have anything to do with them, their
present impasse, or just what they planned to do about it.

"Lovely, hey," Ennis agreed. He began pulling on his
tie, a gesture at once so obvious and revealing that Gretchen
wanted to laugh. She actually felt pretty good—no, make
that *very* good. Better than she had felt since before she'd
arrived here. Throughout the ceremony, she had sat, surrounded by her family, listening to that gorgeous poetry—it

had been quite something to hear it in Hebrew, even if she couldn't understand it—while inside she was poised for takeoff.

Flashing a quick, impersonal smile at Ennis, Gretchen continued walking until she reached the tent where the tables with their white cloths and large centerpieces of white flowers had been set up. The sky had darkened and was now a deep, lapis-like blue.

But all the clouds were gone, and Gretchen could see the first stars begin to shine, weakly at first, in the lovely early June evening.

"What's your rush?" Ennis said as he hurried to catch up and fall into step beside her.

"No rush," she said. "I just wanted to get a drink."

"Can I join you?"

"Suit yourself." She edged closer to the bar and was aware that Ennis remained where he stood. So she had been a bit harsh. But, really, what did he expect, foisting himself on her? Gretchen turned her back on him.

The next few months, she knew, were not going to be easy. Justine was going to need professional help. But having it all out in the open—well, that alone was a monumental relief. Gretchen deeply believed in her own ability to get Justine what she needed; she would not fail her. And simply having said those words earlier—to her sister, her family— made everything seem to shift and realign in Gretchen's vision. How had she not seen it before? All that time, years and years really, of thinking of herself as the freighted, judgmental *less than* instead of the neutral, embracing *different from*.

But no more. Things were going to change. In fact, in her mind they already had. She had decided that next week she was going to quit her job. That book with Ginny would never, ever be written, at least not by her. She had some money saved, and, yes, she could ask her mother for help. Her next job was going to be something that engaged all of her. Next she planned to call her old college friend Wendy Jones, who was pretty high up in the psych unit at Columbia-Presbyterian; Wendy would be able to provide her with some names of therapists for Justine. And Gretchen was going to stop obsessing about her weight. It was such a bore to think about it all the time; she had better things to do.

There were dozens of people milling around the bar; Gretchen was relieved that her father was not one of them. And she could see the receiving line snaking around the rose hedge. She did want to congratulate her sister, but she decided to wait and do it in a more private way. A waiter materialized carrying several glasses of champagne clustered congenially on silver trays. No need to stand at the bar waiting after all.

"Thank you," said Gretchen, helping herself to a glass. Lifting it to her lips, she took a big sip. And smiled. God, but that was good. And she felt the first stirring of a buzz already. By the time she had finished the champagne, the buzz had settled pleasantly around her, emitting tiny pops and fizzes of sensation.

Weaving only the slightest bit, Gretchen found her way to her table, where glass water pitchers and crystal goblets sparkled against all that white; each white bone china place setting was adorned with a place card of heavy white vellum surrounded by a few smooth, white oval stones. The flowers— white roses, freesia, lilies, and a few gardenias—spilled up and over the clear glass vase.

She saw no sign of Ennis (good) or her girls (not so good). There was, she knew, a teen table; a couple of Ohad's relatives would be sitting at it along with Justine and Portia. Maybe Ennis was with them. Gretchen downed the rest of her champagne and was inspecting the inside of the empty glass when another waiter appeared to take it away and replace it with a fresh one. She took a big sip from glass number two and sat down with a little thud. She'd nearly missed the chair.

"Need some help?"

Gretchen looked up to see a man hovering above her. He had nice blue eyes and a neatly trimmed beard. His graying brown hair was pulled back in a short ponytail.

"I'm okay," she said.

"You looked a little wobbly for a minute there. I thought you were going to topple."

"I really can't hold my liquor," she said, gesturing to the champagne.

"Well, I'll be here if you need me," said the man, sitting down. "I'm Mitch; this is my table." He extended his hand.

"Hello, Mitch-this-is-my-table. I'm Gretchen-pleased-to-meet-you."

"The bride's sister?" he asked.

"How did you know? Striking family resemblance?" Her fingers toyed with the stem of her glass.

He considered her for a moment. "Uh-huh. Definitely

some. But my mother, Celia, is a good friend of Lenore's. She's been a widow for decades, so I'm her escort. And she gave me the lowdown on the guests before I arrived. Many times, in fact."

"That explains it. My grandmother probably drew up a detailed family tree and circulated it among the guests. She thinks weddings are the perfect places to make matches."

"My mother too," said Mitch. He reached for an olive that sat in a small crystal bowl on the table.

"What is it about that generation?" Gretchen asked, helping herself to an olive too. The saltiness cried out for another sip of champagne. "They can't help themselves. But I hope I'll be more circumspect when it comes to my own daughters. Stay out of their love lives, you know?"

"How many and how old?" When Gretchen looked puzzled, he added, "Your daughters."

"Right!" she said. That champagne really was making her a bit fuzzy. "Two, and fifteen. They're twins."

"Nice," he said. "I've got one. Daughter, that is."

"How old?" She tried not to guzzle the champagne.

"Fourteen. I don't get to see her much though. She's in Chicago."

"Chicago," Gretchen said reflectively. A fourteen-year-old daughter living in another state probably meant he was divorced. She sat up straighter and brushed her hair off of her face. "I've never been there," she added.

"Me neither," Mitch said.

"Not even to see your daughter?"

"She comes to New York to see me. She says she prefers it that way."

Gretchen busied herself with another olive.

"What about your daughters?

"They live with me," she said. "But their father lives somewhere else."

"Divorced?" asked Mitch.

"Separated," she corrected.

"Ah," was all he said. But it was a knowing, even comforting *ah*. Gretchen decided she liked him.

The table began filling up. Teddy sat across from her, with Martine at his left; Caleb was seated on the other side of Mitch. Some cousins Gretchen had not seen in ages took the remaining chairs. She made the necessary introductions and then the waiter came by to ask whether they wanted filet mignon, poached monkfish, or pasta; orders were taken, and soon the food began to appear.

Gretchen ate hungrily and with pleasure; she'd ordered the fish, which came with roasted beets and quinoa. But she didn't hate herself for her appetite; she just surrendered to it, and as a result, she ate less than when she was constantly battling it. She had bread, but only one piece, and when the dessert came—lime mousse, butter cookies in the shape of wedding bells, petit fours iced in silver and white—she had just a taste of mousse before putting the spoon down. She did allow herself another glass of champagne, though she decided that would be her last drink of the evening.

Mitch was asking her about living in Brooklyn—he

lived in Chelsea—when she felt bold enough to inquire, "So what went wrong in your marriage?"

"There was another man," he said, not appearing to be offended by her question.

"Your ex-wife had a boyfriend?"

He shook his head. "I'm afraid the one with the *boyfriend* was me."

Gretchen didn't get it for a second. And then she did. "So you're . . ."

"Gay, yes."

What, you too? Gretchen wanted to say, thinking of the sexy guy she'd met earlier while swimming, the one she and Caleb had caught kissing Bobby. What were the odds that two attractive men, both encountered on the same day, would turn out to be gay? But all she said was, "Your ex must have been surprised." She felt a slight seep of disappointment spreading like a stain.

"Not really," he said. "I'd felt that way for a long time, and she knew it."

"Then why . . . ?"

"We were best friends. I wanted to be married, have kids. She said she accepted me, but really she believed she could change me."

"She couldn't, though," Gretchen finished.

"No, she couldn't," said Mitch.

"Couldn't what?" asked Caleb.

Mitch turned to look at her brother, and in that quick glance Gretchen felt the current pass between them: a mutual acknowledgment, a kind of recognition.

"I was telling your sister about my ex-wife," Mitch said.

"You can tell me too," Caleb said, leaning in closer. "I'm all ears."

"Would you excuse me?" Gretchen said to Mitch. But Mitch was so absorbed in something Caleb had said that he failed to hear. Gretchen pushed back her chair and steadied herself against the table. She was not drunk, but when she'd finished the champagne, she had ignored her own decision to stop drinking and had moved on to white wine, so she felt a bit woozy as she made her way over to the teen table. Justine and Portia were both there; Justine was talking to one of Ohad's many relatives. Satisfied that the girls were all right, she went off looking for Lincoln. She found him seated at the bride's table, along with her mother, Don, Lenore, and some more of Ohad's relatives. And it looked, amazingly, like everyone was getting along.

"Gretchen!" Lincoln called out, extending his hand. Gretchen moved closer and took it. "You look terrific."

"Thanks, Dad," she said. "So do you." She was puzzled but pleased by his effusive greeting. She could not help but glance at his glass. It looked like it held Coke, but you never knew.

"I decided to stay an extra couple of days," Lincoln was saying. "Your mother says she can get me an appointment with her dentist on Monday, and I was able to change my ticket with no charge. So I thought we could get together, just the two of us. Lunch, dinner—whatever works for you."

"Okay," Gretchen said, surprised. "We can talk about it in the morning."

"Honey, Angelica's about to cut the cake," Betsy said. "Do you want to have a seat?"

Gretchen was just about to slip into an empty seat when a flock of the Israelis—she had trouble distinguishing them, and they really did look like a flock of dark, sleek birds—converged upon the band for what appeared to be a very urgent conversation. After a minute the band started playing "Hava Nagila," and in the space that had been cleared for the wedding cake, the Israelis joined hands and began to do the hora.

This had *not* been part of the plan; Gretchen was sure of it. She looked over at her mother; clearly Betsy was as surprised as she was. The cake on its chrome-and-glass trolley waited in the wings while the dance quickly took on a life of its own, with guests rising from their seats, as if they'd been summoned, to join in. Tables and chairs were pushed back; the music got louder.

Gretchen did not join the dance; instead she sidled over to where her mother stood, and the two of them watched together. Lincoln and Don were dancing side by side; who would have expected that? Caleb and Teddy had joined in and lovely Marti looked as if someone had uncorked her. Angelica was dancing too, her dark hair flipping back and forth, when two of the men dancing on either side suddenly lifted her in a movement so fluid and graceful that it seemed choreographed. They steered her toward an empty chair, and after she'd sat down, they raised the chair high in the air; others quickly stepped in to help them. Everyone cheered and clapped as she was paraded around the floor. Looking game, if mildly alarmed, Angelica clutched the bottom of the chair so she wouldn't fall off.

"This wasn't planned, was it?" Gretchen asked Betsy.

"Are you kidding?" Betsy said. "The hora is hardly Angelica's idea of a good time."

"She looks like she's having fun," Gretchen observed.

"She's adaptive," Betsy said. "She may be controlling, but she can roll with the punches when she has to."

May be controlling? Who was her mother kidding? But Gretchen did not say anything. When the chair was finally set down again, Angelica was out of breath and smiling. Then it was Ohad's turn in the chair, and finally Lenore was the one lifted up, up, and up. She seemed thoroughly delighted as she waved to the cheering crowd.

It took several minutes for everyone to settle down and for the tables and chairs to be restored to their previous positions. Angelica, still flushed, started moving toward the large, pale, five-tiered cake—covered in buttercream frosting and dotted with candied violet petals—that was being wheeled in. Ohad was right behind her.

But then she paused and put her hand on Gretchen's shoulder as she passed. "I think we should talk," she said. "It won't be until after the honeymoon though. I hope that's all right with you." Angelica asking Gretchen if something were all right with her? Asking, not telling, demanding, ordering? Was anyone else registering or even listening to this? She ardently hoped so.

"It's fine," she said. "Just fine."

Angelica kept moving until she reached the cake. She

posed with the knife; Ohad was at her side. Gretchen was making her way back to her own table; she heard the collective sigh when Angelica cut the first piece.

"There you are!"

Gretchen turned. Ennis was standing in front of her, blocking her path.

"Were you looking for me?" she asked.

"I was. You ran away from me before." He moved a step closer.

"I didn't." She stepped back.

"You did!" He looked at her and laughed. "We sound like Portia and Justine, hey? About ten years ago?"

"I guess we do."

"I'm glad she came to the wedding after all. What did you say that got her to change her mind?" Ennis said. He was inching toward her again.

"It wasn't me; it was my grandmother."

"Ah," said Ennis. "Lovely Lenore."

Waiters began circulating with trays of sliced wedding cake; Ennis nabbed a plate and offered it to Gretchen. She hesitated and then asked, "Do you want to share?"

"With you?" He moved still closer, and this time Gretchen did not move away. Instead she offered him a forkful of the cake. "Did we do this on our wedding day?" he asked.

"Don't you remember?" Gretchen instantly felt huffy.

"Of course," he said. "I just wanted to see if you did." He accepted the morsel of cake.

"You know I did," she said in a low but intense voice.

She was slightly drunk, no doubt about *that,* and her earlier good mood was quickly evaporating. An eddy of self-pity lapped at her: their failed marriage, their troubled daughter, the prospect of having to look for a job—again. She willed it not to happen, but she couldn't help it: she started to cry.

"Gretchen," Ennis said, and he tentatively put his hand to the tangle of her hair. "Ah, Gretchen, don't." She had stepped back as if scalded. She didn't want him touching her; it brought back too much. And she didn't want to make a spectacle of herself either. Gretchen looked down at the plate with its barely nibbled slice of cake. "Here," she said, thrusting it into his hands. "You eat it." And she turned and headed swiftly for the house.

"Where are you going?" he called after her. He set the plate down and followed her into the foyer, across the marble floor, up the staircase, down the hall until she reached the door to her room. She was crying harder now, and when she turned to tell him to please, *please* go away, nothing came out but a small hiccup.

"Gretchen, you're getting yourself all upset," he said. He didn't touch her, though she could tell he wanted to.

"No, you're getting me all upset!" she said. "You— showing up here uninvited—"

"Your sister invited me, hey?"

"You shouldn't have come, Ennis," she said, pressing her back to the door. "You have no business being here with my family."

"I *am* your family, remember? I'm the father of your children, and I'm still your husband. We're not divorced yet."

"Too bad you didn't remember that when you were screwing Eve!"

"But that's over, it's done, it's not going to happen again! How many times do I have to tell you? That baby was *not* mine."

"Is that all this is about to you? The baby?"

"Well, it certainly seemed like a big deal. At least to me," said Ennis.

"And to me too!" she shot back. "Believe me, I am so relieved it wasn't yours after all."

"Why?" he said, stepping closer. "Because it means that now we have a clean slate and can start again?"

"Only in your delusional mind, Ennis!" Gretchen said. "I told you: I'm so relieved that the girls aren't going to have to deal with a new baby brother. But it doesn't change anything between the two of us. You still cheated on me; you still broke my heart."

"I want to fix it," he said simply. "Only first you have to let me."

"Too late," Gretchen said. *Is it?* she thought. *It is really?* "I don't care anymore."

"You're lying," he said, suddenly cool.

"Lying?" Clutching the knob in her hand, she pressed herself harder against the door. She could fling it open, go inside, and slam it—right in his face. He would deserve it too. But she didn't. "What makes you think that?"

"Because I think you do care. You care very much."

"And on what exactly are you basing that statement?" She still had her hand on the knob.

"You're still here arguing with me, aren't you? You could have gone inside and closed the door, but you didn't." He looked so smug.

"You're right. I will go inside—right now. Good night, Ennis." She yanked the door open, but he was faster and slipped in ahead of her. They stood facing each other, a pair of boxers in the ring before the fight had begun. "I'm going to ask you to leave quietly," she said. "And I think you will because you don't want a scene any more than I do."

"Do you remember that night in East Meadow?" he said, abruptly changing the subject.

"What are you talking about?"

"That night in your house in East Meadow. You had brought me home for the weekend to meet your parents."

"What about it?" she said, wary.

"Just that they put us in separate rooms, but you snuck out and came down to find me in the den after they'd all gone to sleep. And we tried to be so quiet, not to wake them, but then that dog—"

"It was a Jack Russell terrier, and he belonged to our next-door neighbor," Gretchen supplied. "They let him out at night, and sometimes he came wandering into our yard. He dug up my mother's flowers, and whenever he killed a chipmunk, he left its poor little mangled corpse in front of the door. If we heard my mother shriek in the morning, we knew he'd done it again."

"The dog must have heard us going at it, because it started barking like crazy, and your father came down to find out what all the racket was about and—"

"And there we were," said Gretchen, smiling in spite of herself. God, how much she had wanted him back then! How mad she'd been for his touch, his kiss, his everything. Where had all that gone?

"There we were," he said softly. He shook his head as if to dislodge the memory. "All right, then. I'll go now. Good night, Gretchen."

"No, wait." Were those words really coming out of her mouth? "You don't have to go if you don't want to," she said.

"You want me to stay?"

Did she? Just for now? Or for good? She did not know, but she nodded anyway. While they were talking, she had sat down on the bed, the ridiculous, overdone virginal bed with its poufs and its pillows, its flounces and its flowers. Only right now it didn't seem so ridiculous at all; it seemed an appropriately bedecked and fitting stage for the moment that was about to unfurl if only she would sit still and let it happen. Because it was going to happen; she saw that. She wanted it to. She wanted him. Maybe not in the pure, un-clouded way of their youth. But, yes, she wanted him again.

Ennis moved toward her and once again reached for her hair. This time she didn't push him away but submitted to the caress that quickly traveled from her hair to her cheek, her throat, and then her breasts.

"I missed you so much," he said, burying his face in the soft, abundant flesh that spilled over the top of her bra.

"I missed you too," she said as her arms wound around him, drawing him closer. But then she stopped and moved her face back a few inches.

"Is something wrong?" he asked.

"Justine," she said. "Justine is wrong." Earlier today she had felt confident she could deal with her daughter's problems but now suddenly their enormity loomed like a terrifying wall of water.

"It will be better when we deal with it together," he said, leaning close to kiss her again. "You'll see." Ennis's shoulder knocked one of the eyelet pillows to the floor as he and Gretchen eased their way down onto the wide and welcoming surface of the mattress.

Twenty-five

✦ • ✦

What a glorious evening! Seated near the entrance to the dinner tent, with the sounds of the music still eddying around her, Lenore took stock. Inside, a few people were still dancing. Outside, the lanterns around the tents had been lit; she could see the soft glow they cast on the expanse of white carpet; in this light it almost looked like snow.

Everything about the night had been as wonderful as she had hoped or dreamed. True, there had been that moment right after the ceremony when she'd seen Justine crying. But she seemed all right later, talking to one of those good-looking Israeli boys at the table. And all else had been sheer perfection. That dress of Angelica's—such an unexpected, brilliant choice. The *chuppah*, the exchange of vows, the dinner, the glorious moment of being held aloft in the air like a queen, the dancing that followed. Despite her bad ankle, Lenore had been determined to dance, and dance—or rather sway and rock—and she had: with Lenny Weintraub, Martin Gold, Abe Sandler, and Irving Fishman, among others. She and Irving had been dancing together at weddings for years; he had been widowed long ago, and every time they saw each other, he asked her to marry him. It was kind of a running joke between them. *Lenore, when are you going to marry me?* he'd say, or, *Lenore, you're breaking my heart.* Darling Irving. She did not want to marry him any more than he wanted to marry her. But, oh, how they both enjoyed the routine.

Finally, though, she had to relinquish her place on the dance floor to sit down, so here she was alternating between sips of chilled water and equally chilled champagne.

"Is this seat taken?"

Lenore looked up, and there was Lincoln.

"Aren't you dancing?" she said, moving her chair back so he could join her.

"I needed a break." He sat down and proffered the plate that he held. "Care for a chocolate?"

"Shaped like a heart," Lenore observed.

"And filled with raspberry buttercream. I recommend them highly."

"Raspberry buttercream! That daughter of yours . . ." began Lenore. She took a chocolate.

"And that granddaughter of yours," Lincoln added. "She's quite something."

"Yes," said Lenore. "But, then, they all are."

Lincoln said nothing but helped himself to a chocolate heart. Now there was only one left, and he urged it in Lenore's direction. "For you," he said. "Enjoy."

"Thank you, Lincoln," she said. "For everything. This"—she stretched her arm out—"has been such a truly wonderful evening. And to think that I might have missed it . . ."

"It has been wonderful," he agreed. "More wonderful than I would have thought, given how the day started."

"Days don't always end the way they begin, do they?" Lenore said. "The key can start out minor and switch to major without your having a clue as to how or even when it happened."

"I'd drink a toast to that," Lincoln said. "If I still drank."

"But you don't, do you?" said Lenore. She looked at him intently.

"No," Lincoln said, "I don't."

"I'm so glad," she said, placing her hand over his. Lincoln put his other hand on top of hers, and they sat that way for a while. The jazz band had switched to a slow, sultry number, and most people had drifted off of the floor. But Angelica and Ohad were still dancing, foreheads touching, eyes locked on one another. She was so creamy and fair; he was so dark; what would their children look like? Lenore hoped she'd live long enough to find out.

The music stopped, and the musicians took a bow. The few remaining guests applauded fervently, and then the musicians began packing up trombone and horn, saxophone and clarinet. Hand in hand the bridal couple wandered off. Cases were snapped shut; bits of conversation drifted in Lenore's direction; a mosquito whined near her rhinestone-adorned ear. Absently she swatted it away.

"Hey, Grandma." Lenore looked up to see Caleb and Teddy. "You having fun?"

"The time of my life!" Lenore said. "What about you two?"

"Not too shabby," Caleb said.

"That's all you have to say about it?" Lenore said indignantly.

"He's teasing you, Lenore," Lincoln said. "Can't you tell?"

Lenore squinted up at him. She'd had more than a bit to drink, so the signals were not coming in clearly. He *was* teasing her. That meant that he was in the mood to joke. Lenore was glad that Bobby person had left; he didn't belong at their celebration. Then she shifted her gaze to Teddy, who had his arm slung casually across Caleb's shoulders. Good, this was all good.

"It was great, Grandma. I had a blast," said Caleb.

"Me too," Teddy added. "And Marti—she thought it was perfect." Lenore nodded, pleased to know that the elegant French girl had bestowed her approval. Teddy excused himself to go off in search of her.

"Dad, I'm heading upstairs, but if you want me to drive you back to the motel, I can. I haven't had a drink for hours and I just had a coffee, so it'll be okay," Caleb said.

There was a pause in which no one said anything. Lenore had not seen the motel, but Betsy had told her about it, and she could easily imagine the pathetic carpeting, the pillow that might as well have been filled with sawdust, the leak, because didn't rooms like that always have a leak?

"Though, you know, you don't have to stay there."

"I don't?" Lincoln said. Lenore could feel his hope hovering like that mosquito in the air.

"Bobby's gone, and the room has twin beds. You can bunk down with me. I don't even snore."

"I wouldn't care if you did!" Lincoln said. "Though I guess you should ask your mother and Don first."

"She already invited you, remember? You're the one who insisted on staying in that hellhole."

"I guess I did." Lincoln stood. "But that was then, and this is now." He looked at Caleb. "You think your mother has an extra toothbrush?"

"I'll bet she does," Caleb said. Then he looked at his grandmother. "What about you, Grandma L.? Ready to go up yet? We'll escort you."

"Caleb, I am very glad your mother raised a gentleman, but I do not need escorting. And anyway I'm not ready to go up. The night's not over yet."

"Lenore, you are something else," Lincoln said admiringly. He gave her a quick kiss on the cheek, and Caleb did the same. "See you at breakfast, then. Angelica said they're staying here tonight, and Betsy's got some farewell thing or other planned in the morning."

"Breakfast sounds lovely," said Lenore. "But I don't much like the sound of farewell."

"They'll be back soon enough," Lincoln said. "You know Angelica."

"Maybe she'll be pregnant when she gets back," Lenore said. When she saw the expressions on Lincoln and Caleb's faces, she added, "What? We're family. I can say what I'm thinking, can't I? Or hoping?"

They said good night, and Lenore watched them depart, still not wanting to join them. But after a few minutes she rose and walked out of the tent. Most of the guests were gone, and those remaining strolled along the blue stone path that led to the property's service entrance. Vans were waiting there to take them to where their cars were parked; the valets would then retrieve them. Well, she supposed she ought to go inside after all. Reluctantly Lenore started towards the house. Despite the wide swath of carpeting spread over the soggy lawn, she moved slowly.

"Need some help?"

Lenore looked over to see a young man with a shaved head and most impressive physique. She could tell because the T-shirt he wore might as well have been painted on; as he got closer, she recognized him as the same young man she had seen earlier in the day.

"Would you mind walking me back?" she asked, pointing to her ankle. The small silk scarf had slipped off during the course of the evening, exposing the bandage.

"No problem," he said, graciously offering his arm. It was covered from the wrist all the way up with tattoos, which disappeared under the sleeve of the shirt.

"Can I ask you something?" she said.

"Sure." He smiled affably.

"Did it hurt to get those?"

"The tats?" He extended his other arm, the one she was not holding, and looked as if he were seeing it for the first time. "Yeah. It did."

"Then why do it?" She really did want to know. "I hope I'm not offending you, but I truly am curious."

"They were worth it. Haven't you ever done something that you knew would hurt but that you thought would be worth it?"

So many things, thought Lenore. How could she even begin to list them? What she said was, "I have."

"Well, then you get it, don't you? Pain's not always a deterrent. Pain is sometimes . . . an inevitable by-product of the life you want to lead."

"Yes," Lenore said, delighted by this sudden affinity with a stranger. "Yes, it is."

"Uh-huh." He nodded, seemingly content, and then said, "Well, here we are."

"Thank you," Lenore said. "For your kindness."

Once inside, Lenore realized she was *still* not ready to go upstairs. If she went up, the night—this long-awaited, thoroughly savored night—would be over. A dispiriting thought. She walked into the living room and sank into the down-filled sofa.

"There you are!"

Lenore shifted her gaze. Betsy, her dog tucked under one arm, was in front of her. "Ma, I was worried about you! Wasn't it enough to run off once today?"

"I hardly ran off," Lenore said. "I had something I had to do. Something important." *Even if it hurt.* She did hate being worried about like some doddering old fool. Why, look how sharp she was and what she'd accomplished today: with Justine, Gretchen, and even with Caleb. And Lincoln. Now, that was a windfall, a gift. She had revised her opinion of him totally. How strange after all those years of quiet but seemingly implacable enmity between them. She hoped he was staying in town; she would invite him to dinner.

"Anyway, I'm right here."

"Ready to go up?"

"No," said Lenore, sounding perhaps more strident than she'd meant. "I'm not."

"What do you want to do, then?" asked Betsy.

"Can I sit outside for a bit? On the terrace?"

"It's getting cooler," Betsy said.

"Would you please stop fussing over me?" Lenore said peevishly. "I can sit outside if I want to, can't I?"

"All right, all right," Betsy said. "Come on, I'll get you settled." Betsy slid open the glass doors and helped Lenore outside onto the chaise longue with its striped cushions. "Let me get you a sweater or something," Betsy added, stepping back inside.

"It's not necessary," Lenore grumbled, but she accepted the cashmere throw that Betsy had plucked from the side of the sofa and draped around her shoulders.

"All right, then," Betsy said. "Do you need anything else?"

"No, I'm all set." Then Lenore looked at the dog, still under Betsy's arm. Its mouth was open, and it was breathing heavily, as if in some sort of distress. Such a vulnerable little creature. Pitiful really. But touching too. "There is one more thing, actually," she added. "I'd like to hold the dog for a while. Would that be all right?"

"The dog?" Betsy looked down at the animal perched on her hip. "I thought you hated the dog. Everyone does, you know."

"I know. I did too. But not anymore."

"What happened?" Betsy asked. The dog seemed to understand she was the topic of this conversation, and her lush tail began to stir.

"I don't know," Lenore said. "But something did." She reached for her. "What's her name? Either I don't remember or you never told me."

"Darling," Betsy said. Lenore must have looked confused, because Betsy added, "Her name is Darling."

"No wonder you didn't broadcast it," Lenore said, enfolding the creature in her arms. But the name fit; it really did. "She looks very content."

"There's a reason she's called a lapdog." Betsy straightened up. "Okay, Ma. I'll be back to check on you. And when I go upstairs, I want you to go with me."

"Fine," said Lenore testily. Really, this constant surveillance was wearing. She adored her daughter but would be glad to get back home.

When Betsy had gone, Lenore leaned back against the cushioned chaise and looked up. What a night. The stars were twinkling madly in the sky. There was a moon too, just a sliver of one, delicate as a baby's pinky nail. She recalled ruefully the first time she had trimmed Betsy's nails and unintentionally cut too close to the quick; a bright crescent of blood had instantly appeared, and the sound of the baby's shrieking had shot straight through Lenore's heart. How vivid the memory was even now. Now that baby was long grown, a mother and grandmother too. Time waltzed on.

Then Lenore looked down at the dog, whose eyes held hers for a long minute before she lowered her face to rest on her tiny paws. Her ears went back, and her eyes narrowed to slits. "It's you and me, kid," Lenore whispered. Again the feathery tail responded.

Soon the sounds of the party tapered off. She didn't see Gretchen, Teddy, or Marti; they all must have gone upstairs already. Ohad and Angelica were nowhere in sight either. She heard Betsy's voice from somewhere inside the house, but it sounded far, far away. It was only the help left out here now, collapsing chairs, dismantling tents, breaking down tables. Stacks of dinner plates were being loaded into crates; cutlery clanged into big plastic tubs.

But Lenore didn't really want to see all that, the fairy-tale wedding being taken apart, the coach turning back into the pumpkin. No, she cast her eyes up again to where the stars continued to burn and the scrap of the moon hovered lightly, as if it had just been flung from below.

This was all so different from her own wedding day, which had taken place on a bitter February afternoon in a rented hall in Brighton Beach. But Lenore had not wanted to wait; she was already pregnant with Betsy at the time. She realized she had never told Betsy that; there had never seemed to be any reason. Now she decided that she would, if only to make sure that particular bit of history was not lost to this family that had just been reconfigured, reinvented yet again tonight.

The sounds of the workers grew softer, more muted. Had they finished? Moved off? Or was her hearing starting to go? Because it did seem unusually quiet now. No toads, no frogs. No insects, even. And Betsy was right; it *was* growing cooler. Lenore shivered a little and pulled the throw closer around her shoulders. The dog, responding to the shift in her position, resettled herself, this time tucking her face in the crook of Lenore's arm.

"Good girl," Lenore said. *Wag, wag, wag.* She noticed that the dog's coloring was actually quite nuanced: delicate, sooty markings outlined her face and paws. Using her other hand so she wouldn't disturb her, Lenore patted the small head. The dog's eyes closed. Lenore wanted to look out over the rose garden with its profusion of fragrant blossoms. In the dark, the paler of the roses seemed to be glowing; the rose-covered pergola was almost spectral.

But she felt the overwhelming need to close her eyes. She wasn't tired, no. That was not it. Instead she felt as if two small but distinct weights had been put on her eyelids: pebbles, perhaps, or coins. She could not keep them open for a second longer.

Then she felt an unfamiliar throbbing in her chest— not a pain, exactly, but something demanding, insistent. *Pay attention*, it said. *Watch out.* And one of her feet started to tingle. An arm too, the one on which the dog's head rested.

She didn't want to disturb the dog, so she didn't move. The tingling sensation grew stronger and seemed to assume a sound: she could have sworn she heard it, like an electrical hum, almost melodic in its subtle variations. Her chest was hurting now, her heart convulsing with sinister energy. And she felt cold. Very cold. She shivered but was too weak to adjust the throw. Her fingers twitched briefly and then stilled.

And then quite suddenly it all stopped: the buzzing, the chills, the throbbing of her heart. It was finished, over. The dog, sensing something, pricked up her ears and swiveled her head around to look at Lenore. But Lenore did not, could not, return the look. The dog licked Lenore's arm. Nothing. The dog put her head back down and once more rested it on her paws. After a while Lenore's body began to cool; still the dog did not move or attempt to jump down. She only settled herself more comfortably in Lenore's lap. She could wait.

YONA ZELDIS McDONOUGH is the author of three previous novels and the editor of two essay collections. Her fiction, essays, and articles have appeared in *Bride's*, *Cosmopolitan*, *Family Circle*, *Harper's Bazaar*, *Lilith*, *Metropolitan Home*, *More*, *The New York Times*, *O, the Oprah Magazine*, the *Paris Review*, and *Redbook*. She lives in Brooklyn, New York, with her husband and two children.

A
Wedding
IN
GREAT NECK

Yona Zeldis McDonough

A CONVERSATION WITH
YONA ZELDIS McDONOUGH

Q. How do you set about writing a new book?

A. For me, it always starts with the voice. I literally hear someone whispering urgently in my ear, saying, "Listen, I want to tell you something. Something important. I want you to write it down. And I want you to get it right." And the character begins to tell me his or her story. Often, I feel like I am not writing so much as transcribing; I am the vessel, not the creator. This doesn't happen all the time but when it does it's a marvelous feeling.

Q. A Wedding in Great Neck is told in several voices; whose was the first you heard?

A. Lincoln's. I had such a kinship with him; he started speaking to me immediately. Even though I am not a man, a former substance abuser or divorced, I just felt like I understood him!

Q. So you begin with character?

A. Yes. Character, in my view, determines plot. If you draw your characters well, everything else falls into place. There's a logic to it; what a given character will or won't do is the engine that drives the book. I recently reread John Steinbeck's *Of Mice and Men*. I was struck by how that novel is the perfect demonstration of this idea. Lenny and George are so well-defined that everything they do, the whole tragic arc of the story, issues from their characters. Lenny is big, strong but potentially dangerous; he is also unaware of his power to do harm. First he kills a mouse, then a puppy, and finally a woman. George is the one who cares for him and protects him. His final act is the ultimate expression of that caring.

Q. What other elements do you consider essential?

A. After character, I'm keen on place. Where are these characters? What do they see, feel, smell, hear? Locating them in a credible environment and watching how they respond to that goes a long way to bringing them to life.

Q. Why did you set this book in Great Neck? Do you have a special connection to the place?

A. My dear friend Constance Marks (the book is dedicated to her) grew up in Great Neck, and I've visited a few times. I see it as a kind of quintessentially aspirational, American place, and I find that fascinating. There's a lot of money there, and money engenders longing. Lincoln feels it keenly, and to some extent, I do too.

Q. What is a typical workday like for you?

A. I don't really have a typical day. When I am writing a novel, I try to keep my hand in it every day so it doesn't dry up on me. Even if I can only write two pages a day, that's something. I tell myself that two pages a day = fourteen pages a week = fifty-six pages a month. Pretty soon that adds up to a novel.

Q. Do you have a designated place to work?

A. Yes. For years, it was in the finished basement of my house. The basement had its advantages—it was quiet, it was large, and it was cool in summer and toasty in winter (I don't claim to understand this, but there you have it). Also, my husband had built me a very grand dollhouse, which I filled with the dollhouse furniture I'd had as a child. I love that house, and when I reached an impasse in my work, I would get up and rearrange the furniture and other objects for a while to clear my head. But, despite all its advantages, it was still a basement. No natural light. When my son left for college, we did some reshuffling of rooms, and he asked if he could have the basement room; my daughter ended up in his old room, and I took hers. I had it painted a serene sky blue, and there is a window that overlooks our admittedly tiny backyard. I feel like I have brought the outside in. It's a very peaceful place, and one that is very conducive to writing, musing and dreaming.

Q. Do you need to be alone or have absolute quiet to write?

A. Being both a lifelong New Yorker and a mom, I'd say my tolerance for noise is pretty high. I can tune most things out. I often keep my office door open; I don't need to be sealed away. And I usually have one or two of my three dogs (all small, yappy Pomeranians, like the dog in *A Wedding in Great Neck*) for company while I work. They don't ask for much; the occasional belly rub or biscuit seems to suffice.

Q. Are you working on something new?

A. Yes, I have started a new novel about an unlikely romance between a Christian widow and a Jewish widower. Although they have each lost a spouse, they have nothing else in common and clash from the moment they meet. Yet, despite their differences of both style and substance, these two find common ground and fall in love.

QUESTIONS
FOR DISCUSSION

1. Do you think Lincoln is a sympathetic character? Why or why not?

2. How do you view Justine's actions on the day of the wedding? Is she justified in what she does?

3. How does Gretchen change and grow through the novel?

4. What is Lenore's role in the family in general, and on the wedding day in particular?

5. There are several shifting points of view in this novel but Angelica's, the bride's, is absent. What purpose does this serve?

6. How does the dog affect the different family members?

7. What do you think will happen between Gretchen and Ennis?

8. Are you sympathetic toward Betsy? Why or why not?

9. How do you view the depiction of the wedding itself? Is there an element of satire in the way that it's handled?

10. All the action in this novel takes place in a single day. What is the dramatic purpose of this structure?